CO

Pulling his face upw
intended to be preparati
ignit
her
bo
sol
be
ti
or

s
te
lo
fr
sh

u
S
ha
hi

CHICAGO PUBLIC LIBRARY

**CHICAGO PUBLIC LIBRARY
CANARYVILLE BRANCH
642-646 W. 43RD ST.   60609**

FORM 19

BOOK YOUR PLACE ON OUR WEBSITE AND MAKE THE ARABESQUE ROMANCE CONNECTION!

We've created a customized website just for our very special Arabesque readers, where you can get the inside scoop on everything that's going on with Arabesque romance novels.

When you come online, you'll have the exciting opportunity to:

- View covers of upcoming books
- Read sample chapters
- Learn about our future publishing schedule (listed by publication month *and author*)
- Find out when your favorite authors will be visiting a city near you
- Search for and order backlist books from our online catalog
- Check out author bios and background information
- Send e-mail to your favorite authors
- Meet the Kensington staff online
- Join us in weekly chats with authors, readers and other guests
- Get writing guidelines
- AND MUCH MORE!

Visit our website at
http://www.arabesquebooks.com

Love Everlasting

Anna Larence

Pinnacle Books
Kensington Publishing Corp.
http://www.arabesquebooks.com

DEDICATION

To three very important people in my life:
my sister, Pam, who is the living definition of determination
my brother, Venson, who is the inspiration for all my heroes
with his care, love and respect for women,
and my nephew, Wayne, who brings such joy and happiness into
my life just by existing. Thank you Wayne for keeping me young
and "hip".
I love you guys very much!

PINNACLE BOOKS are published by

Kensington Publishing Corp.
850 Third Avenue
New York, NY 10022

Copyright © 1998 by M. Ann Fields

All rights reserved. No part of this book may be reproduced in any form or by any means without the prior written consent of the Publisher, excepting brief quotes used in reviews.

If you purchased this book without a cover you should be aware that this book is stolen property. It was reported as "unsold and destroyed" to the Publisher and neither the Author nor the Publisher has received any payment for this "stripped book."

Pinnacle and the P logo Reg. U.S. Pat. & TM Off.

First Printing: May, 1998
10 9 8 7 6 5 4 3 2 1

Printed in the United States of America

One

The Church of All Saints in Fort Worth, Texas, was filled to capacity. Even though the numerous windows of the two-story white brick structure indicated gathering darkness outside—brought on not only by the approaching evening hour but also the gloom from the earlier thunderstorm—the excited guests didn't mind or care. This was the event of the season: the wedding of Gerald Forrester and Heather Chadwick, the union everyone had been waiting on for years. The level of anticipation among the guests was so high they didn't even ooooh and aaaah over the lighted slim white taper candles situated at the ends of each pew, the white ribbons and white silk panels strewn elegantly across the altar and the cross, the white springtime flowers that adorned the walls and doors, and the subdued lighting that gave it a surreal scene of romance.

It was a quarter till six, fifteen minutes before the appointed time for the couple to become one flesh. On cue, the wide double doors at the back of the church opened, signifying the start of the ceremony. The whispered conversations of the guests ceased as the only living grandmother on either side was led to her seat on the second row from the altar, at the front of the church. The parade of honored family members continued with the organist playing soft music as a pleasing background.

While the family members were being seated, Heather Chadwick, the bride-to-be, paced the length of her makeshift dressing room. Her arms were wrapped around her middle, and her head was down. Anxiety marred her usually smooth forehead.

The door opened and Nachelle DuCloux, Heather's best friend, flew into the room. "Heather, Evelyn sent me in here to check on you. Why aren't you dressed? They're seating the family. You gotta hurry!"

Heather turned around at the sound of her friend's voice and stared at her. After one year of marriage, Nachelle still radiated with happiness. Her beautiful brown skin had a natural, healthy glow, her facial features were soft, and even the beginning pudge of her belly from the first trimester of pregnancy didn't detract from her shapely figure. Heather sighed, her shoulders slumped, and she second-guessed herself for the zillionth time that day. *Maybe I can go through with it. Surely if Nachelle and Steven were able to overcome all the odds stacked against them and live happily ever after, then I can succeed with this marriage game, as well.* As quickly as the thought formed, it vanished. Fear gripped and took control of her.

Placing a detaining hand on Nachelle's arm, Heather stopped her friend from unzipping the garment bag the Bob Mackie wedding dress was hanging in. "I've decided not to go through with it." She spoke quietly, her hazel eyes begged for understanding.

"What did you say?" Nachelle whispered, staring at her friend as if she'd lost her mind. "Surely you didn't say what I thought you said?" A perplexed look settled on Nachelle's beautiful face.

Heather dropped her hand and her head. It was evident Nachelle didn't understand her decision, didn't understand the panic and terror that caged her. Moving away from Nachelle, she walked toward the window. Pushing the heavy red velvet curtain aside, she looked unseeingly at the rows and rows of high-priced foreign cars silhouetted in the early evening light. "Nachelle, I can't fake it anymore. I just can't do it." She turned her back to the reminder of the number of people waiting just down the hallway to see her and Gerald tie the knot. With agitated hand movements marking her words, she tried to communicate her dilemma to her confidante. "I love Gerald. Lord knows I do, but I don't want to get married."

Nachelle walked up to her friend and took her hands. Bringing her hands and Heather's to rest on her chest, Nachelle looked deep into Heather's eyes. She saw the fear and confusion that resided in Heather's eyes. Lowering her voice to a parenting tone, she spoke quietly. "Heather, Gerald is lined up with the pastor. The guests are here, the reception is all set, and the honeymoon is a memory waiting to be created." Nachelle stroked Heather's clammy arms. "You're just having the usual last-minute jitters that everybody has. It's natural."

"You don't understand, Nachelle. I can't marry Gerald." The more she said it aloud, the more final it became. The more right it felt, the less fear she felt.

"Heather, you just said you love Gerald and I know . . . you know . . . he loves you."

"So, why can't we go on like we've been doing? Why do we need marriage to validate our love?"

"Marriage is the next natural step, and soon after that you'll want to create life together." Nachelle rubbed her stomach and smiled a rainbow of a smile.

Breaking free from Nachelle's touch, Heather resumed her pacing. Her wild hand movements punctuated her distress. "Nachelle, I understand the progression of love and life and so on. But, my heart and my mind aren't matching on this initial step to marry."

"Heather, I understand what you're going through. Right before Steven and I got married, I thought I was going to be sick. I was nervous, and my hands were sweaty, and I started thinking about all the things I was giving up and all the compromising I would have to do. I started thinking about Harlan and how my relationship with him almost destroyed me and my career, and then I thought about how my marriage to Steven would impact my career. I wondered if I was making a grave mistake by marrying the boss. All sorts of crazy thoughts passed through my mind, and I almost bolted." Nachelle grew misty eyed, reliving the day she became Mrs. Steven DuCloux. "Then, the music started flowing and the next thing I knew, I was walking down the aisle in a daze. But, one look at Steven's face when I stood next to him, all the doubts and questions and insecurities disappeared. I haven't regretted the decision, and now I can't imagine life without him." Nachelle went to Heather and hugged her. "The same thing will happen to you. One look in Gerald's eyes, and you'll feel safe and loved. Everything will be all right."

"I want to believe that, Nachelle," Heather mumbled, pulling out of Nachelle's embrace. With teary eyes, she spoke her fear. "I want to believe our love will endure."

"It will." Nachelle smiled, and Heather tried to believe her. While Nachelle sought a tissue for Heather to wipe her eyes and nose, Heather thought about Nachelle's words. She wanted to believe in the fairy tale. She closed her eyes, visualizing herself and Gerald as husband and wife. She pictured them with children. Would the kids be light in color like her or dark brown like Gerald? Would the kids be short like her or tall like Gerald? She smiled at the image her mind conjured of a family of six—she, Gerald, and the four kids they had discussed having—relaxing at the park with a picnic basket and swings or cheering Daddy on to victory on the courts or helping Mommy with her puppet business.

As Heather daydreamed pleasant thoughts, Nachelle went to the wedding dress, slipped it off the hanger, and approached her friend. "Hands up."

Heather opened her eyes and followed Nachelle's command. She allowed Nachelle to slip the dress over her head, being careful not to disrupt the stylish hairdo. Moving behind Heather, Nachelle adjusted the crisscross straps in the back and with eyes glowing, moved around in front of Heather. "You look beautiful!" Grabbing one hand, she led Heather to the full-length mirror. "Oh, Heather. You look absolutely captivating."

Staring at her reflection in the mirror, Heather initially saw a young bride in a floor-length white satin dress. The wedding dress was more like an evening gown than a traditional wedding gown. It was cut like a slip and featured an abbreviated train. It molded her body but only enough to hint at the curves beneath. As she continued to stare at herself in the mirror, the image of a thirty-two-year-old bride gave way to the memory of a five-year-old child's image of a parade of men coming in and out of her mother's—and her—life. Calling themselves husbands yet staying no longer than a roommate. Some of the "husbands" had been nice to her, some had been indifferent, acting as if she didn't even exist, and some had been mean, treating her as if she were the one who stood in the way of their long-term happiness with her mother.

It was those images that caused Heather to back away from the mirror, shaking her head no. *No, I'm not going through that. I won't do that to our children, and I won't do it to us. I won't kill this love of ours by marrying.* Ignoring the shoes Nachelle held out to her, Heather started shimmying out of the dress as if her life depended on it.

"Heather, what are you doing?" Nachelle asked, surprised.

"I'm doing what I should have done months ago. I'm calling off this wedding. I'm not getting married. I won't be able to bear it when our love dies." Another childhood image popped in her head: a young child in the playground at school. The other children circled her and teased her about being the daughter of the most married woman in Texas. *No, no way she was getting married today.*

"What are you talking about? Heather, you can't do this to Gerald."

"I can and I am." With her mind made up, there was no budging her from her position. The expensive wedding dress fell to the floor. Heather stood in her underclothes, looking around for her street clothes.

Nachelle grabbed her friend by the arms. Talking tough and straight, she said, "Heather, think about what you're doing! Think about all the money and time that's been invested in this day. Think about Gerald! He'll be heartbroken."

"No, he won't. I'll explain everything to him later. He knows I love him." Heather stared at her friend, believing the words she spoke.

Nachelle persisted, softening her approach. "Heather, I know you're afraid. I can feel you trembling. Let me go get Gerald. I bet once you've talked to him, you'll be ready to run down that aisle to him."

Heather's hazel eyes flared brilliantly, making them glow like tiger's-eye marbles. "I do want to talk to Gerald, but not for that reason. I want to break the news to him. It will be better coming from me."

Nachelle ran a hand across her brow. She couldn't believe Heather was doing this. She grasped for the last remaining person who could possibly change Heather's mind. "What about your mother? Have you thought about her?"

Heather spoke vehemently. "If it weren't for her, I wouldn't be in this mess in the first place." Nachelle had no way of knowing Heather was referring to her childhood issue. Although they had been friends for over ten years, Heather hadn't shared the binding influence her mother's lifestyle had had on her. Now, anger at her mother drove her. "I went through all this fuss only to get her off my back. I just wanted her to quit pressuring me. I wanted her and Gerald to quit ganging up on me. But, it's time—past time—I was honest with myself. I don't want to do this."

The door opened and Evelyn, the wedding consultant, popped her head through the door opening. The perky smile on her face dropped when she noted Heather was still in her undergarments. A frown appeared when she noticed the tears and smeared makeup on Heather's face. She closed the door behind her and walked into the middle of the rectangle-shaped room where Nachelle and Heather stood. "Okay, now I'm worried. The groom just entered with the pastor, and we have no bridesmaids to stall with for more time." Evelyn had thought it the weirdest thing when Heather had adamantly refused to have bridesmaids, not even Nachelle as a matron of honor. She had been unwavering in her desire to have only her, Gerald, and the preacher at the altar. That had been a new one for Evelyn, but she was paid to do what her clients wanted and since that was what the young lady wanted, then so be it. The young couple was also paying her to run this day with an iron fist to make sure they stayed on schedule—to the reception by eight, to the airport by midnight to catch a plane to New York for a short, two-day honeymoon in Niagara Falls, Canada. The "real" honeymoon—two glorious weeks in Egypt—would come when the NBA season ended. "You have one minute to get yourself together and out there."

"Please go get Gerald!" Nachelle commanded.

Having worked with the prospective bride and groom and their closest friends and families for months now, Evelyn had come to know them quite well. In all those months, she'd never heard Nachelle speak with such force or urgency. That was when she knew something was terribly wrong.

Evelyn responded without delay. "I'll notify the guests there will be a . . ." She paused, staring pointedly, hopefully, into Heather's eyes. Reading Heather's facial expression, she finished with a slight catch in her voice. ". . . delay."

The tall, slender woman backed out of the room as quickly as she had come in. Her fingers were crossed, but with more than twenty-five years in the wedding business, she knew when a marriage would or wouldn't happen. This one wouldn't. Of course, all along, she had detected some foot-dragging on Heather's part. It was just a shame that Heather hadn't dealt with whatever problem she had before now. Sighing deeply, the wedding consultant headed for the side entrance, the one closest to where Gerald stood waiting for his bride. Cracking open the door, she surveyed Gerald's straight back and serious expression. It saddened her to look at him, for she had enjoyed working with this fun-loving couple and had thought they were perfect for each other. Shaking her head and stiffening her spine, she took a deep breath and entered the sanctuary.

Moments later, a hard knock sounded throughout the bride-to-be's dressing room. Nachelle opened the door to allow a concerned Gerald in. "I'll be hanging around if you guys need me." She shut the door behind her.

Upon entering, Gerald didn't say anything for several moments. He stood stone still, staring at the woman who would soon be his wife. As it always did when he looked at her, his heart swelled and the blood raced through his veins. He smiled and gave silent thanks for the wonderful angel who had fallen into his life. For yet another time, he wondered how he had gotten so lucky. With his dark brown eyes reflecting love, he recommitted her being to memory. A mere two inches over five feet, she was short by any standard, but her diminutive height was magnified by his six-foot-eight-inch stature. Although compact, she was stacked just right: small but full breasts, a slim, tucked waist, curvaceous hips, and a slammin' behind. She was light in color with yellow undertones, and not just her mouth but her entire face seemed to smile constantly as if she never had a bad day. Her eyes were her most arresting, most captivating feature. Hazel in color and very expressive, very alive, always sparkling as if she had just cried or was beginning to cry. Indeed, Heather's whole being was sparkle-made-human and very animated. It was that aura of liveliness that had attracted him to her the very first night they met at an NBA All-Star party in Houston six years ago. No doubt it was one of the things that made her successful in her work as a self-employed puppeteer who wrote, directed, and acted out her own productions. Yes, she was perfect in his eyes, and in a few minutes she would be his wife. His chest swelled with pride.

Gerald walked to Heather with his arms stretched out wide. "Hey, baby, what's up? Evelyn said you needed me." He hugged her briefly and kissed her forehead before putting a little space between them. Holding her within the circle of his arms, he stared into her face and realized all was not right. The usual smile that greeted him was still there, but some of the luster was gone as well as the usual shine in her eyes. Were those dried tearstains marking her cheeks?

Gerald frowned, and a handful of fear gripped his heart.

"Gerald, I need for you to please understand what I'm going to tell you." Heather put a comforting hand on his chest and used the other arm to circle his waist, drawing them closer. The pleading in her eyes matched her pleading words.

"Baby, what is it? Are you sick? You not feeling well?" Gerald put a massive, basketball-palming hand to her forehead. It almost dwarfed her face. "If so, we can just have the preacher come in here. I won't make you stand."

Heather shook her head. "No, Gerald, I . . . It's not . . . I feel fine," she ended weakly. Earlier, she had thought it would be a simple thing to share with him her desire for a postponement, but it was turning out not to be so. Gerald had looked so handsome in his coal-black hand-tailored tuxedo when he walked into her room. He had looked so happy. She hated to think she was going to make him unhappy, even for just a short time.

Trying to ignore his own growing anxiety and feeling of foreboding, Gerald lecherously wiggled his brows and parted her robe at the lapel. "You just want Big Daddy to give you a quickie in sin before it becomes legal for us to make love, huh?" Leaning low, he planted a kiss on the roundness of one breast.

Despite the bad news she needed to share with him, Heather smiled at his foolishness, then whimpered as his kiss turned into a flick of a tongue against her nipple. *Gosh, I really love this man! How in the world am I going to explain this decision to him?*

Pulling his face upward, she kissed him on the lips. It was intended to be preparation for the bad news, but the kiss instantly ignited a desire so strong they couldn't ignore it. Heather arched her body against him, needing to feel the strength of his manhood. Gerald slipped the satin robe from her body, returning her kisses with equal passion and caressing the soft, smooth skin on her shoulders, her breasts, her derriere. Each took and gave as if they both knew this session of lovemaking would have to last a lifetime. When suffocation threatened to overcome them, they parted only to come together again in a full body hug.

"I think I'd better leave before we get this wedding way off schedule." Gerald spoke to the top of her head. Taking deep breaths, he tried to slow the beats of his heart and shut out the ringing in his ears. She did this to him. Without intending to, she turned him on, making him ready for love anytime, anywhere. She always did and always would have that upper hand on him. But, now, there was an even more important task at hand. Holding her protectively, tenderly, against his chest, he whispered in her hair, "I love you, Heather." Gerald dropped his arms and stepped back from her. Using a finger to flick her nose, he smiled. "Now let's go show the world how much we mean to each other."

Heather turned her back to him to hide the tears in her eyes. Picking up her robe, she wrapped it around her and turned to face him. She spoke slowly. "Gerald, I love you very much. That's why it's so hard for me to tell you"—Heather took a deep breath and gripped his biceps—"I can't marry you. Not now."

Gerald sucked in a breath and stepped back from her as if she had slapped him. With rapid eye movement, he searched her countenance for signs that she was teasing him as she so often did. But only the serious side of her personality existed, the side she rarely showed. He had no reason to think that she wasn't being straight with him.

"Gerald." Heather took a step toward him with a hand held out in supplication. "I need more time." Her eyes bored into his, translating her misery and asking silently for his understanding and forgiveness.

He didn't pick up on her nonverbal messages, only the words she had communicated to him. *She doesn't want to marry me.* The words echoed throughout his head. *She doesn't want to marry me.* That earlier feeling of danger had been a premonition, a warning that had done no good to ignore.

"Why not?" he asked in harsh softness. His eyes stung, and his throat hurt from trying not to act like a kid and start bawling. He swallowed several times and didn't care that Heather saw his weakness. His openbook, upfront, and sharing personality didn't allow him to hide his emotions from friends and family.

Of course, on the basketball court, it was different. He was paid to keep his head on straight. He was paid handsomely to maintain a professional demeanor, to concentrate on the mechanics of the game. He allowed himself the luxury of emotions after the final buzzer, and that was when the crowd witnessed the true Gerald Forrester.

But, now, standing in front of the one woman who held all power, he had no choice but to let her know how deeply she had cut him. His eyes told her he was hurting, for the words wouldn't come. His eyes told her there was nothing she could do to erase the pain except retract those damning words.

Heather accurately translated his eye messages, but she was too tied up in her own fear to consider a change of direction. She just needed to make him understand that she needed more time. "Gerald, I want you to understand. It's important that you listen to me." She advanced on him.

Gerald didn't trust himself to speak.

"Gerald, you know how much I love you." Heather shook his arm as if that would break him out of his muteness or help him understand her position.

"Apparently not," he croaked, casting her hands off his arms. Clearing his throat, he took one last swipe at his eyes.

"Honey, you know that isn't true. Just a year. Give me one more year and I promise I'll be ready." Heather begged for her life. Standing up on tiptoe, she framed his face with her hands.

Even though she was touching him, Gerald was as still as a ceramic figurine. He thought about the previous six years—one year of engagement, two years of dating exclusively, and three years of dating off and on, more on than off. In those six years, he had always been the one to suggest the next step, the next level of commitment. Although Heather had always eagerly agreed, he couldn't forget the fact that he had been the initiator. Now that they'd reached the final level and she was balking, he couldn't help but wonder, What now? There was nowhere else to go. "And when that year is up, and you're still not ready?" Gerald queried. His voice was deceptively low. His plan was not gone, just temporarily shelved.

"But I will be ready. I promise," Heather petitioned fervently, her eyes sparkling brightly with the promise.

The lump in Gerald's throat finally dislodged, and he looked at her with new eyes. If he'd been honest with himself, he would have seen this coming. Over the past few months, as "the date" had come closer and closer, he had noticed Heather acting more uptight. She hadn't been teasing him as often, nor had she been sliding into any of her good cartoon character roles. By the world's standards, she had been withdrawn and sullen. When he'd asked her about her out-of-character personality change, she had attributed it to the contract she had signed with the Fort Worth Independent School District.

He had bought that for a while because her contract with FWISD to provide puppet shows to pre-K, kindergarten, and first grade students on various childhood topics was her largest account—and she was determined to do a bang-up job, so that it would lead to contracts with other school districts. Granted, as a self-employed person, her livelihood depended on her alone and understanding that, he had supported her.

But, as the performances smoothed out and became more routine, and she still hadn't eased up, he'd begun to suspect that it was premarital jitters. He knew it was natural for women to get them. Hell, men got them, too. Although he'd had a moment of uncertainty at last night's bachelor party, the feeling had passed when he'd conjured up a picture of Heather's lovely face. All insecurities and doubts had been buried with the night.

Apparently, the same didn't hold true for Heather. He had hoped that whatever gray cloud she was holding on to would blow away with his caring support. He had hoped that she would have faith in them. Apparently, the love and care that he so unselfishly gave was not enough. So, the hope that he had carried with him the last couple of months petered out. If his love, his caring, and his sensitivity weren't enough for her, he had nothing else to give her and, that being the case, it truly was over. No matter what time period Heather attempted to put on it, the final act of committing themselves one to the other would never come to be.

Before they wrote "the end," he had to know one thing. Repressing the tears that burned his eyes, he lowered his head to stare into hers. Quietly, he asked, "Is it me? Am I not Prince Charming enough for you?"

Heather gasped and her eyes widened. "No, Gerald,

that's crazy. You know that has nothing to do with it. You know I love you."

"You keep saying that, but your actions don't prove it!" He hadn't meant to raise his voice, but he was out of control. There was no gate to hold his anger, confusion, and heartbreak at bay. He didn't care that anyone loitering in the hallway could hear his angry retorts. "How can you love me when you don't trust me?"

"I do trust you," Heather beseeched.

"If you do, tell me the real reason you don't want to marry me. Is it because I was born on the wrong side of the tracks? Is it because I get confused as to which fork to use at a formal dinner party, or because I don't know the difference between Russian and some other country's caviar? What is it, Heather? For once, be up-front with me about this whole marriage thing."

"I don't give one hoot about your social skills or your lineage—and you know that, Gerald." Heather was breathing deeply. The last thing she had wanted was for Gerald to take blame. He was the most caring, supportive man she had ever met, and it was important to her that he understand *he* was perfect. *She* was the one with faults and hang-ups. Laying a solicitious hand on his arm, she pleaded with him. "Gerald, please, honey, it's not you. It's me. *I* have some issues I need to work out. I just need some time."

Holding up one long, slim finger, Gerald stated, "I'm going to ask you one more time. What are those issues?" As swift as an eye blink, he went from anger to petitioning. Throwing out his hands, he asked, "What can I help you with?"

Heather looked at the ground, up at him, and then back down at the ground. She couldn't verbalize it. Gerald would think she was crazy, and then he wouldn't want to marry her. No, she couldn't take the chance of losing him. Better to put him off for a year, get over this fear of marriage, and then come back to him as a whole woman. "Gerald, let me present it when I feel ready, please. I don't want to talk about it right now. I'm asking for only twelve months."

Taking a deep breath, Gerald ripped off his silk bow tie. "Fine. Take all the time you need." The cummerbund joined the tie on the floor. He turned and started for the door.

Heather ran past him and blocked the door with her body. Splaying her arms and legs out wide, she cried out for his understanding. "I'm sorry, Gerald. I know my timing stinks. I wanted to talk to you months ago. To share my concerns. But you were so caught up in the wedding. Both you and Mother. And I just . . . didn't. I'm sorry."

Gerald stopped short of the door, just short of her. With a wasted expression on his face, he placed his hands on his waist. He didn't know what to do. He'd never felt this bereft, this lost in his life. He felt like he was reenacting the scene in *Indiana Jones* where the hero was within a baby's toenail length of securing the Holy Grail, within an eyelash distance of achieving the greatest treasure ever, only to have it snatched away in an instant. They had been so close to happiness, and now it was as far away as Pluto. Yet, even now, staring at her petite body plastered against the door, even now with her actions twisting the life out of his heart, she still had the power to thrill him, to evoke in him feelings of love. Well, it wasn't to be. She'd made it clear that she didn't want to marry him. Not now. Not in any amount of time. Fighting the overwhelming sense of loss and the accompanying pain, he took a deep breath, squared his shoulders as if fortifying himself for a long, tough battle, and walked toward her. "You know what, Heather? There's no sense in continuing this. You've made it clear that we're through."

Heather tottered on the brink of anger. "I didn't say we're through. I said I'm not ready for marriage." Why didn't he understand she just needed a little time? Why was he being so difficult?

"Same thing, isn't it?" Gerald took another step toward the door. "At this point in our relationship, it's either get married, stand still, or quit. You should know by now that only one of those choices will make me happy. The key question is, how much do you love me? Are you willing to trust me, trust us, with whatever problem you think you have?" Gerald shook his head no. "Obviously, your love isn't deep enough for that." He reached around her without touching her and turned the doorknob. "I'm leaving. It's over," he said with a catch in his voice, a lump in his throat, and a knife in his heart.

"Gerald! No, it's not!" Heather flung herself at him, wrapping her arms around him. "Don't leave. We're not through."

Extracting himself from her smaller figure, he steadied her against the wall with his hands on her shoulders. "Honey, we've been through. I was just too dumb or hopeful to realize it."

Tears filled Heather's eyes. She slumped against the wall with one hand reaching out to him. "Gerald, how can you say that? I love you."

It took all Gerald's self-control and discipline to keep from going to her to comfort her. He opened the door. But before it swallowed him from her sight, he turned to stare at her one last time. In a voice as hard as cement, he said, "You can keep the ring. I don't want any reminders of us." He slammed the door shut behind him.

He took four giant steps, rounded the corner, and almost collided with Nachelle, Steven, Evelyn, and Marilyn Wolfe, Heather's mother. His sudden appearance and disheveled state surprised them.

"Gerald?" Nachelle spoke in a gasp.

Gruffly, he spoke. Unshed tears made his eyes shine brightly. "There won't be a wedding. Evelyn, handle the guests. Tell them to enjoy the reception. I'm out of here."

Before anyone could ask any questions, his long legs took him to the entrance of the church. The heavy glass doors didn't make a sound when he roughly pushed them open. Soon his shocked audience saw him running down the long driveway.

Nachelle turned a frightened, anxious face to her husband.

Steven, always in control except when it came to his wife, took his beautiful, pregnant wife by the shoulders. "You'd better go check on Heather. She's going to need protection from 'well-meaning' guests." Taking long strides, he started tracing Gerald's footsteps. With a tight expression on his face and a tenseness in his voice, he threw over his shoulder, "Evelyn, you'd better go do what he said. I'm going after Gerald."

Following Gerald's footsteps, Steven ran as fast as he could. But, with Gerald's superior physical shape, longer legs, and the adrenaline that was pulsating through his body, Steven knew there was no way he could catch up to him on foot. Spotting their family car, he fished around in his jacket pocket for the keys and within minutes he had the Mercedes-Benz sedan pointed in the direction he'd seen Gerald headed.

He drove for about a mile, zigzagging through the quiet residential neighborhood in search of a speeding human bullet. "Think, Steven, think. If it were you, where would you go?" It was no good to try to project himself into Gerald's place. It was too painful to even contemplate. Although he and Nachelle lived a happy life now, there had been a time when that had not been the case. There had been a time when he had almost lost Nachelle due to his own stupidity. That had been one hell of an episode for him, and just thinking about it made him shudder. *Gerald isn't thinking, he's just probably reacting, trying to outrun the pain,* he thought. Deciding to take a chance that somehow Gerald's subconscious was leading him home, Steven headed his car in the direction of the nearest freeway.

In this northeast section of Fort Worth, the closest freeway linking Dallas, where Gerald lived, to Fort Worth, where Heather lived, was Interstate 30. After completing a few long blocks, Steven turned onto the service road of the freeway. His supposition had been on the mark, for after a short time, he happened to glance in his rearview mirror and saw Gerald's lithe, lean body turn the corner onto the service road, running as fast as Michael Johnson.

With a screeching of tires, Steven stopped his Benz and reversed it. Ignoring the ogling of the passengers in the other cars, he drove backward on the access road of I-30, giving thanks that at this time of day traffic was light. He prayed that the cops wouldn't see him and that no cars decided to exit. Fortune was with him, for soon he was parallel to Gerald. Not that Gerald acknowledged his presence. He shot past Steven, running, head down, arms loose. Putting his car in forward, Steven caught up to Gerald and shouted his name through the open window. Several seconds passed before Gerald finally looked up.

"Get in! You'll get killed running on this busy freeway."

Gerald stopped running.

Steven slid to a smooth stop and popped open the front passenger door. He noticed that somewhere along the way Gerald had shed his coat, tie, and cummerbund.

Hands on his hips, head hanging low, Gerald walked around in small circles. He sucked in huge gulps of air. After a while, he leaned over from the waist, hands on knees, legs bent, chest heaving. Steven recognized that "time-out" posture from the court action.

"Gerald, come on. Get in."

Gerald straightened and tilted his head back toward the sky. He stood like that for several seconds and just as Steven had made up his mind to get out of the car and forcefully stuff Gerald in, the three-time NBA MVP slid his long body into the car. Sitting low on his spine, he leaned his head against the window and cried silently.

Without confirming his assumptions about Gerald's destination, Steven merged with the other speeding cars, heading east toward Gerald's house. He accelerated quickly, zooming Gerald away from the physical source of his pain.

They drove the distance in silence, with Gerald wrapped in misery and Steven as quiet as a chapel in a hospital. He figured that when Gerald was ready to talk, he would.

Within thirty minutes, they pulled into the driveway of Gerald's house on historic South Boulevard in South Dallas. They entered the house—a three-story frame building with maid's quarters in the back built in the forties for a rich, white Jewish family who vacated it in the sixties when blacks started moving in the surrounding area—via a side entrance, still in silence.

Throwing the extra key, which he had unearthed from a planter beside the door, on a side table, Gerald gestured for Steven to come in. Steven did so, mentally noting it had been a while since he'd been at Gerald's house. He remembered this was the den, one of the rooms Gerald spent the most time in when he was at home. He remembered Gerald telling him he could come in this haven of soft almond-colored leather furniture and blond wood tables and relax with music, plants, and pictures of Heather—the three things that kept him sane, the three things that kept him from living the media hype. And, now, looking around the room, refamiliarizing himself with Gerald's private space, Steven noted there was indeed a lot of candid as well as posed pictures of Heather: Heather by herself, Heather at one of her performances, Heather and Gerald together on the first night they met, Heather and Gerald at a formal banquet, the four of them—Heather, Gerald, Nachelle, and Steven—at some after-five function, Heather in bed asleep, Heather on a swing, Heather, Heather, Heather, everywhere. Steven prided himself on being an observant man but realized he'd never before noticed just how many pictures of Heather Gerald possessed. *The man's got it bad,* Steven thought. He immediately chided himself, for he admitted he had it just as bad for Nachelle. He would give up his life for her, and he imagined Gerald would do the same for Heather. So, for her to dump him . . . A shaft of pain and fear shot through Steven when he imagined Nachelle turning her back on him. He immediately commiserated, for he remembered the pain and fear he'd gone through when he thought he'd lost Nachelle, and then he gave thanks for the happiness, the completion, he experienced when they finally got together to make their lives one.

Steven returned to the present with a slight shiver shaking his body.

As if returning to earth himself, Gerald, sitting in one corner of the sofa, looked up at Steven, who hovered over an easy chair. Taking a deep breath, Gerald said, "Thanks for the ride. I guess I wasn't thinking." He stood up as if yanked by a string. Moving around the room, his head low, he mumbled, "I needed to get away. I needed some air."

Steven felt awkward. What did you say to a man who was hurting from a broken heart? "I understand."

"Do you?" Gerald twisted around to stare at his friend. Even though their busy schedules—Gerald's basketball games and media and personal appearances and Steven's CEO position in his family-owned computer company—kept them apart, the friendship they had formed as a result of having women who were best friends allowed them to speak with truth and passion.

"Yes, I do," Steven replied defensively. "You of all people should remember how Nachelle and I almost didn't come to be. Don't you remember, you took her out of town with you? You shielded her from me, remember?"

Gerald was silent for several seconds. Finally, he confirmed Steven's statement. "That was so long ago—or, rather it seems like it." He sighed.

"Well, I can tell you I went through hell trying to find that woman. So, don't tell me I don't know how it is to love and hurt at the same time."

Suddenly drained, Gerald slumped into a chair. "I just thought this would really be it. That we would finally get together permanently." Gerald slumped further into the soft cushions of the leather chair. He threw his head back and closed his eyes. Speaking more to himself than to Steven, he remarked, "We've been together for so long and I love her so. . . ." Gerald choked up and silenced the hurtful words.

The ringing of the telephone prevented Steven from having to say or do anything. Hurriedly, he went to it. "Hello."

"Steven, oh, good," Nachelle gushed. "I was hoping y'all would be there. I tried to stop Mrs. Forrester and the girls from leaving, but they're on the way to the house. I just wanted you to know. How's Gerald?"

Steven was silent, trying to think of a way to answer Nachelle's question without Gerald picking up on the conversation. Steven covertly glanced around to where Gerald sat. Gerald was gone.

"Steven, you can't talk, can you?" Nachelle sighed. "Well, I can surmise that he's probably falling apart. Oh, gosh, I wish I was there. But, Heather is a basket case, too. Her mother really lit into her. Marilyn was so angry, I thought she was going to have a heart attack. Poor Heather just sat there and cried. This is the biggest mess!"

"Yeah, it is," Steven spoke absently into the mouthpiece. Frowning, he looked around the room, wondering where Gerald was.

"Well, I've got to go. I'm going to try and sneak Heather out of here. Most of the guests are gone to the reception to help themselves, but there are a few nosy family members hanging around and, of course, Heather is in no shape to speak with them."

"I won't see you at home later, will I?" Given all that had happened, Steven had the overwhelming need to hold his woman and child close in his arms tonight.

"I don't think so, but I'll call you later. Gotta go."

"Nachelle!" Steven yelled into the phone.

"Yes, honey. Make it quick." He could hear her restless movements and knew she was in a hurry to get back to Heather.

"I love you . . . very much."

A moment of silence passed. In an emotion-filled voice, she whispered, "I love you, too, honey. I'll see you soon."

They hung up, miles apart but close in each other's hearts.

Steven walked to the doorless entrance and almost collided with Gerald.

Gerald had a garbage bag in his hand. "Excuse me," he mumbled as he proceeded to peel the pressed opening apart and shake air into the bag. Circling the room, he picked up every picture of Heather and dumped it in.

Steven stared at him with his mouth open. "What are you doing?"

"Cleaning house. She's made it clear she doesn't want me, so I'm reciprocating." Gerald spoke boldly, a guise for his hurt feelings. "Trash. Trash. Trash." With each word, he threw framed pictures in the garbage bag. "That's all it was. Our relationship. Trash, disposable trash. This is what it amounts to."

Steven watched with stupefied wonder as Gerald circled the huge room. He picked up and discarded pictures that sat on bookshelves, the entertainment center, the top of the Bose speakers, the coffee and end tables, the ledge of the windows, practically everywhere there was a flat surface. When he reached the picture of the four of them, he threw it to Steven with a cryptic, "Here, give this to Nachelle. Tell her it's for her memory book of the wedding that never happened."

When his chore was complete, Gerald sat down hard on the sofa and placed his head in his hands. He stared at the garbage bag at his feet. The short burst of anger had taken him only so far. He hung his head and wept.

Steven was saved the problem of having to say or do something to comfort Gerald because his mother and sisters, all three of them, walked in and immediately huddled around him.

Linda, Gerald's youngest sister and the one who lived with Gerald in his luxurious house, dismissed Steven.

"Thanks, Steven. We can take it from here."

Two

"Wake up, sleepyhead. Here's breakfast." Nachelle used her knee to nudge the mattress. Bending from the waist, she slowly lowered the natural wood breakfast tray with the white ceramic tile facing to one side of Heather's bed. With her hands free, she was able to reach over and shake Heather's shoulder. When Heather only moaned softly, Nachelle shook harder and pulled the pillow off her head, throwing it to the floor.

"Aauugh," Heather moaned. "I don't want to get up," she mumbled as she blindly searched for the missing pillow. The rich smell of coffee and raisin nut toast hit her, and she changed her mind. She slowly opened her eyes and rolled over simultaneously. Frowning, she sat up against the headboard and accepted a full cup from Nachelle. "Thank you." She closed her sleep-heavy, hazel-colored eyes and dropped her head back, savoring the taste she had grown to rely on.

Nachelle moved off the bed toward the wall of windows, which looked out onto the two-lane street below and that allowed a person to view the outline of downtown Fort Worth. Looping the silk panels around tiebacks, she allowed the morning sunshine in. As Heather sipped her first cup of the morning coffee, Nachelle surveyed the surrounding neighborhood. She had grown to enjoy this neighborhood, which was a far different feeling than her initial response eight years ago when Heather had first moved in.

Back then, when Heather had first mentioned her new address, both Marilyn and Nachelle had been appalled. They had tried to change Heather's mind about the location. Not only was the building dilapidated, but Heather's neighbors would be derelicts and homeless people. Indeed, the entire neighborhood had been abandoned by the shipping and trucking companies who had elected to move to newer industrial areas. Their appeal to Heather to seek safer accommodations had fallen on deaf ears. Heather had been determined to make this her home. It had taken her years and plenty of money—hers and her mother's—to make the two-story, gray brick building safe, habitable, and warm, but she had done it. She had designed the second floor into her living quarters, consisting of a living area, two bedrooms, three bathrooms, a kitchen, dining room, and patio balcony. The bottom floor held her office, a conference room, and a theater, complete with lobby, backstage, and concession area.

A year or two after Heather had moved in, other African-American artists had started buying the surrounding buildings in a four-by-four-block radius. The abandoned warehouses started turning into places of commerce, and for some, housing. Today, this community was a haven for the artsy crowd. But, it was also known for its unique art, talent, and cafés.

Pushing open one of the windows, Nachelle leaned forward to take a big sniff of the aromatic smells coming from Ali and Malcolm's Art Café. The two brothers owned the combination art gallery and café on the corner, a half block from Heather's. Ali was setting out patio furniture in preparation for the Sunday morning brunch crowd. No doubt Malcolm was in the kitchen, along with their mother, preparing the wonderful Caribbean dishes they would serve to their hungry guests. The food was good enough to bring people from as far away as I-20 to the south and Weatherford to the west. It helped that the café had live jazz and gospel music, as well.

The stopping of a forest-green Nissan Pathfinder at the traffic light caught Nachelle's eyes. She squinted, trying to see past the light tint to make out the form. Could it be Gerald on his way to speak with Heather? The light changed, and the truck turned away from Heather's building. Nachelle let out a disappointed breath. Someone with a truck like Gerald's had her hoping and wishing for a speedy reconciliation for the lovers.

Sighing, she turned away from the window and moved back toward the bed. Deciding to take the sunshine, after the overcast gloomy day yesterday, as a sign of hope for Gerald and Heather's relationship, Nachelle gingerly sat on the bed and helped herself to another cup of the vanilla nut coffee.

Heather opened her eyes when she felt the bed shift. She had been so deep in thought, she had forgotten Nachelle was with her. "Thank you for everything, Nachelle. You're a dear friend." Heather didn't try to hide her depression from Nachelle.

Nachelle covered one of Heather's hands. "Don't be silly. That's what friends are for. Besides, you've been there for me countless times. Remember the split-up with Harlan, his drug addiction and subsequent death, and Steven's betrayal before we got married?"

"Oh, please, I'm not keeping score." Heather managed a slight smile. It didn't last long. She leaned her head against the headboard and realized she felt drained, tired, and achy all over. She didn't think she had another tear left in her, but every time she pictured Gerald's stricken and broken face, she grew tense and emotional all over again. "I really didn't mean to keep you all night. Steven's probably ready to strangle me."

Nachelle offered a wry smile. "Don't worry about Mr. DuCloux. I called him after you fell asleep, and he insisted I needed a change of clothes and some toiletries. I'm sure he just wanted to see for himself that we were both okay. Anyway, he came by around three this morning."

Heather sat up straight, remembering Steven had driven Gerald home from the church yesterday. Anxiously, she asked, "Did he say anything about Gerald? What did Gerald say when he drove him home? How's Gerald doing?"

Nachelle drained her cup to gather some time to think about how she would edit the conversation she'd had with her husband late last night—or rather, early this morning. Steven had informed her that Gerald had washed his hands of Heather. He told her about Gerald's miserable state and about him throwing away Heather's pictures. Nachelle's heart had sunk low in her chest upon hearing Steven's story. She was at a loss as to how to help her friends get it together.

Heather continued with her questions, prohibiting any type of response from Nachelle. "Has Gerald called? Please don't tell me I slept through Gerald's phone call."

"No, you didn't. The only person who has called is your mother." Nachelle decided there was no time like the present to figure out where her friend's head was so they could work out a game plan. Seriously, softly, she asked, "Do you really expect him to?"

"Of course," Heather replied indignantly. "He loves me." She adjusted the T-shirt she used as a sleeper and picked up the clock to check the time. "Surely he's awake by now."

"Probably—but, Heather, again, do you honestly expect him to call?"

Heather looked Nachelle squarely in the face, picking up on her meaning. Even though uncertainty clouded her eyes, Heather replied positively, "Yes, I do. Gerald loves me."

"No doubt about that. I don't know too many men who are willing to give a woman their name and access to their fortune unless they love them." Scooting closer to her friend, Nachelle pierced Heather with a direct stare. "Heather, I know things are muddled right now. I know you made a difficult decision yesterday, and I know it must have been tough on you to have to tell Gerald. But, have you given any thought to how Gerald must be feeling at this point? Have you considered what's going through his mind?"

"I know, Nachelle, I know. That's why I need to talk to him. I just want to reiterate that I still love him. That hasn't changed." Heather spoke beseechingly.

Nachelle took her friend's hand in hers. "I understand, Heather, but have you considered how embarrassed Gerald must be? He had his teammates there, his family and friends from Atlanta. He must feel humiliated and angry and hurt. Given that, do you really think he's going to call you again?"

Heather thought about the picture Nachelle painted, and fear entered her heart. Was it possible she had turned Gerald against her forever? Was it possible he would never speak to her again? She shook her head to rid herself of the negative feeling settling in the depths of her heart. Keeping a courageous, hopeful front, she replied, "Gerald has to know nothing's changed between us, except that I need more time."

"You told me last night he said it was over. What if he's serious about ending your relationship? What if he's truly made up his mind that it's over? In that case, he wouldn't wait for you. He wouldn't care about the time you need."

"I'll straighten all that out with him when I speak to him." Heather was determined to keep a happy face. She would not let Nachelle scare her into thinking Gerald meant what he had said last night. "I'll send a formal apology to everyone who attended, if he wants me to. I'll even pay for everyone's expenses. I just need more time."

"Heather, you can't fix everything with money. You can't fix a broken heart with money. You can't wipe out pain with money, and you certainly can't re-win someone's trust with a big bankroll."

Heather was silent. With eyes downcast, tracing the pyramid patterns in her sheets, she tried to digest Nachelle's words. She didn't want to hear what Nachelle was saying. It was poison to the nice, neat plan she had developed for her and Gerald. A plan that involved keeping their relationship the way it had been the last couple of years—and then, after she'd been through some counseling for this fear of marriage that paralyzed her, getting married.

"You keep saying you need more time. Why? Why do you need another twelve months? What will make you ready a year from now? What if a year's not enough? What then?" Nachelle blew out a heavy breath. "Heather, please, I'm not trying to confuse you. I just want you and Gerald to be as happy as me and Steven. Making a lifelong commitment is a challenge, but it's also one of the most rewarding things I've ever done."

Wanting to share her fear with Nachelle but unable to verbalize it, Heather lowered her head into her hand and spoke sadly. "It's very complicated, Nachelle. I just don't want to marry right now. I need some time to straighten a few things out."

"What things?" Nachelle lost her patience. She stood and paced the airy room, gesticulating wildly. "What could possibly be so important that it would make you hurt someone you love?"

Heather opened her mouth to blurt out the truth. That she was afraid of marriage, that she didn't want to marry Gerald because she loved him too much, that if she married him, she would kill their love. She conjured a mental picture of them after two years of marriage, and she visualized them splitting up. And, then, like her mother, she would be on to the next man and the next and the next. She couldn't conceive of a life without Gerald. He was everything to her and as long as they kept their relationship the way it was, she could rest comfortably knowing everything would be all right. But to marry and wonder when the breakup would occur was a hurtful situation she dare not attempt. *Gerald is a patient man,* Heather told herself. *He'll wait for me. Right now he's angry with me, but he never stays mad at me for long because he loves me.*

Heather closed her mouth, swallowed the truth, and replied, "Nachelle, I don't want to talk about it right now. I just want to talk to Gerald."

Nachelle returned to the bed and stood over Heather with her hands on her hips. "Whatever it is that's got you spooked, that's preventing you from enjoying the happy ever after, you'd better clear it up and quick. Gerald is a wonderful man who deserves better than how you treated him yesterday." Nachelle picked up the dirty dishes they'd left scattered on the bed and placed the cups and saucers on the tray. "I'm sorry if that hurt your feelings—but, Heather, you need to face whatever's holding you back and defeat it, or you'll never know true happiness. You're right to be honest with Gerald, but he deserves to be happy. *You* deserve to be happy. Think about that." Nachelle thought about

Gerald collecting and trashing the pictures of Heather. To put a spur under Heather's saddle and get her moving, she wondered if she should tell Heather that Gerald's patience was used up. That she was out of time for happiness if she didn't do something real quick.

As Nachelle opened her mouth to speak what she knew, the phone rang. Both women stared at the phone as if it were an intruder. After the first ring, Heather actually put a hand out to answer it, then withdrew her hand, motioning for Nachelle to answer for her.

Nachelle put down the breakfast tray and walked around to Heather's side of the bed. "Hello." A second passed. "Good morning, Mrs. Wolfe."

Heather shook her head vigorously. She was in no mood to take any more of her mother's harsh words or tears. She, herself was just beginning to unwind, to shake the tenseness that had been with her since yesterday. She didn't want or need her mother's drama.

Taking Heather's cue, Nachelle lied, "She's not available. I can have her call you back." A moment passed while Nachelle nodded her head. "I promise I will give her both of your messages." Nachelle paused, listening to Marilyn Wolfe talk. "I don't know if she'll call you back before you leave for church. All I can do is give her your messages." The natural wood, cathedral-shaped clock sitting on the bedside table ticked off the seconds as Nachelle listened to Mrs. Wolfe on the other end of the line. "I see. Well, I'll be sure to tell her that you'll be by after church to see her. Yes, ma'am. Goodbye."

Heather almost groaned out loud. She rolled her head back against the headboard and closed her eyes. At some point today, she knew she was going to face her mother again, and she was not looking forward to it.

"Well, young lady, I guess you heard that," Nachelle warned, using a schoolmarm voice. She smiled, looking at Heather's comically distorted face. "It's not nice to make faces at your mother."

"Yeah, well, it's not nice for mothers to harass their daughters," Heather retorted.

Nachelle laughed. "That's what you get for being an only child."

"I didn't have a thing to do with that," Heather protested. Picking up the handset, she hit the speed dial for Gerald's number. As a testament to the close-knit circle of people she loved and trusted, Heather had only seven numbers programmed into her speed dial for three people: three numbers for Gerald, home, work, and car; two for Nachelle, home and work; and two for Steven and Nachelle's second home and office in Atlanta. In her eyes, no one else was worth loading into her speed dial capability.

Linda Forrester, Gerald's kid sister and another "star" in the family, a guard for the WNBA, answered on the second ring.

"Hello, Linda. I need to speak with Gerald." She was desperate to hear his voice, and that desperation reflected in her own voice.

"Well, he doesn't want to speak to you ever again." Linda slammed down the phone with such force, Heather had to shake her head to clear the ringing.

Shocked at such a vehement response, Heather stared at the phone as if it had disconnected on its own. Her anger flared, and she quickly redialed. "Linda, put Gerald on the phone. Let him speak for himself."

"Gerald isn't here, and even if he was, neither I nor Mama nor Donna or Theresa—none of us—would let you speak with him after what you did to him, you little spoiled rich girl. How . . . ? Who do you think you are to treat my brother like that? He loved you, and you treated him like last week's trash."

Weary and close to tears, Heather put her head in

her hand. "Linda, you don't understand. I'm not going to discuss mine and Gerald's business with you." She sighed. "Please, *please*, tell me the truth. Is Gerald there? If he is, please put him on the phone."

"I told you," Linda said in an ice-cold voice, "he's not here, and he left explicit instructions that if you called to tell you he doesn't want to speak to you."

"I don't believe you. Gerald would never say anything like that," Heather obstinately replied. "Not about me, anyway."

"Oh, wake up and join the rest of us in Realityland, Heather! You hurt him deeply—and now you expect to talk to him? Get a grip and make a note of this. He's through with you. No more stringing him along, no more dogging my brother out, no more nothing. It's over!" Linda spoke with the force of a bulldozer.

"Linda, put Gerald on the phone," Heather demanded.

"Don't call back here again." The dial tone signaled the line had been disconnected . . . again.

Anger guided Heather out of bed. She untangled the raw silk sheets and comforter from around her body and descended the two steps to the main floor of her bedroom.

Nachelle stared at her openmouthed. "Heather! What did Linda say?" Trailing behind Heather, Nachelle was worried and concerned. She could detect the heightened brightness in Heather's eyes, telling her that her friend was on the verge of tears.

"Who do I think I am, indeed?" Heather flung open her mirrored walk-in closet doors and stormed to a built-in chest of drawers. Pulling open a drawer with pastel and solid-color undergarments, she yanked out a pair of undies and a matching bra. "She's fixin' to find out just who I am."

Even with all the money she had at her disposal due

to her biological father's accidental death when Heather was two, and her mother's uncanny ability to marry men with more and more money, Heather had a meager wardrobe consisting of jeans, silk and cotton sweat suits, cotton shirts, and linen dresses and suits for social and professional occasions. If she had to dress up in after-five attire, as Gerald's profession occasionally called for, she always went to Nachelle's closet. Even though the fancy evening dresses were a size eight and Heather was a six, she always managed to make them work.

"I can't believe she had the audacity to hang up on me!" Heather stormed into her adjoining bathroom and without letting the water level out, stuck her toothbrush under the flow. Talking around the paste and brush, she spoke in muffled phrases: "Can you believe she . . . had the nerve to tell me . . . Gerald doesn't want to speak to me anymore? That she thinks . . . I dogged her brother out. I love Gerald—I would never do that."

Nachelle screwed up her face. Sometimes she wondered about her friend. Heather worked with puppets eight to ten hours a day and concerned herself with the cares of little people. Cares that involved no broken hearts or broken commitments or facing adult fears, but cares like learning to share and obey and learning the ABC's and 1-2-3's. She worked in a fairy-tale land, and sometimes she didn't come out of fairy-tale land. She honestly didn't understand that she had indeed humiliated Gerald in front of five hundred people. She actually believed that because they were in love, everything would be okay, and things would return to status quo. Nachelle didn't know what to do but speak the truth.

"Heather, you did do Gerald wrong," Nachelle said softly, trying to balance Heather's anger with reason.

Heather stopped brushing and gave Nachelle a bland look. "I admit my timing is bad. I should have stood up to Gerald and Mother and told them I didn't want to get married, but I—"

"Heather, you hurt Gerald, plain and simple. Steven told me Gerald threw away all the pictures of you in his house. Gerald told Steven he never wanted to see you again."

Heather's light eyes got round and large. "That can't be. I . . ." Bending low, she quickly spat out the paste and rinsed her mouth. "Gerald would never say that. He loves me. He just needs time to cool off."

"I don't know, Heather. You certainly know Gerald better than me, but just how long do you think he'll allow himself to be strung along? How many wedding delays do you think he's going to tolerate? He's not going to let you play him too many more times."

"I love Gerald!"

Nachelle sighed. "Sometimes love isn't enough. Especially when that person who claims they love you disappoints you time and time again. Eventually, love is replaced with anger or hate or worse, indifference. Believe me, Heather, I know. Remember the ordeal I went through with Harlan. All the lying, the half-truths, the two-facedness. It eventually turned my love to cold indifference. If you're not careful with Gerald, he could turn his back to you. After you accepted his engagement ring, you put him off for months before selecting a wedding date—and then on the day of the wedding, you tell him you changed your mind. That's not good, Heather."

Indignantly, Heather remarked, "Thanks for taking their—his—side. It's good to know my very best friend doesn't even support me."

"Don't even try it, Heather. You know I love and care for you, but you need to hear the truth." Nachelle walked to Heather and put an arm around her shoulder. "All I'm saying is be more cognizant of Gerald's feelings." Nachelle kissed her on the cheek and turned to leave. "I'm going to put the breakfast stuff away. Do you want to go over to Ali's for a real meal? You know, I *am* eating for two."

Staring at her reflection in the mirror, Heather didn't respond immediately. She focused on Nachelle's words and Linda's strong actions. *Could they be right? Am I the one that's out of step? If so, that's all the more reason to help Gerald understand my position.*

"Heather . . . ?"

"Did you say Gerald threw away my pictures?"

"Yes. Steven was there when he did it."

Heather looked away from Nachelle to stare into the half-dollar-sized hole in her sink. Her home was a mixture of old and new, and in the bathroom she had elected to have an old washbasin, complete with rubber stopper on a silver chain and white ceramic hot and cold handles. As she stared down the blackness of the drain, she wondered if she had indeed flushed her relationship with Gerald down a hole. Had she dealt him a blow that would forever shatter their happiness? She admitted she had taken it for granted that he would rebound from this as he'd done from previous fiascoes—on and off the court. Now, she wasn't as sure. For the first time since Gerald left her yesterday, she wondered if she would ever see him again.

Turning back to a waiting Nachelle, Heather shook her head. The anger she'd felt earlier, after Linda's call, had evaporated and was replaced with fear. It was that emotion which drove her to speak and act quickly. "No, no. I'll pass on lunch. I'm going over to Gerald's house."

Without another word, Nachelle left to clean up the breakfast mess, and Heather stripped and stepped into the glass-encased shower stall. As the water cascaded in rivulets down her naked body, her head swirled with all the information Nachelle had told her. Did she really stand a chance of losing Gerald? *Have I really screwed up this time?* she thought. *I know I've pulled some stupid things in the past, but Gerald's always forgiven me. I've just gotta get to him and talk to him. And, then, no more delaying. I'm going to start counseling. Oh, what's the name of that black female therapist I met at one of the elementary schools? Yolandia something.* She hastily decided to check for Yolandia's business card downstairs in her office on the way out. That way she could prove to Gerald she would be ready in a year. The more she thought about her hastily constructed plan to convince Gerald to give her another chance, the more her need to see and speak to him increased. Throwing herself into manual overdrive, she quickly finished her shower, and donned a pair of heavily starched jeans, a simple white T-shirt, and multi colored espadrilles.

Heather sped through the bedroom, oblivious to the bright sunshine and light morning breeze that billowed her beige curtains and made the ethnically designed room—done in shades of brown, black, and white— brighter. In the living room, she spied her wallet on the low, cream-colored marble coffee table. Descending the two shallow steps in one bound, she snatched it up and hurriedly looked through it for cash and identification, a habit she'd picked up from Nachelle after being stranded late one evening with no cash, no credit cards, no change, and no gas. Here, in the living room, as in the bedroom, a wall of windows looked out over the now-awake neighborhood. Even though her head was elsewhere, and she was in a rush, Heather automatically rocked in time with the jazz notes floating up from the street and through her open windows.

Ordinarily, this was her favorite time on a Sunday

morning, during one of her favorite months of the year—April. Ordinarily, she would have taken the time to sit on the couch with a cup of coffee and listen to the world downstairs come alive.

Even though a mightier goal awaited her, she couldn't resist one quick peek out of the window. Heather smiled as she noticed Ali and Malcolm, both artists in different mediums, treating their guests as if they were family. Although they had a handful of customers now, within the next thirty minutes, a conglomeration of artist-types, buppies, and liberal white folk would be crowded in there to look at the latest art by the talented brothers and to get a hearty Southern breakfast or Caribbean lunch dish at a reasonable price. A wave of nostalgia overwhelmed her as she thought about the past Sundays when she and Gerald would order breakfast, playfully argue about who would pick it up, and then eat lazily at the windows, enjoying the meal and the music without the hustle and bustle of actually being part of the crowd. A shuddering sigh escaped her body, and she turned from the scene below before the threatening tears flowed.

Skirting the camel-colored sofa piled high with huge African print cushions and pillows, she snatched her keys off the matching marble sofa table. Again, she took the two steps leading to the landing and the yellow and burgundy kitchen in one step. Noticing Nachelle was not in there, she went to the right toward the guest bedroom.

"Nachelle. Nachelle, I'm gone," she called out.

Heather walked into the bedroom and saw Nachelle's open garment bag lying on the queen-sized bed. The steam from the bathroom alerted her to Nachelle's whereabouts. Walking to the open door of the guest bathroom, she poked her head in, waving the steam aside. "Nachelle, I'm leaving. I'm gone to Dallas to see Gerald."

"Okay," Nachelle shouted from the shower stall. "I'm going home, but I'll be there all afternoon—so call me when you get back or if you need me to pick you up, okay?"

"Will do."

Heather shut the heavy wooden door to her private living quarters and locked the two locks. She had several employees who had keys to all of the locks downstairs, but for her private living rooms, she, Nachelle, and Gerald were the only ones who had keys. Running down the two flights of stairs to the first floor, she made a sharp right and entered her office. After rummaging about for several minutes, mumbling the entire time about getting organized, she finally stumbled upon the business card she'd thought about upstairs. Pocketing it, she headed for the garage and within minutes was headed east toward Dallas. In her candy-apple-red Porsche, she would be there in no time.

Three

Gerald listened patiently as his baby sister succinctly told him of her conversations with Heather. He felt like a two-faced liar. It was true he didn't want to see or speak with her, yet he couldn't suppress the thrill that shuddered throughout his body, knowing she had called. He looked affectionately at Linda, the youngest of his mother's four children, and could have hugged her for being so protective of him, but he was a grown man and needed to deal with this on his own.

"What did she say after you told her I wanted no contact with her?" Gerald was fatigued. He'd been up most of the night, trying to come to grips with the truck that had run over and flattened his world. The sun was beginning its ascent by the time his wrecked mind had quit agonizing over the final scene between he and Heather. His troubled mind had allowed him to garner a few hours of sleep before waking him again to the reality that he was a single man. Now, he felt like an empty seashell, devoid of the desire to eat, think, feel, to *be*. He was a mannequin with living flesh, all thanks to Heather . . . and his own stupid belief in love.

Sighing, he set the grocery sacks on the kitchen counter. The entire Forrester family had return flights to Atlanta late that morning, but he knew his mother wouldn't let any of them leave without a full breakfast in their stomachs. So, instead of lying in the bed thinking about his bleak future, he'd gotten dressed and headed to the grocery store.

"She said she didn't believe me, that you would never say anything like that. I told her she was tripping. I told her she had hurt you enough, and she wouldn't get a second chance." Linda paused and following Gerald's lead, pulled out a chair and sat down at the kitchen table. "You won't like this part, but I called her a name."

Gerald's eyes got big, and he lowered his head into his hands. "Oh, Linda." Gerald shook his head. As children and young adults, Mrs. Forrester had tanned their hides good if she heard them cussing. She had extracted that bad habit out of them early and considering that, Gerald imagined Linda hadn't used any sailor terms. But knowing how direct Linda could be, he had no doubt she had gotten her point across.

Smiling, he walked around the table to massage his sister's shoulders. "Linda, Linda, Linda. You're a mess, but I love you, kiddo." He kissed the top of her head. "But, please, don't call the woman I love any more names, okay?" Gerald paused. "So, that was it?"

"Yeah, it doesn't take long for me to get someone straight."

Gerald had his back to her, unloading the grocery sacks, but he whipped around at her words. They shared a secret smile, both remembering a scene from their childhood.

As the two youngest kids in the Forrester family, they shared a relationship so close and special that they had gotten to the point where they could almost read each other's minds and finish each other's sentences. The discovery that they both had a natural gift and talent for basketball had added Super Glue to their already tight relationship. Many an evening, while their mother was at work from three to eleven as a nurse at the VA hospital, Donna and Theresa would prepare dinner while Gerald and Linda would be outside playing hoops.

One particular evening as they practiced jump shots and free throws, Suzanne, a pretty girl in Gerald's junior high class and his then-girlfriend, stopped at their driveway to cheer Gerald on. Soon, Gerald started showing out and pointwise, was beating the pants off Linda. Suzanne, feeling sorry for Linda, started rooting for her. Linda had immediately turned to her and in a very direct, rude manner, had told the girl if she was her brother's girlfriend she had better support him in everything—and that meant not rooting for the other team, no matter what. Before Linda was through "schooling" Suzanne, the girl had run home crying.

As the years progressed, there had been other times when Linda had to set some girl straight, and Gerald had to beat up some boy on behalf of his sister. They protected each other and watched each other's backs.

The chiming of the doorbell interrupted their brother-sister remembrances. Linda rose to get the front door. "Who could be visiting so early? Don't they know it's Sunday? They ought to be at somebody's church." She mumbled all the way down the hallway to the front door. She could barely make out the figure through the stained glass door, but she could see it was a very short figure, and her feet stalled. "I'll be damned!" she whispered, hoping her mother was still upstairs showering and dressing so she couldn't hear her cuss on the Sabbath.

Linda yanked open the door and scowled at Heather. "You're a hardheaded little something, ain't you?"

Heather attempted to brush past Linda, but the other stronger and taller woman stopped her. As a paid professional athlete, Linda made it a point to stay in shape, which meant she was firm and solid. With her superior height of six-feet-one, she dwarfed Heather's petite figure.

Heather should have been intimidated, but she was on a mission. "Is Gerald upstairs? I know he's here because his Pathfinder's parked in the driveway." She made another move to slip past Linda.

Linda wasn't having it. She threw out an arm and blocked Heather's movement. "I don't wanna have to kick your butt this morning."

Feisty Heather didn't miss a beat. "And I don't wanna have to scratch your eyes out. Now, get outta my way." She may not have grown up in the tough environment Gerald and Linda had, but she was no marshmallow.

"Linda." Gerald's voice from down the hallway interrupted their standoff. "I'll handle it."

Throwing a disappointed glance at Gerald, Linda turned back around to Heather and whispered under her breath, "You're lucky."

But Heather was no longer focused on Linda. Her eyes drank in the sight of Gerald. He had bags under his eyes, but other than that, he looked the same. His smooth, sable-brown complexion glistened in the morning light, and his Mavericks team sweat suit silhouetted his tall, lean figure. Like most of the guys in the NBA, he wore an almost bald haircut, and his defined features—thick dark eyebrows, full lips, strong square chin, chiseled cheekbones, and deep-set Hershey's-Kiss eyes—made a lie of his age. Although he was thirty-five years old, he looked to be in his twenties. Just looking at him made her long to be in his arms, stroking each other and telling each other that everything would be okay.

"Linda, I got it." Gerald put his hands on Linda's shoulders and steered her away from the door.

Gerald stared at Heather, trying to disguise the love

he had for her. But it was no good; it showed in his eyes. He was an open, honest man with not a deceptive bone in his body. He couldn't lie to her about his love, but he wasn't open to anything she had to offer.

"I called this morning." Heather swallowed hard. "I need to speak to you, please, Gerald." Heather put a hand on his arm. "I have to speak to you."

"Let's go outside," Gerald offered gruffly. He stepped around Heather, being careful not to touch her, for he knew if he did, he would be lost. For this discussion, he needed to keep a straight head.

Stepping onto the wooden porch, Gerald headed for the small grouping of furniture in one corner of the large porch. The floor was painted forest green to match the trim and shutters. It was a nice contrast to the white railing, which ran in an L around the front of the house. The porch furniture, two white wooden rockers and a small patio table, had been found in the attic. Mrs. Forrester had painstakingly repaired and repainted the chairs and had then arranged the grouping. On the other end of the porch, she had hung a swinging bench for lovers. When he could steal a moment, Gerald loved to sit in one of the rockers with the setting sun as his backdrop. He used those precious moments to focus on his goals and life after basketball. After this discussion with Heather, he wasn't sure if the rockers or the porch would ever bring him peace again.

Gerald selected one of the patio chairs and turned it so it faced not the other chair but rather the front yard and the serene street beyond.

Heather took the other chair. "Gerald, first let me say I'm sorry about yesterday. I realize I was wrong for treating you so poorly. I apologize for treating your feelings so casually. Please forgive me."

"I forgive you, Heather, but I meant what I said." He wanted so desperately to look at her beautiful face, but to do so would court disaster. He recognized he was still weak with love for her.

Heather was silent for several seconds, trying to figure out where to go from here. On the drive over, she had played out countless scenarios in her mind, but now the words weren't flowing. *Maybe if I consider this a scene in one of my productions, I can say the right words to get him to open to me.* Visualizing them as characters in one of her plays, she continued. "You have a right to be mad at and disappointed with me. I'm disappointed in myself as well. I should have been honest with you months ago about not wanting to get married."

Gerald remained silent, staring at his hands clasped in front of him between his powerful, lean thighs. His back was as straight as an ironing board.

"I do want to make you happy, Gerald. I do love you. But I realize I can't come to you incomplete. I want our marriage to be solid for years and years to come."

Still no response from Gerald. He focused on trying to maintain some degree of frigidity. He didn't want to give in to his emotions. He needed to make the best decision for him, and to do that he needed to shelve his feelings.

"Why did you accept my ring if you weren't ready for marriage?" Gerald asked in a hurt-filled tone of voice.

"Because I love you. That's why I accepted your ring. Because you make me happy."

Gerald tilted his head toward her. His handsome face was screwed up in confusion. His eyes showed her just how deeply he was hurting. "How can you love someone and hurt them so deeply? What is your definition of love? Maybe that's the problem. Maybe we're operating off two different definitions of the word 'love.' "

Heather shook her head no. Falling to the floor on one knee, she laid her hands on top of his. "No, Gerald, no. That's not true. We share the same idea of love. I

LOVE EVERLASTING 51

love you, and I know you love me. I can see it in your eyes." She moved her hand to cup his cheek. He leaned back as if she held poison ivy in her hand.

At that moment, unable to stand her closeness, unable to smell her feminine scent, which was so uniquely Heather, he grew angry at her for hurting him. He felt the need to strike out verbally at her. With a hard set to his face, he spoke with ice in his voice. "You're right, Heather. I do love you. And I was ready to prove it yesterday. You hurt me, Heather. You embarrassed me in front of my family and friends. You selfishly thought of only yourself. Now, I've made up my mind to think of Gerald. And I've decided it's over. There's nothing you can say or do to change my mind." Gerald stood up to erase the smell and feel of her. "I don't ever want to see you again. It's over. We're through."

Heather stood and took steps toward him. The look he gave her stopped her from progressing. "Gerald, I had hoped that once you cooled down, you would change your mind about splitting up. I don't want that."

"Well, we don't always get what we want, now, do we?" Gerald spat the words out. He paused and stared at her bowed head. "Good luck on fixing the things that kept us apart. I wish you success."

If nothing else, Marilyn had taught Heather to go after what she wanted. She appealed to Gerald's love. "Gerald, can we at least take it slow? You said you forgive me, so let's just back it up and start over again. All I'm asking for is a little more time. Surely you can grant our love that much, right?"

When he shook his head negatively, Heather felt her heart fall to the floor.

"You said you love me and I love you. I don't understand your reluctance, your desire to turn your back on me, on us," Heather cried out. The tears brimmed her lids and spilled over, down her cheeks.

"Because a guy can take only so much rejection, Heather. You've hurt me for the last time." Gerald's anger evaporated as quickly as it had formed. Sadness engulfed him.

"When have I hurt you before? What are you talking about?"

"Oh, so you don't remember my catching you out with what's-his-face right after we had decided to date exclusively? You don't remember my seeing . . . um . . . um . . ." Gerald struggled, trying to remember the names. Snapping his fingers, he remembered. "Carl's car at your place after midnight? And for months after we got engaged, you sidestepped the issue of setting a date for the wedding. Didn't you realize what a terrible position that put me in, having to try and explain to family and friends that 'Yeah, we're engaged but we haven't set a date yet.' Do you realize how shattering that was to me?"

Taking another step toward Gerald, Heather held out her hands. "I explained those things to you. I told you I was out with Michael only to explain I could no longer see him, that I had decided to make a commitment to you. That night was our last night out together. And, Carl, yes, he was over after midnight and, yes, we were together, but he was helping me with the lighting and audio for the big production that weekend. There was nothing sexual going on. It was work! And if you had taken the time to come in instead of zooming off, you would have seen it for yourself." Heather was breathing hard. She wanted to make sure she got her point across. Her happiness depended on him understanding. "As for the delay in setting the date for the wedding, I was waiting to hear about my school contract. I didn't know what my schedule was going to be. Hell, Gerald, you know how long it took for them to get me a final schedule of performances. You were at my place when it came in the mail."

"Yeah, I've heard all this before, and again I'm telling you that if you really cared, if you really loved me, you would have handled each one of those situations differently. You would have thought about the impact on our relationship." Gerald ran a hand over his near-bald head and took a deep breath. In a softer, more gentle tone, he repeated his decision. "No, Heather. It's over. I'm taking my heart to the shop to get it repaired, and when it's whole again I'm keeping it under Fort Knox security. Thanks for the valuable lesson in life and love."

Gerald walked to the door. His heart was as heavy as his footsteps. With his hand on the door, he turned his head to speak over his shoulder. "Linda was right. I don't want to see you again. Don't call me. Don't try to see me. Don't come to any more games. Wipe my name out of your vocabulary. It's over."

"Gerald, you can't mean that!" Heather ran to him but stopped when Gerald turned a hate-filled face to her.

He held out a detaining arm and pointed a finger in her face. "I do, and I'm dead serious." Gerald opened the door and shut it before he witnessed another tear roll down her cheek, or before he ran to her. Putting the lock on the front door, he simultaneously locked his heart. With tears in his eyes, he ran up the stairs to his room. He closed and locked that door as well.

On the front porch, Heather stood still, staring at the door, not believing that Gerald had left her . . . for good. That look on his face made it clear he didn't want anything to do with her ever again. The hot scalding tears came faster and heavier, blurring her vision. That look of hatred was engraved in her heart and mind. Had she really been the one responsible for turning such a fun-loving, peaceful, patient, and kind man into a man who could throw such an evil look at her. *God, what have I done?* Heather questioned herself. For him to turn his back to her permanently meant she had really hurt Gerald. The thought made her sick. Angry with herself for being too afraid to trust him with her fears, she fished in her pants pocket for the therapist's card. Sadness washed over her as she stared at the plain white card.

Looking up at Gerald's bedroom window, Heather wiped her eyes. "I'm sorry, Gerald. I really am. I promise I'll make it up to you. I will."

Stuffing the card back in her pants pocket, she walked down the front walkway toward her car. "I'm not giving up on us," she whispered to herself. Turning to speak to his bedroom window, she spoke as loud as she could. "I'm not giving up on us, Gerald. I love you. I'll be a better woman the next time we talk."

Heather gunned her sports car and made a quick U-turn at the dead end of the street. She stared at Gerald's house as she zoomed by it and although she couldn't be sure, she thought she saw the drapes in Gerald's room part as she drove on. She wasn't a block from his house when she pulled over. Tears rising from the bottom of her heart blocked her vision.

Four

Heather carefully, methodically, packed the female puppet named Aretha into the black leather carrying case that she had specially designed for her lifeless friend. Chris, one of her male employees who was a trained actor and singer, worked next to her, packing the male puppet named Marvin into his private case. Another employee, Vandy, also a trained actor and singer, worked behind them, collecting the props, organizing them and piling them systematically into a box for carrying. The three associates worked quickly, efficiently, with very little dialogue between them. They usually reserved the debriefing aspect of the performance until arrival back at the Twelfth Street Puppet Company, the name of Heather's puppet troupe and, coincidentally, the address of her home and theater.

The three of them—Heather, Chris, and Vandy—had met years ago when they all did a stint of teaching for the FWISD at its high school for the performing arts. When Heather had gotten her business off the ground, almost eight years ago, Chris and Vandy had been thrilled to work for her, developing scripts, acting as the legendary singing puppets, and singing on the cassettes and videos Heather produced. They had been excited to learn that they would be helping to educate children while at the same time entertaining them.

Heather considered them friends as well as business associates and, therefore, she had asked them to sing at her wedding. Although the wedding hadn't happened a little over two weeks ago, Chris and Vandy had been respectful enough not to ask Heather any questions, even though she still wore her engagement ring. They cared for her and felt when the time was right, she would talk to them.

Rising from his kneeling position, Chris spoke in a deep voice. "I think that does it. I'll start moving these things out to the van."

The auditorium of M. M. Walton Elementary School picked up his voice and circulated it throughout the now empty rows of seats. Fifteen minutes earlier, the auditorium had been filled with three classes of thirty children, each ranging in age from four to six years old. The kids had been a great audience, very interactive, very bright, and captivated by the movements and songs the puppets performed. From their perspective, it had been a great show.

"Thanks, Chris. I'm going down front to get the feedback forms. Vandy, would you check around backstage one more time to make sure we got everything?" Heather headed for one of the side steps leading to the main floor of the auditorium. Like most public school auditoriums, the stage was set high off the main floor to allow all in attendance to see clearly. The rows and rows of seats angled upward toward the back where the entrance and exit doors were situated.

As Chris and Vandy scurried off to complete their assignments, Heather went to pick up the evaluation forms the pre-K and kindergarten teachers had completed and left on a chair in the first row. Heather smiled as she riffled through the sheets, eyeing the high marks they had received. A thrill of excitement raced through her body. *Soon I can approach other school districts about offering this same lineup of programs. With these wonderful recommendations, the sky's the limit,* she thought.

"Yes, it was that good." A voice spoke from the depths of the auditorium.

Heather's head popped up, and she eyed the stranger who approached her. As she continued to stare at him, she realized she knew him from somewhere. She just couldn't remember . . . from where. "Thank you." She smiled her professional smile.

"Unfortunately, I'm as bad as the children at times. I forgot to turn in my evaluation. I hope since I caught you before you left, you won't put me in detention." The stranger smiled, showing a mouthful of white, even teeth. In fact, his teeth were so aligned and so translucent that he could have easily been a model for Pepsodent. He was tall, at least six feet, and caramel in skin color. His sharp, defined features were arranged handsomely on his face, and his goatee was perfectly trimmed. Suit, shoes, and shirt were made of high-quality materials, and the suit fit his lean body as if it had been made expressly for him. The jewelry on his finger, wrist, and cuffs sparkled as if it had been recently polished. By any standard, he was extremely good looking and . . . he smelled wonderful. "Even though I wasn't able to stay for the entire performance, I enjoyed the part I saw. I'm very impressed." He held out the evaluation sheet, still smiling with his teeth and his eyes.

Heather's genuine acceptance of his praise made her face light up. Her smile transformed from professional to sincere, making the twinkle in her eyes as bright as a firecracker exploding. "Thank you very much. We want to make sure we're living up to the school's expectations."

"Oh, but you are, Ms. Chadwick! I'm going to make it my business to tell anyone and everyone who asks me that this is one program worth keeping in special curriculum programs and in the budget."

It snapped! This was one of the school district's program administrators for program development. Even though she couldn't remember his name, she remembered his face from the countless meetings she'd had with FWISD administrators when pitching her concept. This man was one of the people responsible for her securing this contract and for her getting it renewed year after year after year. It did her heart good to know he was pleased with their work.

"Thank you very much for that vote of confidence. It means a lot to hear you say that." Heather's voice was full of pep and cheer.

"I mean every word of it." The man smiled deep into Heather's eyes.

Vandy spoke from the back of the stage. "That's it, Hea—" She stopped when she noticed Heather talking to a very suave, very good-looking man. Her single blood propelled her to join them down front on the main floor.

As Vandy advanced on them, Heather said, "This is Vandy Wright. The voice of Aretha, the puppet, and one of the best jazz singers in town. She has opened for great artists like Koko Taylor, Herbie Hancock, Jonathan Butler, and the list goes on. Chances are, if you've ever been to the Caravan of Dreams for the Jazz Explosion, she was one of the featured artists. She has a voice that'll make Whitney Houston sit up and take notice. And personally"—Heather hugged the younger girl around the waist and keeping a hand on the small of her back, smiled at her—"I don't know what I'd do without her."

Vandy returned Heather's smile, then turned to extend a hand to the administrator. "It's nice to meet you, Mr. . . ."

"Patterson. Warren Patterson." They shook hands.

Inwardly, Heather's mind clicked. *Yeah, that's his name. Whew! Thank goodness Vandy showed up. This could have been embarrassing.*

"Mr. Patterson was just saying how much he enjoyed the performance. He's promised to be an advocate for us. Isn't that great!" Heather's enthusiasm was catching, and Vandy caught it—but for not entirely the same reason.

"Oh, wonderful!" Vandy batted her long, inky black lashes at the tall, good-looking man. "Then hopefully we'll see more of you." At the tender age of twenty-nine years old, she truly had made a name for herself in the music industry in the Dallas/Fort Worth metroplex. But she wanted so much more. Her goal was to secure a contract with a national, reputable music company. She wanted lights, fame and fortune, and her every waking thought and nighttime dream was on how to achieve that goal.

Vandy attributed her current success to her extensive vocal range maintained by her adherence to a strict code of ethics: no smoking, no drinking, no drugs, low fat intake, no dairy products, ten glasses of water or more per day, and most importantly, hours and hours of vocal practice daily with her voice instructor. But to reach the level of success she aimed for, she would have to work harder at the business side of the music industry. That side leaned not toward talent but rather focused on looks and who you knew. So, recently, she had begun to work out her size-twelve body as religiously as she worked out her voice. By summer, her goal was to be in a size ten and, by the end of the year, her goal was to be a sexy size six. Vandy knew she'd never be a petite Toni Braxton, but at least as a six she would be able to catch and keep the eyes of a talent scout or a music producer. And since God had already blessed her with provocative features, she need only continue her extensive skin care regimen so that her unblemished, deep chocolate-brown skin would continue to be an asset. Fortunately, her agent and vocal instructor had inroads into some of the record companies and with her current success and determination, it would be only a matter of time before it was her time.

Oh, yes! She was determined to achieve her goal before she reached age thirty—but, of course, every woman climbing the ladder of success needed a play period, and this charming, desirable man would be a good playmate during recess.

Pointing a long manicured finger at both women, the man laughingly replied, "Only if both of you promise to call me Warren."

They all chuckled as the women agreed to his request.

"Warren, it was nice seeing you again. We've got to go now, but hopefully we'll see you again real soon." Heather added his evaluation form to the small stack and held out a hand.

They shook hands, but after the customary two, three, or four pumps, Warren continued to hold her hand. "Oh, you can bet on it." He squeezed her hand lightly and slowly slid his hand away from hers.

Internally, Heather questioned the action. She and Gerald had been together a long time, but not so long that she didn't recognize a flirty action. She looked questioningly at Warren, but seeing only kindly interest in the depths of his brown eyes, she brushed aside her initial thoughts and pegged him as a warm, caring person who was willing to help another person succeed.

Besides, he had shaken the hand on which rested a huge diamond engagement ring, Gerald's pledge of commitment, which Heather refused to take off even though Gerald had rebuffed her calls and her personal visits for the past two weeks. Suddenly, Heather felt weepy and weak for Gerald's attention and love. *Not here, Heather. Not now,* she coached herself. She wouldn't break down in front of her professional colleagues. She wouldn't wallow in the fear and depression that had been her constant companions these past few weeks. She just wouldn't.

Straightening her shoulders in defiance of her pain, she headed for the stairs.

Warren and Vandy walked behind her, talking of mindless piddle. Just as the two women started to climb the stairs leading to the backstage area, Warren's deep voice arrested them.

"Oh, please"—Warren reached in his breast pocket, pulled out a gold business card holder, and he handed them each a card—"take one. Call if you ever run into any trouble with any of the schools."

"Oh, thanks," Heather gushed. Yeah, she'd been reading too much into his actions. He was just a friendly, caring brother.

"No, no. Thank *you.*" Warren spoke to Heather, looking deep into her eyes. "Bye, now." He turned and walked toward the doors at the rear of the auditorium.

As the women exited the school from the back door, laughing and giggling about their new, handsome fairy godfather, Warren Patterson exited the school through the front door, smiling at his creativity and craftiness. His plan, converted from his head to action, would work well after all. Now, the only thing he needed was patience to see his plan through. And that, he recognized, would be the hard part, for he was not normally a patient man.

After unloading the van at the Twelfth Street Puppet Company and placing everything in its proper place, the trio of workers debriefed the earlier performance, then split up to enjoy their weekend. Carl, a dedicated father and husband, headed to his east side home where his wife and two children eagerly awaited his arrival so they could begin whatever weekend adventure was on the calendar. Vandy made a beeline for the gym to meet her personal trainer for a strenuous workout. Heather dashed upstairs to her apartment to throw some clothes and toiletries in an overnight bag and then to the airport to catch a quick forty-five-minute flight to Houston.

Three hours later, she drove a rental car shaped like a box, with no tape cassette or CD player, to the Summit in Houston where the regular season game between the Dallas Mavericks and the Houston Rockets was being played.

It was early, nearly four hours before tip-off, but she knew from experience that the team was already present, either in their locker room, psyching themselves out, or talking to the team doctor, or on the court, autographing pictures and programs for the season ticket holders, or practicing shots.

Her plan, which she'd hatched days ago after a visit with her therapist, Yolandia Parks, was to show up for the game and somehow demand that Gerald speak to her. She would then plead for their love and insist that he give her and their relationship another chance.

As she parked the rental car, she wondered if her plan was reasonable, given the fact that Gerald had refused over the past two weeks to speak with or see her. Still, she was determined. She even had an ace up her sleeve.

It was customary for team members to leave a list of names of family and friends at the box office for complimentary tickets to the game. Knowing this, Heather walked to the box office, confident Gerald had not changed his standing list for tickets. For although he possessed many wonderful qualities, he was not an attention-to-detail man, except on the basketball court. She knew her name was still on his ticket list.

"Hi." She smiled grandly at the high school boy who worked behind the Plexiglas window. "I'm Heather Chadwick. Gerald Forrester left me a ticket for tonight's game."

The young guy slowly closed the *Teen Rap* magazine he'd been reading and, frowning, glanced up at her. "What?" he asked with the attitude of someone who had been greatly inconvenienced.

Heather noticed he had braces on his teeth, wore a huge high school class ring, and his chestnut-brown skin was a little ashy. "I said"—she leaned forward to speak into the round hole in the middle of the glass—"my name is Heather Chadwick. Look at your comp list for Gerald Forrester."

He pulled a shoe-box-sized box from a bottom shelf and started looking through it. "You said Gerald Forrester?" he queried in a man's voice.

"Yes. I'm Heather Chadwick, his fiancée." Heather offered him her friendliest smile and placed her ringed hand on the counter to back up her lie.

The boy frowned deeper, not at all impressed with Heather or her ring. "We get a lot of groupies at this window, claiming they're somebody's fiancée or girlfriend or whatever. Most of 'em are lying." He looked pointedly at Heather. "Most of 'em are skeezers or gold diggers." He rolled his inexperienced brown eyes at her, then pulled out a list with tickets wrapped inside. He pulled the rubber band off the bundle and straightened out the list. "Let's see if you fit the bill."

Heather wished she could reach through the glass and shake some respect into the young boy. Instead, she reined in her anger and said in a stilted voice, "I can assure you I'm not a groupie, a skeezer, or a gold digger. I have been on Gerald's list for the past six years."

The young boy wasn't interested. Using his finger to scan down the list, he moved his lips as he silently read the names. Slowly, he progressed until finally he reached the bottom of the page. Satisfied that he had pegged her right, the young boy pulled up his head and stared her directly in the eyes. "It ain't here." He gave Heather a knowing look.

Heather was shocked. No way would Gerald delete her name! First of all, he wouldn't have had the foresight, and secondly, that would be like an official act of cutting her out of his life forever. Although technically they were no longer betrothed, she knew they still loved each other. She knew Gerald loved her and wouldn't treat her so coldly. Despite the comfortable April temperature, a chill swept over her, and she shuddered. Standing on tiptoe to get a better look at the list, she frantically commanded in a high-pitched voice, "Look again." She leaned her head against the thick glass window. "You must have overlooked it. It's Chadwick. C-h-a-d . . ."

"I know how to spell it. And it ain't here," the boy insisted, crossing his arms over the list. The frown never left his face.

"But, it's got to be there," Heather screamed in a louder voice. Inwardly, she told herself this was a mistake. *Gerald wouldn't do this. Gerald wouldn't shut me out of his life. He can't turn his love off like a water faucet. He loves me!*

Seeing Heather's determination, the young boy quelled the nasty remark that was on the tip of his tongue. "Here"—he forcefully pasted the list against the Plexiglas—"see it for yourself, Ms. C-h-a-d-w-i-c-k."

Heather quickly scanned the list and not seeing her name, looked again, slower this time. For the past six years, her name had the number-one slot on his list—even for games they knew for sure she wouldn't be attending, Gerald never took her name off. It was always her name, his mother's, then Linda, Donna and her husband, Ted, along with Theresa and her husband, Tyrone, plus his nieces, nephews, and a few close friends. It had been that way for six years. Now, her name was gone. His mother's name was first on the list . . . and hers was completely gone.

Heather hurt. It felt like someone was squeezing her heart, trying to drain all the blood out of her. Dazed, sick to her stomach, and with tears in her eyes, she turned away from the window, giving the rude young boy her back. With the back of her hand, she swiped at the tears that fell silently. Heather threw back her head to look at the clear blue sky above the skyscrapers, above the Summit. How, after six wonderful years together, could he within a two-week window wipe her out of his life? How could he dismiss her existence so efficiently? How on a day so clear and beautiful could her world become so cloudy and gloomy? How could he do this to her? Now, what was she supposed to do? How was she going to prove to him she loved him and wanted his forgiveness? How was she going to convince him to keep their love alive?

Behind her, the boy replaced the tickets inside the list and rubber-banded the packet. He flipped over the magazine and began reading. Already, she was out of his mind.

Heather turned around to stare at the boy's bent head. *Skeezer. Gold digger.* His nasty words circulated through her mind. She didn't care about his assessment of her, but she did care about Gerald's, and his action frightened her. But whether she wanted to admit it or not, she was her mother's child, and whatever Marilyn Chadwick-Wolfe went after, she got. That strong will had been passed on to Heather. *Gerald's going to learn that he can't put me out of his life. He ain't seen nothing yet,* she thought. She was determined to fight for him, for their love.

Turning her back to the fear of losing Gerald, she swallowed the thick lump in her throat, straightened her shoulders, and headed for the box office window. She stood there a second, being totally ignored by the young boy. Impatiently, she rapped on the window. "Hey, I know you see me standing here." She matched his previously rude tone.

Reluctantly, the boy looked up from the story he'd been reading. "Got another superstar's name you wanna use?" the boy asked brusquely.

Heather reached into the breast pocket of her faded denim jacket and pulled out a wad of money. "Give me the best ticket you have for tonight's game." She threw three fifty dollar bills under the slot.

The wad of money earned the young boy's respect and admiration. His eyes lit up. He sat up straight, and he actually smiled at her. His nasty disposition was replaced with one of eager helpfulness, when he quickly gathered the bills and then searched his computer for the best available seat. "I can put you nineteen rows up. It's not as good as the seats his guests will have, and he probably won't see you, but it's a good seat, smack dab center court, visitors' side. I wish I could afford it."

"I'll take it," Heather responded dryly.

The boy quickly printed out the ticket and handed it and her change to Heather.

"Keep the change," she mumbled as she stuffed the ticket and the rest of her money in the front pocket of her jeans. She had already turned and didn't see the boy kiss the fifty dollar tip he'd just received.

With slow steps, Heather made her way back to the rental car. Shortly, she pulled out of the parking lot at

LOVE EVERLASTING

the Summit and headed for the nearest hotel. As she drove, she thought about her next step. Without a guest pass, she wouldn't be able to talk to Gerald before or after the game. She had really counted on being able to see him before the game so they could talk about the future. So he would know that she still supported him, still cared for him and his career and, most importantly, still wanted a relationship with him. She sighed. *I can forget that for now, but I'll come up with something. Maybe as I watch him play, I'll be inspired to come up with a crafty way to get to him.* Feeling less fearful and more hopeful, Heather checked into the Doubletree Hotel. A short nap, a change of clothes, and a renewal of spirits was in order.

The game was exciting, and although there was no way for Heather to let Gerald know she was in attendance without getting arrested, she still enjoyed watching him play. She always did! She loved the way his muscles rippled beneath his team jersey. She admired his long, lean legs as they covered the court at almost superhuman speed. She revered his level of concentration, his ability to put the crowd, the music, even the half-naked dancing girls out of his mind to focus only on the next shot, the next play. The way the sweat poured off his body, staining his uniform, reminded her of their marathon lovemaking sessions where wet sheets and deep breathing were standard—the reminder of which had her almost willing to risk arrest. She loved this man, and now she was beginning to doubt his love for her. In the scheme of things, having her name removed from the list was a minor thing. However, it was enough to put a hole in her confidence and make her think that maybe . . . just maybe . . . he really didn't love her anymore. *I just need to speak with him,* she thought, *I need to let him know the few counseling sessions I've had are going well, and I'll be ready to be his wife in a year.*

Heather looked at the game clock. The game would be ending very soon, and she was no closer to coming up with a plan to see him than when the game started three quarters ago. She felt herself toppling over into a state of depression.

An eardrum-splitting cheer went up, making Heather snap her head back around to the clock then to the action on the court. Gerald had just made a two-point shot, putting the Mavs ahead by one, with fourteen seconds left on the clock. Another cheer went up when a forced turnover by the Mavs brought the action downcourt to their basket—and again Gerald Forrester, small forward, received the ball and with an almost clear path, slam dunked it, securing the Mavs' victory.

Simultaneously, the final buzzer sounded, the visiting crowd went hog-wild, and the Mavs entire team and coaching staff came off the sidelines. Heather joined the Mavs fans in cheers of congratulations and shouts of joy. Soon, she and the other thousands of fans filed out into the aisles and headed for the exit doors. Heather tried not to think about the privileges she would be enjoying now if she had been listed as one of his guests. But it was a futile gesture. By now, Gerald would have made his way to her and kissed and hugged her in victory. Then, with the other guests, she would have waited patiently for the team to meet, interview, shower, and change clothes before ending back at the hotel for a postgame celebration.

Suddenly, she stopped. An idea hit her. *That's it! The hotel. When the team plays in Houston, they always stay at the Renaissance. I'll meet him at the hotel. Surely, when he sees how determined I am to speak with him, he'll agree to talk to me. He won't turn me away.* As the idea gelled in her mind, she picked up her speed and once outside in the cool night air, she raced to her car.

It didn't dawn on Heather until she entered the beautiful pink-marbled and green-planted lobby of the Renaissance that she didn't know which room Gerald occupied. The front desk treated any sports team staying at their hotel like demi-gods, protecting their privacy as they would protect the privacy of the President of the United States. The hotel operators had restrictions on which calls to pass through and which ones to terminate. Deciding her best course was to hang out in the lobby and wait for the team bus to arrive, she ordered a white wine from the side bar and selected a seat facing the front doors.

Two hours and two glasses of wine later, not one of the team players or coaching staff had walked through the front door. Heather looked at her watch and then allowed herself to get antsy and nervous. *Where are they? They should have been here by now.* Heather stood and walked to the bank of phones. Talking into the receiver, she tried her best impersonation of a frantic wife of one of the players. It got her nowhere. *The operators have been trained well,* she thought as she hung up the phone. Looking around, she saw a housekeeper come through an unmarked door—and at that moment it dawned on her that, depending on how booked the hotel was, the team would sometimes use the back entrance of the hotel. Disappointed in herself for not thinking of it initially, Heather slipped into the door the housekeeper had come out of. A few minutes later, she found herself wandering through a maze of hallways at the rear of the hotel. Just as she thought she had gotten lost and would never see the light of day again, she ran into a larger hallway leading to a loading dock. Peeking her head out of the door, she spotted the team's bus. It was empty. Turning around, upset that her lack of thinking had quelled her last opportunity to see Gerald, she nearly bumped into Alexander Hawkins, a teammate of Gerald's.

Alexander held her by the shoulders, steadying her. "Whoa, there . . . oh. Hi, Heather. How you doing?" He hugged her quickly and then held her at shoulder's length. "I didn't mean to almost run you over. I left my bag on the bus, and I'm in a hurry to get back upstairs. A bunch of us are going out to celebrate the victory at some new hot spot. Silly me, forgot my deodorant in my bag." He winked and made a move to walk through the door.

Heather stopped him with a hand on his arm. "What room is Gerald in? I need to see him."

"He's right next to me. Room 1612. See you."

Heather was elated. She could have kissed Alexander, but his long legs had already taken him outside toward the bus. She yelled at his back anyway. "Thanks, Alexander, and have fun tonight."

"Will do." The night air carried his response back to her.

Heather raced through the maze of hallways, surprised at how familiar they had now become. Or was it because she was now on her way to see Gerald? Impatiently, she waited for the elevator and when it finally came, she squeezed through the door as it started opening. As the glassed-in cage whirled her upward, she checked her appearance in the mirror and made adjustments where needed. Then, she mentally rehearsed what she would say to Gerald. The dinging of a bell announced her arrival at the sixteenth floor and before the doors could open wide, she again squeezed her small body through the opening. It was a matter of moments until she reached room 1612. Her heart thudded loudly in her chest as she paused, her hand poised in midair, to catch her breath. She knocked. She was both apprehensive and excited.

A few moments passed, then a gruff voice called from inside the room. "Who is it?"

Heather's response was to knock again and step out of view of the peephole. With a kiddish smile on her face, she thought she would surprise Gerald.

A few seconds later, she heard chains rattling and then the click of a dead bolt being released. The door opened slowly and when it was several inches wide, she jumped in view of the door.

The surprise was Heather's. A beautiful, dark, exotic-looking woman with a brickhouse body clad in a Frederick's of Hollywood outfit was faintly outlined in the crack of the door.

"What do you want?" the woman asked. Her voice sounded as if she had just awakened. It was deep and sexy.

"Who is it?" Gerald's equally deep and sexy voice asked from within the darkness of the room.

Heather was speechless. Her brain went numb, only feelings and emotions were still alive. Unconsciously, she moved backward, away from the door, shaking her head. "No. No. It's not possible. Gerald loves me," she said softly, in a mantra, as if trying to make the beautiful creature in front of her disappear. "He loves me."

Time ticked off seconds in its usual rhythm, but to Heather it felt like the world had slowed to a snail's pace. She continued to stare at the girl eyeing her up and down, trying to dissolve the evidence in front of her. "He loves me," she repeated with less conviction.

Gerald's tall silhouette appeared behind the woman. That image of the two of them, clad in next to nothing, in a darkened room, was the catalyst needed to shake the fuzziness from her mind and the inactivity from her limbs. Hurt replaced numbness.

Squinting against the bright lights in the hallway, Gerald edged the woman away from the door to jerk it open. Looking out of one half-opened eye, he frowned, then seeing who stood a mere foot from his door, both eyes opened completely.

"Heather!" he breathed. "What are you doing here?" He was as shocked as Heather was surprised.

"What are *you* doing?" Heather asked in a frightened voice. Taking tiny steps toward him, she pleaded, "Gerald, please, please, tell me I'm not seeing what I'm seeing."

Gerald stared at her, still struggling with the hold the shock had on him. "I . . . um . . ." He tightened the towel wrapped around his middle then flicked on a light near the door, all the while staring hard at Heather.

"Gerald, how could you do this?" Her eyes searched his, trying to understand what this meant. "I thought you loved me. I thought I was special, that we had something special." A lone tear rolled down Heather's light-colored cheek.

A frown darkened Gerald's little-boy features. He wanted to run to Heather and smother her in his loving arms, but he was afraid of the power she had to hurt him even more than she'd already hurt him. Although he took a small step forward to carry out his initial desire to hold her, to replace the nameless woman in his bedroom with her, he stopped himself. "I didn't expect you. I thought it was one of the guys . . . you know . . . playing around."

"Gerald . . . what about us?" Heather had come within inches of Gerald's still form.

Shaking himself out of the hold her presence had on him, he put his senses in perspective. "Heather, you're the one who dropped me, remember? So, don't try to make me feel ashamed or embarrassed or wrong for what I'm doing." *So, why then do I feel like I'm cheating on her?* he thought. *Why can't I enjoy this beautiful woman who's so ready to do anything I ask her to do?*

"It took you only two weeks to get over me? It took

only two weeks to replace me with a . . . a bimbo? To take my name off the list?" Heather was openly crying now. "Maybe I was the fool, thinking you loved me when all along you couldn't have. Not if you could so easily jump from my flesh to hers."

Gerald ran a hand over his almost bald head. "Heather, you just don't get it, do you? This has nothing to do with feelings. This has nothing to do with love."

"And that's supposed to make me feel better?" Heather screeched.

Gerald felt awful about Heather finding him with whatever-her-name-was. But, why should he? He was the one left standing at the altar. He was the one who'd had to return to Atlanta among family and friends and apologize for her actions. He was the one who had written checks to reimburse people for their travel expenses and had returned gifts and had hung his head whenever someone mentioned wedding or marriage or even the word "relationship." He was the one who had gotten into a fight with a teammate after his teamie made an ugly comment about being jilted. If he needed to ease his sorrow in another woman's flesh, why shouldn't he? "You're the one who dumped me, Heather," he said again. Suddenly, he grew angry at Heather and himself—angry at the power she still had over him and angry at himself for letting her have that control. "You are so damned selfish. You can't always live life on your terms, Heather Chadwick. As far as I'm concerned, you've made your decision and I've made mine."

Gerald stepped back and made a move to close the door. Another moment in her presence and he didn't know what he'd do—either throw her down on the carpet and make wild, desperate love to her or beat her with harsh words.

Heather placed a hand on the door. "Gerald, wait,

please—I know I made that decision." She pleaded with her body, her eyes, for his understanding.

"What decision, Heather?" Gerald looked at her with hard eyes. "Look at you, you can't even say it aloud. Let me help you—" Yelling at the top of his lungs, Gerald shared his pain with the world. "Heather decided she didn't want to marry me!"

"But, it doesn't change, it'll never change how I feel for you." She placed a hand on his chest. It was the soft touch that made him jump back away from her. Heather noticed his retreat from her, but tucking her hurt feelings aside she begged him, "I just asked you for more time. I *am* going to marry you, Gerald! I love you."

Heather watched as Gerald turned to stone, his body stiff, his face brutally cold.

"I used to love you. I don't anymore. Not since you made your choice." Pointing a finger at his bare chest, Gerald spoke harshly. "Since you didn't choose me, I don't choose you. I'm a free man to do what I want, when I want, and with whom I want." Gerald looked over her head as two burly security guards came barreling down the hallway. "Now, I think you'd better leave." He pointed a finger at the approaching men. "Those brothers don't look like they're playing."

The hotel security guards reached Heather and Gerald at the same time as Heather turned to meet their glaring gazes.

The biggest of the two men asked, "Mr. Forrester, is this groupie bothering you?"

"I'm not a groupie," Heather spat out. "I'm his . . ." Heather turned beseeching eyes to Gerald.

Gerald wanted to supply the word that two weeks ago would have made him happy, but he didn't. The pain was too raw, the anger and humiliation ran too deep.

Heather held up her hand with the diamond engagement ring. Her voice was deathly quiet. "Gerald? This means nothing to you?"

"Gerald . . ." A plaintive wail came from deep inside the room, reminding both Gerald and Heather of the other woman. "I'm getting cold and lonely."

Gerald didn't react to the invitation. He turned his dark brown eyes to the security guard, who had a steely grip on Heather's upper arm.

"Don't touch her. Let her go," Gerald commanded the security guard.

He obeyed at once.

Heather felt a ray of hope spring within her. A smile started to spread on her face.

"You can escort her out of the hotel, but don't touch her," Gerald finished.

Hope died; the beginning smile vanished.

"Sure thing, Mr. Forrester. By the way, you played exceptionally well tonight. I mean, you play like a champ every time, but tonight . . . tonight you played as if the devil hounded your heels. What was it that spurred you on?"

Gerald looked deep into Heather's eyes. Without batting an eye, or skipping a beat, he replied, "Pain. It was pain that drove me."

"Sorry to hear that, Mr. Forrester. Hopefully, it's something the team doctors can take care of."

It was on Gerald's lips to tell the guard it had nothing to do with physical pain. That type of pain he would welcome over the pain of getting a good jab in the heart by the woman he would have laid down his life for.

"Well, sorry for the disturbance, Mr. Forrester. We've posted a guard by the elevators, so you don't have to worry about any further disturbances. And again, good game."

Softly, Heather pleaded, "Gerald, you don't have to

do this. It's not too late for us. We can make it work, Gerald."

Gerald stood back and slowly closed the door, never losing eye contact with her. As painful as it was, his decision was made. He loved her and would die loving her, but she would never be willing to commit herself totally to him.

A nudge from the guards reminded her she was now standing and looking at a closed door. The tears started as soon as she walked away from the door of room 1612.

Five

"She doesn't do impressions anymore, and you know how she's always smiling and has that bright, perky cheerleader attitude?" Nachelle paused, not really expecting Steven to answer her question. "Well, she hasn't smiled in days. She just mopes about unless she's getting ready for a show. It's like the real Heather has been gutted, leaving just a shell of her former self." The urgency in her voice matched her urgent movements. She leaned forward, sitting on the edge of her seat with one knee bouncing up and down. The phone was cradled between her shoulder and her ear, and she anxiously doodled on a yellow legal pad. Wrinkling her brow, her voice dropped an octave to reflect a mournful tone. "Steven, I don't know what to do."

Throwing down the pen in frustration, Nachelle swiveled her chair around, hoping the night lights of downtown Fort Worth might spur her creativity and help her generate some ideas to help Heather rise from her depressed state.

The floor-to-ceiling windows offered a perfect frame for the teeming Friday night activity. In the last few years, the city council had taken funds and dumped them into this previously neglected portion of downtown. Old office buildings and warehouses had been transformed into specialty shops, clubs, and restaurants that now pulled in more traffic than one could shake a stick at. The Fort Worth offices of DuCloux Enterprises sat smack dab in the middle of the five-block area. Nachelle mindlessly watched the coming and going action below her. Her focus was on Heather's deepening despondency.

Hundreds of miles away, in the Atlanta office of DuCloux Enterprises, their family-owned and managed computer company, Steven covered the mouthpiece of his phone, issued a short command to his secretary, and then returned to their conversation. "I'm sorry, baby. Dorrie just laid a pile of papers on my desk. Guess who it's from?"

In the background Nachelle could hear Steven riffling through papers.

"Who?" Nachelle suppressed her irritation with her husband. She had been waiting all week to talk to him about Heather and her problems. She wanted to use him as a sounding board, but it appeared his mind was focused solely on business, as usual.

Sometimes she wished his brothers were the ones responsible for running the company. They, like Steven, worked long hours. They, like Steven, were committed to the continued success of their family's company, which had been in the DuCloux family for generations. However, the key difference was Steven was the CEO and as such, a large percentage of responsibility for the company rested on his shoulders. To perpetuate DuCloux Enterprises' well-being, Steven traveled extensively doing deals for the good of the company. Not only did he travel between Atlanta and Fort Worth but also to foreign countries and major domestic cities. Nachelle counted herself lucky if she saw him four times a week.

In contrast, Steven's brothers had the advantage of living and working in Atlanta full-time, doing moderate traveling. Their wives and children could rely on them to be home for dinner or soccer practice or piano recitals or whatever else was going on in their lives.

Nachelle often wondered what was in the cards for their future—more so now since she was pregnant. Would the birth of their child settle Steven? Would it change his focus, his priorities? Would she and their child have the same advantages as her sisters-in-law? Would she be able to schedule family dinners? Would she be able to count on his presence at childhood birthday parties or his help with science projects or his being available to take their child to the park? Would she and Steven be able to continue their romantic affair? It scared Nachelle to think about those things because she knew how committed Steven was to DuCloux Enterprises. But she also knew Steven loved and coveted her and their yet-to-be-born child. Still, as the competitive environment in the computer business heated and as changes in the industry continued to reshape their company's objectives, she wondered if she would continue to win out over the company.

For even now, sitting in the privacy of her office on executive row, Nachelle tried to squelch the growing resentment she felt toward his family, the company, and the fact that she and Steven saw less and less of each other as the company grew more and more successful. Ignoring that fear for the time being, Nachelle tuned in to Steven's words.

"Nathaniel! He's suing us for 2.5 million dollars!" There was a pause while Steven read on. A few seconds later, he exploded. "I can't believe it! The man is saying we discriminated against him due to his age, that we unjustly fired him. Can you believe this shit?"

Nachelle's mouth fell open, her irritation with Steven, the DuCloux family, and DuCloux Enterprises forgotten.

"You're kidding?" Her voice escalated. "We didn't fire him. He quit!"

"I know that, but that's what this letter is saying. That he was fired." Disgust was evident in Steven's voice.

"Oh, that's the most ridiculous thing I've ever heard." Nachelle was floored. She couldn't believe Nathaniel. Then again, when she thought about what a snake in the grass he'd been, she could believe he would do something this devious.

"Man . . . I can't believe this. This is crazy," Steven disgustedly exclaimed.

Nachelle could just imagine Steven shoving papers around and pacing around his office. She could picture the tension grooves carved in his forehead and around his mouth.

Steven erupted. "What in the hell does he hope to accomplish? What in the world is he thinking?"

When her initial surprise and anger abated, Nachelle could think more clearly about the situation. She thought about the last conversation she and Steven had had with Nathaniel. That had been a little less than a year ago.

Nachelle and Steven had just returned from Las Vegas, where they had an impromptu wedding. Nathaniel had been waiting in Steven's Atlanta office, having been advised beforehand by Dorrie, Steven's secretary, that Steven needed to speak with him.

When they'd entered the office, Nathaniel's face had told them he was not happy about Nachelle's appearance. Unknown to Nachelle and Steven, Nathaniel had worked hard to set up Nachelle so Steven would have no choice but to fire her, leaving the field wide open for him to step into the number-two position at DuCloux Enterprises as the chief financial officer. His plan had worked, for Steven *had* fired Nachelle, and Nathaniel *had* been named to the coveted spot. Nathaniel had been on cloud nine, for that position plus the unquestionable support of Steven's father—Adolphus DuCloux, the patriarch of the family and previous CEO, now retired, but still an important decision maker concerning the company—would allow him to obtain his ultimate goal: power. Nathaniel knew he would never be the CEO of the family-led company. However, he knew true power was not always in a title, and since he had been Adolphus's right-hand man and good friend, he knew he would have the power. Steven would simply be a figurehead like Queen Elizabeth of England. And Adolphus would continue to think Nathaniel was a genuine friend, when in reality he was using the old man.

But, unwittingly, Steven had thrown a wrench into Nathaniel's plans when he went in search of and found Nachelle, married her, and brought her back into his life and into the company in the number-two position at DuCloux Enterprises. Nathaniel had been furious when Steven communicated his demotion from CFO to vice president, working under Nachelle. His anger intensified when his threats, cajoling, and negotiation skills had not reversed Steven's decision. Nathaniel had finally rejected Steven's job offer and walked out, tendering his resignation verbally.

That had been the last time they'd heard from Nathaniel until now.

Nachelle massaged her temples, trying to stop the dull headache from becoming razor sharp. Between Heather's problems, the changes her body was going through as a result of the pregnancy, and the loneliness she felt without Steven being near, and now this, she didn't know if she was coming or going.

Forcing herself to focus on the immediate problem, she used her calculator brain to analyze the situation.

"Why now? Why are we just now hearing from him? He quit a year ago."

"Hell if I know." Anger colored Steven's words.

Nachelle's grip on the telephone tightened, thinking about the question she needed to ask Steven. She didn't know how he would accept the possibility that his father might have known some of Nathaniel's thoughts or feelings about the resignation. It was no secret that the two of them were closer than the teeth on a zipper. "What do you think your father's going to say? Is he still friends with Nathaniel?"

"I don't know." Steven sighed deeply. "I have no idea. Dad and I haven't spoken Nathaniel's name since the day he walked out."

Listening to the background noise that the speakerphone cleanly picked up, Nachelle imagined Steven stalking around his office, running his hands through his wavy salt-and-pepper hair in frustration.

"Honey, I think you need to stop by their house on the way home tonight. Adolphus needs to know, and we need to know what, if anything, Adolphus knows about this." Nachelle spoke softly, hoping her offensive words would land gently.

It was obvious they didn't. She heard his heavy steps lead him to the telephone. Judging by the loud grating sound that made her jump back, she could imagine Steven had snatched up the phone.

"Are you saying you think Dad has something to do with this? That's crazy, Nachelle. I know you and my father don't get along, but how could you even think Dad would hurt the company he worked so hard to build?" She heard him breathing hard and fast.

Although Steven couldn't see her actions, Nachelle splayed her hands out in defense. "I'm not saying your father instigated this or that he's in cohoots with Nathaniel. All I'm saying is you or the attorneys need to speak with Adolphus so we can approach this lawsuit from the right angle. Who knows Nathaniel better than Adolphus?" Nachelle coolly defended her position, refusing to meet his anger.

Nachelle heard his deep breathing and knew he was trying to get a grip on his emotions. In a calmer voice, he agreed. "Yeah, I guess you're right." Steven released a tense breath. "I'm sorry I yelled at you, baby. I guess I'm just tired."

"I understand, honey." Nachelle quietly released the breath she'd been holding. She was glad Steven had agreed with her quickly. She had no desire to add an argument with her husband over his father to her burgeoning list. "Why don't you just mention it to your Dad and then let Legal handle it. You have enough to worry about."

"You're right about that," Steven said.

Nachelle could almost hear his smile on the phone.

He continued. "You're so smart. What would I ever do without you?"

"Let's hope we never have to answer that question." Nachelle returned his invisible smile. Her words were as soft and warm and inviting as his.

"Indeed." Steven paused to reclaim his seat. "So . . ." Dropping his already deep voice to a new low, he asked, "What are you wearing?"

Nachelle laughed. She loved this man of hers, and suddenly that much needed laugh removed all the doubts, fears, and resentment she'd harbored earlier. Those negative ugly emotions had been replaced with overflowing love. She, Steven, their marriage, and the baby would be just fine.

Teasingly, she answered, "I ain't telling you because you never answered my question." Her smile belied the reprimand in her voice.

"What question?" Steven asked as serious as an IRS agent during tax season.

"See, you weren't even listening when I was telling you about Heather. Now, I'm never going to tell you what I'm wearing."

They both laughed.

"All right. All right. I'm sorry, baby. I promise I'm listening now. What's going on with Heather and Gerald? Hey, isn't the game on tonight?"

Nachelle could hear the TV in his office. He must have turned it on. "Steven, you'd better listen to me this time or . . ." It didn't do any good for Nachelle to shake her finger at the phone, but she did it anyway.

"Baby, I'm listening. I promised you I'm listening, didn't I? Go ahead."

Nachelle sighed expressively and kiddingly threatened him. "Okay, Steven. I'm going to tell you again, but this is your last chance."

"Uh-huh."

She could tell by his absentminded expression that she had lost him, but she needed to get her concerns off her chest. Talking—even to her husband, who had his head in the game—would help her make heads or tails of Heather's mess.

"I said Heather's depressed, and I don't know what to do. She doesn't find enjoyment in the things we used to do. I even spoke with Chris and Vandy, and they said her performances have not been up to snuff. I mean, it's still good enough for the audience, and they wouldn't know the difference unless they had seen her previously, but this thing with Gerald has really upset her."

"I'm sorry to hear that. Is she still going to counseling?"

"Yes, but that takes time. In the meantime, she's going downhill, and I don't know what to do." Nachelle

LOVE EVERLASTING

was no fool. Even though Steven had turned the TV down low, she knew he still had one eye glued to the tube. "How does Gerald look? Is he playing well? Does he look depressed?"

"No, he looks"—Steven realized he was caught—"fine." In a shame-filled voice, he conceded to her smarts. "He doesn't look like anything is out of the ordinary, but judging by the stats, it looks like his game is off a little. He's not making his shots. Maybe he'll pick up in the second half."

She decided to punish him later. "Heather flew to Houston a week ago to try to talk to Gerald. She went to the game and then to his hotel room afterward. Some . . . *woman* was in his room."

She had Steven's full attention now. The game was forgotten. "Oh, yeah?"

Nachelle continued, playfully smug in her ability to attract his full consideration. "It broke Heather's heart. What should I do, Steven? I need a male perspective."

"Wow, baby, that's something. I wonder who she is?" Steven's eyes automatically focused on Gerald as his mind processed the information. "It didn't take him long, did it? But, then, I'm sure those high-profile guys have their choice of women."

"Heather said she was beautiful."

Steven guffawed. "I'll bet."

"And what does that mean?" Nachelle's hackles rose.

"Come on, baby. How many of these professional athletes have you seen with an unattractive woman? You have to admit they usually have beautiful babes on their arms, and most of them have exotic features or are light-skinned or have long hair—and all of them are fine. You know, women who look like Heather. And we won't even talk about the ones married to white women." Steven paused to switch the TV to CNN during the commercial break. He hated to hear those sportscasters with their ridiculous comments, unless, of course, it was Ahmad Rashad or Dr. J. Now, those two brothers could talk some sports. "Look, all I'm trying to say is they can have their pick of any woman, and if they don't feel like picking then they let the most aggressive of the beautiful women pick them."

He flipped the channel to a local station when he realized CNN was a replay of an earlier news broadcast. "I can understand your wanting to help your friend but, sweetheart, get real. She embarrassed him, she broke his heart. *She* made the decision to end their relationship. She needs to be adult and live with her decision."

Nachelle retorted, "Could you be a little more cruel, please?"

"Naw, baby, come on, now," Steven pleaded in a singsong voice. "You asked for a male's perspective, and I'm giving it to you. Don't be mad at me, please, baby. I'm already lonely and missing you. I don't want you to be mad at me. I'm sorry, okay?"

Nachelle huffed and waited several seconds to let him squirm. "Apology accepted," she muttered.

"Thank you, baby. Now, let me clean it up." Steven flipped back to the game. "She hurt Gerald deeply. It's going to take time for him to get over that. Right now, the best thing she can do is give him some time, some space. She needs to go on with her life just like Gerald is doing, and after a while, if she decides to approach him again when the pain isn't so raw, then she can, but only"—Steven paused for emphasis—"only to apologize for hurting him. At that point, he'll make it clear if he wants to be bothered with her again."

"Hmmm. That's not bad advice from someone who took only one class in psychology."

"Yeah." Steven was again focused on the action on the screen. A foul had been called on Gerald, and he was now in the referee's face, arguing about the call. "He'd better get out of that referee's face before he gets a technical."

"I assume you're talking to the TV, and if that's the case that means this conversation is over." Nachelle tried not to sound emotional, but she felt lonely and sad. Here it was Friday night, and while other couples were making plans for the weekend or were already enjoying each other, she was in the office in Fort Worth, working, and he was in their office in Atlanta, working—hundreds of miles apart, and he hadn't even said he loved her. *I am not going to get emotional,* she told herself. *I am not going to think about the lack of quality time we have. I am not going to think about how sad and depressed Heather is and how that could have been or might still be me.* She knew some of her roller-coaster emotional outbursts were attributable to her pregnancy, but she also knew a large part of it had to do with her and Steven's current circumstance. *I am not going to worry about what's going to happen to us. We have this second, and I'm going to enjoy him shouting in my ear.*

"Oh, man!" Steven stood up, his boisterousness loud and clear through the phone line. "Nachelle, baby, turn on the TV. Gerald's acting like a madman." Steven didn't even hear her earlier comment. He hollered an obscenity at the TV. "Gerald just got a technical! That's the first technical he's gotten in a long time."

The word "technical" pulled Nachelle from her misery. "Gerald? A technical?" She couldn't turn on the TV fast enough.

"Baby, are you looking at it? Do you see the replay?"

NBC was good enough to show the complete play from the foul action to the call to Gerald arguing with the referee. She didn't know enough about the technical rules of the game to know if it was a legitimate call or not, and she really didn't care about that part. She was interested only in Gerald's actions.

NBC switched to live action in time for the couple to see Gerald's subsequent actions. Simultaneously, the couple exclaimed, "Oh, my, God! He pushed the referee!"

Nachelle saw but couldn't believe it. Gerald actually put his hands on the ref and pushed him. "I can't believe it. Gerald's never been that aggressive toward the refs before."

Even though he knew the referee was correct to eject Gerald from the game, Steven was outraged. Gerald Forrester was a premier player who combined street ball with the technical, rules-ridden court game. Watching him play was entertainment at its best. "The Mavs might as well go home with Gerald out of the game. Damn! This was going to be a good game."

Nachelle shook her head slowly, her brow wrinkled in consternation. "Why did Gerald do that? He's never done that before. He's usually so in control on the court." Nachelle pressed her face into the TV when NBC graciously repeated the replay, this time from the play to the call to the push. The startled comments of the sportscasters were a background to her own surprised words. "What in the world was Gerald thinking, putting his hands on that ref? He must be out of his mind." Unlike Steven, Nachelle had forgotten to put her phone on speaker. She forgot he was on the line. "Why did he do that?" she asked the TV.

Nachelle rushed back to the phone, intent on calling Heather to speak to her about Gerald's actions when she realized she'd left her husband dangling. "Oh, honey, I'm sorry. I forgot you were on the line." Turning around to face the TV, she asked, "What's up with Gerald?"

"I don't know. Man, I can't believe this. It's only the

LOVE EVERLASTING 89

first quarter of action." Steven watched the fourth replay of the scene. Obviously, NBC was just as confused and surprised as the rest of the spectators. They panned the camera toward his coach, who was not a happy camper. "Awww, man. This is not good. Something's up with him. I wonder if this has anything to do with the breakup with a certain petite, light-skinned, light brown-eyed honey named . . ."

"Heather Chadwick." Nachelle finished the sentence for him. She made a quick decision. "I'm going to call Gerald. I'm going to find out what's going on."

"Nachelle, didn't we talk earlier about giving Gerald some time?"

"Well, yeah, but we were talking in reference to Heather. Gerald and I are friends, too. Can't a friend call on a friend she's concerned about?"

Silence greeted her comeback.

After a second, she demanded, "I just don't want his game impacted by his separation from Heather. Don't you agree?" she asked coyly, knowing full well Steven loved the game and enjoyed watching Gerald razzle and dazzle.

Steven's continued silence on the other end of the line let her know he wasn't fooled by her concern for Gerald's game. Although they had been married only a year, they could read each other very well.

Moments later, Nachelle almost felt Steven's sigh as it wailed through the receiver. "Nachelle, you don't have to talk to Gerald. I'm telling you it's classic 'fightin' the pain' behavior. Trust me, I've experienced it myself with a brown-skinned, *fine*, almond-eyed beauty named Nachelle DuCloux, whom I love dearly."

"You went through destructive behavior like that because of me, honey?" Nachelle puzzled through Steven's revelation.

"Yeah, every man who's ever loved but suffered pain

because of loving deals with that pain in his own way. For me, it was throwing myself into work, driving myself day and night. I didn't eat or sleep. I practically lived at the office but, in all honesty, that didn't work. Nothing worked until I could have you in my arms again."

Nachelle smiled, her eyes grew misty. Her heart filled with love. "Oh, Steven. That's so sweet. I love you so much."

"And I love you too, baby. Very, very much."

"So, why are we apart? It's killing me for us to be separated so often." Nachelle hadn't meant to bring up her issue, but she couldn't help it. She wanted Steven near her. She wanted his arms around her at night, she wanted his sexy morning smile and early morning lovemaking. She wanted him. Pure and simple.

Steven matched her wistful tone. "I know, baby. I know. I feel the same way. Once we completely merge the Fort Worth and Atlanta offices, things will be better. Until then, we'll just have to make the most of the times we do have together."

"You're right."

"Tell you what. This meeting in the morning should be over by noon. I'll catch the first available flight to Fort Worth, and we'll do something special when I get there. How does that sound?"

Nachelle smiled grandly. "It sounds like heaven, but are you sure? You still have that meeting early Monday morning, don't you?"

"Yeah, but I'll talk to Donald. They're scheduled to leave Aspen Sunday afternoon, so he can have the company jet detour here, pick me up, and we can be back in Atlanta late Sunday evening. It'll be fun hearing my beautiful nieces chatter on and on about their first ski trip."

Nachelle laughed, picturing the scene Steven painted.

His older brother, Donald, had three girls all under ten years old, and they adored their uncle Steven. They would indeed talk his head off. "Okay, honey. I'll see you tomorrow then." Nachelle grew excited; she would see Steven after all. A feeling of euphoria and giddiness filled her.

"Yes, you will. Drive careful on the way home and don't forget to call me when you get there. And make sure security walks you to your car. I'm sure there are plenty of people on the streets tonight, but you can't be too safe."

Nachelle's heart warmed at his caring comments. "Yes, sir."

"I love you, Nachelle, and I can't wait to see you tomorrow."

"I love you, too."

Nachelle hung up the phone, smiling and feeling warm all over. As she packed her briefcase, she thought about their love, their developing child, and the future after their commuter marriage had ceased. She felt great and wanted to share her good fortune with the world, starting with her best friend.

Gerald should be home this coming week. I'll call and see if I can meet him early next week. But, for now, I need to speak with Heather. She needs to know about Gerald, Nachelle decided.

Putting action to her thoughts, she picked up the phone and dialed Heather's number. On the fourth ring, Heather's answering machine picked up.

After the recorded message played out, Nachelle left a brief message. Frowning, she replaced the receiver and wondered where her friend was that evening.

Six

Ten blocks from Nachelle's downtown office, Heather stood outside The Menu, waiting for her dinner partner to show up. Although Nachelle teased her for being late almost everywhere she went, business appointments were another thing altogether. When it concerned business, she was either early or right on time.

Heather checked her watch for the third time. *A quarter till seven. Where is he?*

The mere thought seemed to trigger the appearance of her dinner guest. Warren Patterson screeched his burgundy-colored sedan BMW to a halt in front of the valet.

Heather smiled as he exited the highly waxed car, and she walked toward him with a hand extended. Given the fact that he was in a position to help her secure additional business, she dismissed the fact that he was almost twenty minutes late.

Like their meeting at the auditorium a week ago, he was impeccably dressed in the latest fashion "do" for men. His lightweight tan jacket had a high lapel with five buttons. The crease on his matching slacks could probably slice through sourdough bread with ease, and his tan, basket-weave loafers looked as if they had just come out of the box. Gold jewelry sparkled at his neck, on his hand and wrist.

"Hello, Heather. I'm sorry for being late." His smile reflected friendship as he took her hand and lifted it to his lips for a light, breezy kiss.

Only the flicker of her lashes hinted at her surprise at his action. Gerald had kissed her hand at their first meeting so many years ago. She smiled at the thought of their first date, but that thought quickly gave way to thoughts of her current situation, and the smile slipped along with her forced business attitude. *I won't think about Gerald or our problems tonight,* she vowed. *This is a very important business appointment that will require all my concentration and good manners. I won't think about Gerald!* No sooner had she made the pact with herself than a concerned voice inside her wondered if she would be home in time tonight to see him play at least the last two quarters of the game.

"You look very lovely tonight."

Warren's deep voice brought her back to him. She noticed he openly appraised her from head to toe and when his eyes met hers, they signaled his approval.

Heather gently extracted her hand from his and readjusted her smile. Something about his look made her feel quite uncomfortable and suddenly, she grew self-conscious. *You're being silly, Heather. It's just been a long time since any man other than Gerald paid you a compliment.* Fighting the urge to check herself, she cleared her throat. "Thank you. Shall we?"

Heather cocked her head toward the entrance and with his hand on the small of her back, guiding her, they entered the elevator, which took them down, beneath street level, to the restaurant.

"Have you been here before?" Heather asked Warren as they stepped off the elevator and into the lobby of the elegant restaurant.

Decorated with expensive artwork, leafy green plants, water fountains, crystal ornaments and lighting, and with formal black and white linen for the tables, The Menu was not Heather's style. With the unusual circular, multi-tiered layout of the restaurant, without even entering the main room or seeing the menu, Heather guessed this eating establishment was more along her mother's style—upscale, high-dollar, exotic meals served in small portions in a formal setting.

"Yes, as a matter of fact, I know one of the investors. I was fortunate enough to attend the private opening."

"Oh, how nice," Heather managed, hoping her disapproval didn't show through her thin veneer. Without even venturing into the main serving floor, she already knew this was not a place she would visit again. No, she was much more comfortable in a place where she could put her elbows on the table, stick a knife in the ketchup bottle, and use one fork or even better, her fingers. The Menu reminded her of her childhood, and she had no desire to revisit that period in her life.

While Warren conferred with the maître d', Heather gave in to the urge to check her appearance. Turning toward the mirror near the elevator, she decided the black linen dress was okay. Maybe she was just a tad underdressed, but she would pass. She had selected a simple, black sleeveless A-line linen dress with a V front and V back, with the ends of the Vs linked by a petite gold chain. The dress stopped right above the knees and perfectly outlined her curvaceous petite body. She had paired the dress with two-inch sling backs. Her minimalist makeup would have to do in the darkened atmosphere, and the short curls on her head were holding up nicely. *If I'd known it was this type of place, I would have stopped by Nachelle's office and had her check me over and fix me up.* Heather sighed. *I wonder why he picked this place anyway? With this dark lighting, I won't be able to take good notes but, then again, it is quiet. Yeah, that's it. We can get in some really good discussion time tonight.* Heather bobbed her head in conclusion and turned to ascertain Warren's whereabouts. He was still at the maître d's post and looked to be in a heavy discussion. *Gerald would never have brought me to a place like this. He knows how I feel about dressing up and being around certain types of people. There I go again, thinking about Gerald. I've got to stop that.*

"Why the sad look? You're far too beautiful to ever have that look on your lovely face." Warren cupped her chin, bringing her face up so he could peer into her light brown eyes. His eyes held more than a hint of personal interest.

Heather circled his wrist with her hand and removed his hand from her face. The tightening of her stomach muscles made her keenly aware of how uncomfortable she felt with him touching her "Oh, I was just thinking about a personal situation. Nothing important," she lied. "Is our table ready?" she asked with a bright, cheerleader smile.

"Yes, it is." Warren moved aside, and Heather could see the maître d' standing politely by.

She followed the black-tuxedoed figure to a table in a far corner. They walked past several guests who were in various stages of their meals. Heather recognized a few and nodded her head in acknowledgment or spoke a pleasant hello. *Friends of Mother's . . . just as I suspected.*

At the small round table, the diameter of which could fit in an efficiency apartment with room to spare, Warren seated her. When he sat down, their knees bumped under the table and Warren had to readjust his legs. The surface space wasn't much healthier. There was barely enough room for two plates, two glasses, and silverware, let alone her elbows. Heather's suspicions were confirmed. The restaurant's ambiance was directed more to intimate dinners than business discussions. She would have to make the most of it.

"Again, let me apologize for my tardiness. I was trying

to resolve a matter with a friend who stopped by unannounced." Warren was the only one who knew that was a lie. His bedmate had come over right after work and instead of leaving after they had both been physically sated, she had insisted on staying with the intent of sharing a quiet, romantic evening with him at his place. He'd had a difficult time getting her out of his town home and had finally had to resort to physically hitting and pushing her to get her out. "I give you my scout's promise that I won't be late for future dates."

Again, that uneasy feeling that he was perceiving this dinner in a different vein than she registered in the depths of Heather's stomach. She chose to ignore her suspicions for the moment and concentrate on getting him as an ally for her business. However, she did make a mental note to talk to Nachelle about it later. "Oh, that's quite all right. I understand." Heather smiled. "Friendships are very important and should be cherished." She tried not to think about the friend she'd lost in Gerald.

Warren smiled openly, warmly, with no hint of a romantic interest. "I agree. I hope we can be friends."

Heather returned his smile. "I'd like that." She questioned her earlier feelings. *Maybe I've been off base with my assessment. Maybe I'm reading too much into his touches, words, and mannerisms.* She decided, staring into his friendly, coffee-bean-brown eyes, that he was just exhibiting rare traits found in people today. He was caring and gentlemanly and also happened to be one of those touchy-feely persons. She brushed away his earlier comments and gestures and focused on the moment. "You know, I've got to ask you this and I hope you don't think I'm being nosy or offensive, but . . . what is the name of that cologne you're wearing? I just love it."

"It's called Warren Patterson."

Heather wrinkled her brow in confusion.

Warren chuckled. "Back home, there's a perfumer who creates unique fragrances based on your body's natural scent. It's a little pricey, but worth it since you don't have to worry about someone else smelling like you, as with over-the-counter fragrances. But, thank you for the compliment. I'm glad you enjoy it."

The appearance of the waiter halted their conversation. Efficiently, he took their drink order and then the thin, young black man scurried off.

"Perhaps you can accompany me the next time I go home so he can create a fragrance for you. A woman as lovely as yourself should have her own." Warren spoke slowly, deeply, and pinpointed her with a direct stare.

A silence settled at the table. Confusion once again reared its head. Heather wasn't sure now about her earlier assessment. His eyes and voice were sending a message of more than business, more than friendship. Deciding to roll with the changes in Warren's behavior by maintaining her focus on being friendly yet businesslike, she cleared her throat. "Where is home?"

"New Orleans. Have you ever been?" Warren leaned forward and in the already cramped space, that action brought their faces within a ruler's length of each other.

"Yes, I have." Heather leaned back in her chair to regain her personal space. "A few times. My fiancée"—Heather paused to look at the engagement ring sparkling on her ring finger—"and I love to visit there for weekend getaways. We always have a great time."

The bright, cheerful countenance she had worked so hard to construct for this evening cracked as a vivid picture of Gerald with that other woman flashed through her mind. She felt a well of tears bubbling within her, seeking release, but as swift as a heartbeat, she closed the lid on the well. *I can't dwell on that tonight. I've got to stay focused on winning this man over to my side so he feels comfortable recommending us for more contracts,* she told herself. *More business means less time to think about Gerald . . . and what he might be doing.*

Eager to latch on to anything for a diversion, Heather opened the eleven-by-fourteen inch menu and asked, "What do you recommend?"

"I eat only fish so I can recommend only the fish dishes. I've had the salmon with potato pancake. It was delicious. The smoked trout encrusted with almonds is excellent as is the pan-fried haddock." Warren reached over and took Heather's menu. With a smile, he silkily coaxed, "Why don't you let me order for you?"

"Oh, okay," Heather replied, surprised. This was a different experience for her since in all the times she and Gerald had gone out for meals, he'd never once ordered for her.

As if he had been spying on them from a secret watch place, the waiter appeared with their drinks as soon as Warren closed his menu. The waiter quickly set down their drinks, took their dinner order from Warren, and quietly left.

Warren picked up his wineglass and held it high in the air. "A toast to a lasting relationship."

Heather met his eyes and murmured a repetition of his toast. They clinked glasses and took deep sips.

"Ummmm. That's good." Warren closed his eyes in appreciation of the deep burgundy red wine he'd ordered.

With his eyes closed, Heather studied him up close. He really was a handsome man. His caramel skin glowed more yellow than brown in the light from the single votive candle on the table. In the same scarce lighting, his carefully trimmed goatee seemed darker and his aquiline features more sharp. Sitting this close to him, she noticed an aged scar, which ran parallel from his temple to right about the opening of his ear. Just as she started squinting to study the scar, Warren opened his eyes.

His dark brown eyes seized her. His voice was oddly deep and devoid of any emotion. "Something the matter?"

"No, no. I was . . ." Heather nervously laughed. "I'm embarrassed to admit I was staring at your scar."

Warren smiled, showing his evenly capped pearly whites. The abrupt change from deep and dark to light and friendly happened in a flash. "I was a very precocious child. I got into anything and everything, including climbing a tree at the age of three and falling out of it. I landed on my head and here's"—he used his middle finger to trace the downward angle of the scar—"the permanent reminder."

"Ohhhh. It looks like it may have hurt pretty bad back then."

Chuckling, Warren admitted, "It did, but the butt whipping I got from my grandmother for climbing her pecan tree hurt more."

Heather joined his laughter, secretly envious that she hadn't had an adventurous childhood. Her mother had held her captive to the life she had designed for Heather, without Heather's input. While other neighborhood children played outside with bats and balls and bicycles, and turned cartwheels and backflips and wrestled on the well-manicured, lush green lawns, Marilyn had made Heather practice her ballet or the piano or study whatever foreign-language book was lying around at the time. Marilyn was determined to make Heather a black American princess whether Heather wanted it or not. By the time she was eight, Heather knew she didn't want that lifestyle. She knew she wanted to use her dormant, unchallenged creativity in the world of the arts—either acting or dancing or singing or all of the above. Although Heather made constant pleas to Marilyn to sign her up for acting and voice and tap and modern dance lessons, Marilyn had refused, saying over and over again, "I'm preparing you for a charmed life. Be grateful." Heather had finally quit asking and had retreated to the fantasy world she had created and practiced in her mind.

Warren's deep voice interrupted her recollections. "So, tell me about your childhood, Heather. Was it a happy one?"

Heather dropped her eyes, staring at the bloodred liquid in her wineglass. How did she tell this friendly stranger that, until she went to college, her life had not been her own? How did she explain that she had learned early in childhood to cover up the "real" Heather and instead, show the world her superficial, bright, sunshine-yellow face, which hid the pain? "I had an interesting childhood. I didn't lack for anything." *Anything except love, stability, and the freedom to be me,* she thought silently.

"That's an interesting answer." Warren looked her dead in the eyes. "I sense there's more to it than you're letting on. You're doing a good job covering it up, whatever it is, but I have extrasensory skills"—Warren smiled, lightening the gravity of his words—"and can see right through your lying lips to your pained heart. As you can see, I have big ears, so when you feel the need to unload, I'm here for you."

"Thank you, but everything's fine." Desperate to change the subject before she made a spectacle of herself, she remarked, "I didn't know this restaurant existed, and I'm a native of Fort Worth. How did you, a non-native, discover it?"

"Oh, so, that's your way of saying you don't want to talk about the past anymore, huh?" Warren winked at her. "Okay, I'll play along for the time being, but I'm not through with you yet, Ms. Chadwick."

Warren emptied his glass before continuing, "Actually, that same friend I was helping this evening is one of the investors in this restaurant. Her best friend opened this place about six months ago and judging by the reservations book, I think it's going to be a success. Of course, that makes her very happy since she plunked down quite a few dollars."

With a playful lift of her brows, Heather kidded, "Oh, so that explains why we were able to be seated immediately. You're connected."

Warren nodded and winked like a used car salesman. "You got it." Sobering slightly, he added, "And don't you forget it."

Heather wasn't sure if she should laugh or not. Fortunately, she was saved from having to decide on any type of response. The waiter appeared at their table with their dinner, that looked and smelled delicious.

While the waiter served them, she decided that Warren was a very complex man. One minute he was friendly and warm, the next, dark and shadowy. One minute she felt they were both on the same path toward a productive business relationship, yet the next, she felt he was venturing off down the wrong path—the path toward a personal relationship. One minute he teased, the next he was serious. He was a confusing man, quite opposite from Gerald, who was very readable and quite clear in his presentation. Gerald was wonderfully open, wonderfully sincere, and full of trust and love. A person never wondered where he or she stood with him. He would tell or show you! *There I go. Thinking about Gerald again. Will it never stop?* she asked herself. Deep in her heart, she knew the answer was no. She loved him and missed him terribly. *Maybe if I hurry through this meal, I can still get home in time to catch some of the game on TV.*

Warren interrupted her thoughts of Gerald. "How's your dinner?"

"Delicious! I never would have thought about putting salmon and a potato pancake together. It's very good."

"Do you cook?"

"Oddly enough, that's one thing my mother let me slide on. Probably because she herself was not a good cook." Heather chuckled, remembering the first time she ever saw her mother in an apron. "When I was, oh, probably a preteener, my mother decided she was going to cook Thanksgiving dinner. She had her latest boyfriend over and my grandmother and a few other friends of hers. It was a disaster. She had forgotten, or didn't know, she should remove the wax paper from the pie shells. So we had wax-paper pecan pies. Then, she put the macaroni in the pot with the ham hocks and the greens in the pot with the milk, butter, and cheese. When she dropped the turkey in a pot of boiling water, my grandmother put her foot down and took over. Thank God Grandma was there to save the day . . . and the dinner."

Both Heather and Warren were laughing outright. Heather continued. "And can you believe the man still asked my mother to marry him? I guess that just goes to show some men don't necessarily put food at the top of their hierarchy of needs."

"The woman I marry need not worry about cooking. My mother and grandmother made sure I learned my way around a kitchen. As a matter of fact, next weekend I'm having a few friends over for a casual affair. You'll have to come over and try some of my authentic New Orleans-style gumbo. I guarantee you'll be back for more."

"Ummm. It sounds good. But, do you mind if I call you to confirm? I need to check my calendar." In the back of her mind, she also wanted to find out where Gerald would be. If the Mavericks were playing at home, she might be able to sneak into Reunion Arena and force a conversation with him.

"Sure, I'll give you my home number before we part for the evening."

"Before I forget, I brought some brochures and pamphlets about the Twelfth Street Puppet Company." Heather sat up, eager to get the business discussion on the road so she could hightail it home to watch Gerald. "I'm interested in investigating the needs of other school districts—"

Warren held up a hand. "I refuse to mess up a good meal with talk of work. We'll have time during coffee and dessert to talk shop."

"Sure." Disappointed, Heather ducked her head and inhaled her food. It really was good, but one sneak peek at her watch confirmed she would not be able to see the entire game. It was already under way. She would just have to find a polite way out of coffee and dessert, yet still pump him for information about the needs of the nearby school districts. *Of course, if I don't get everything I need tonight, I can always call his office and make an appointment.* She was beginning to think she should have done that in the first place. She was beginning to think he was an odd sort of man.

Heather snuck a peek at Warren. His head was bent over his plate, allowing his black wavy hair to glisten in the candlelight. She noticed he didn't have a wedding ring on his finger and, considering he looked to be in his mid to late thirties, she speculated on why not. Was he a divorcé, a confirmed bachelor, or so complex that no woman stayed around long enough to figure him out?

Suddenly, Warren raised his head and caught her staring at him.

Heather smiled slightly. To cover up for her poor

manners, she asked the first thing on her mind. "Have you ever been married before?"

"No. Why do you ask?" Warren put down his fork and leaned back in his chair.

"I was just wondering." Heather picked up her fork and finished the last bite of food.

"You mentioned a fiancé earlier. He doesn't mind your meeting men for dinner?"

"Oh, no. Gerald . . ." Heather didn't know how to finish the sentence. She was going to say Gerald knew how committed to their relationship she was, but she would have been telling a lie. Gerald had turned his back to her. Gerald had booted her out of his life. Gerald had had another woman in his hotel room. "Gerald understands a business meeting is different from a personal meeting."

"I see. I must meet this Gerald." Warren sat forward, quietly sucking his teeth. "I would like to meet the man who let a beautiful woman out for an evening with another man."

That perpetual smile showed on Heather's light face, and she murmured her thanks. The waiter must have been tuned in to Heather's psyche, for he appeared again out of nowhere, saving her from tongue-tiedness. Silence reigned at the table while the young wait-person poured them coffee, then dished up a scrumptious-looking whipped cream and chocolate pastry dessert.

Warren took a sip of coffee and remarked, "Now, I'm ready to talk business."

"Heather, sweetheart." The familiar sound of Marilyn's soprano voice stopped Heather from returning to the topic she'd been waiting all night to talk about. "You haven't returned any of my calls. If you were younger, I'd spank you."

Heather stood up and walked into her mother's embrace. She kissed Marilyn's smooth, unblemished, fifty-something-year-old cheek. "Hello, Mom. How are you?"

Marilyn, draped in black like her daughter, resembled a short Diahann Carroll. She was two inches taller than Heather, slender, like her daughter, and dark in color, unlike her daughter. She had beautiful brown eyes with specks of gold and brows that were perfectly arched. Her full lips were glossed in Riviera red, and her fingernail polish matched her lips. Marilyn could easily have led a life as a model if not for her height impairment. "Better now that I see with my own eyes that you're still living. You've been ignoring me," she reprimanded her only child.

Heather didn't meet her mother's challenge. She turned instead to Roger Wolfe, her mother's seventh . . . or was it eighth? . . . husband. Heather had lost count. "Hello, Roger. How are you?" She lifted her cheek for his kiss. "In town for anything special?"

"A benefit for the Democratic party tomorrow night," his tenor voice reported. Roger was the perfect accompaniment to Marilyn. His Apache Indian lineage showed in his heightened cheekbones and coal-black hair and mustache, while his African-American heritage showed in his ebony skin and full lips. Standing at average height for a man, he overcompensated for his lack of height by maintaining a trim physique, running ten miles every morning. He, like Marilyn, believed in physical fitness. As usual, he looked utterly handsome in his hand-tailored dark suit, crisp white shirt, and power tie. When Marilyn first told Heather she would be marrying the distinguished senator, Heather had rolled her eyes, thinking he would be like the other men her mother had married: pretentious, stuffy, and rich. But, after her first meeting with Roger, she wondered what was up with her mother. Roger was completely unlike the other men her mother had brought home. He was very subtle in the way he bent Marilyn to his will, yet he was sensitive to Marilyn's needs. He was the only one of her mother's husbands who encouraged Marilyn to let Heather live her life her own way. And for that he won an A++ on Heather's report card. Heather honestly liked and respected Roger, and she secretly hoped her mother's marriage to him wouldn't end anytime soon.

"Ummm," Heather murmured as she turned toward Warren at the table. "This is Warren Patterson. Warren, my mother and her husband."

Marilyn rolled her expressive eyes at Heather as if to say, "I thought I taught you how to make a proper introduction." Smiling like the queen of a country, she leaned forward and offered Warren her hand. "Let's try this again, shall we?" Marilyn said in a schoolmarm voice. "I'm Mrs. Marilyn Chadwick-Wolfe, and this is my husband, the Honorable Roger Wolfe, senator, from this wonderful state and chairperson for the Black Congressional Congress."

"The pleasure is mine." Warren bowed over and kissed Marilyn's hand. Straightening, he shook Roger's hand. "Nice meeting you. I admire your political agenda."

Roger nodded in thanks.

Marilyn wasted no time delving into Warren's business. "And where did you meet my lovely daughter?"

"Through the Fort Worth school system. I work as a program manager for Special Curriculum. It was my pleasure to approve the hiring of Heather's puppet company for our elementary schools. She's done a fabulous job. You should be proud of the beautiful and talented daughter you raised."

Heather could almost see Marilyn's chest puff out. The smile she bestowed on Warren shone in her eyes, and it almost created a halo above her head. "Why, thank you." She paused before continuing. "Well, you men talk for a second while I have a private word with my daughter." As she spoke, she clamped a hand around Heather's upper arm and dragged her off behind a leafy potted palm tree.

Looking into her mother's timeless, dark brown face, Heather could detect the brewing storm beneath the carefully madeup surface.

"What are you going to do about Gerald?"

"Mother." Heather dragged the word out as if it was a song. "Please. Don't start here."

"Why not here? You won't return my calls, so I've got to talk to you somewhere." Marilyn patted her perfectly coiffed hair—not that it needed any attention. "Now, what's going on? Have you two reset the date? Have you commissioned another wedding dress yet? You know you can't use the same one."

Heather's brows drew together in a scowl. "Why not? I had it on for only a second." When she thought about the insanity of pursuing that topic, she shook her head hastily and said, "No, never mind. I don't even want to discuss that, and I can't tell you anything about me and Gerald. Things are still the same."

"What does that mean?"

"It means . . ." Heather blew out an exaggerated breath. "Mother, do we have to discuss this here and now? Warren and I are trying to discuss business and obviously, you and Roger have a romantic evening planned, so why don't we get together tomorrow and discuss it. Okay?"

"Not okay!" Marilyn exclaimed. "You've been putting me off, and now that I have you, young lady, I'm not letting you off the hook." Marilyn's eyes blazed with determination. "Have you apologized to poor Gerald? Have you come to your senses? He loves you and, honey, if you can find a man who loves you, you'd better grab him and quick. Gerald, especially! He's a millionaire, for gosh sakes! This is the dream I've had for you ever since you were born."

It was on the tip of Heather's tongue to point out to her mother that that was the problem—it was Marilyn's dream and not hers and, secondly, that it was Marilyn's marital history that had scared her on her wedding day. Instead, she clamped her lips together and wriggled out of her mother's grip. "Roger is signaling for you to join him." Heather walked away from her mother and rejoined the men at the table.

Roger placed a fatherly arm around her shoulder and squeezed gently. "Heather, I was just mentioning to Warren that we have extra tickets to the party tomorrow night. He's already indicated he's free, so perhaps you can join us as well?"

"Oh, Roger, thanks, but I've a business engagement tomorrow evening." Heather cast an apologetic glance at both men.

It was obvious by the downcast look on Warren's face that he was highly disappointed. "Well, perhaps some other time then?" He spoke to the senator.

Heather shrugged a shoulder noncommittally and added, "Please, don't let my not going stop you from attending."

Roger reached into the breast pocket of his suit jacket and drew out an envelope. He handed the envelope to Warren. "We'll see you tomorrow evening then. I believe our other guests have arrived, so we'd best be moving on." Turning to Heather, he kissed her on the cheek and said, "Drive home safely and call us in the morning." He put a hand on Marilyn's back while mother and daughter hugged quickly, then guided his wife away from the table.

Turning her head over her shoulder, Marilyn called out, "Heather, please, don't forget we haven't finished our conversation. Do call me in the morning."

Heather waved and expelled a deep breath. She loved her mother—but, Lord, she could be a pest.

"You're quite the enigma, aren't you?"

For that brief moment in time, Heather had forgotten Warren existed. She'd been so deep into worrying about how she could put her mother off her trail. Whirling, she turned around to fully face Warren and saw that he held her chair for her. Sliding into the chair, she asked, "I don't understand what you mean."

"You don't?" he teased. "Come on. You give the impression that you're a commoner when in reality you're rich. You're nobility as far as black people in Fort Worth go. Now, I understand the connection. Your father was a great businessman in Fort Worth history. Everybody's heard of Everett Chadwick. He's an icon in Fort Worth business journals, and there's even an elementary school named after him. Now that I know, I can see the resemblance between you and the pictures I've seen of him. I should have guessed prior to this." Admiration glowed in Warren's face.

"It's true my father owned a string of grocery stores, but unfortunately, he died when I was very young, and I don't know very much about him. I am, however, very proud of the fact that a school was named after him. My mother and I attended the dedication ceremony so many years ago. But I prefer to make the Twelfth Street Puppet Company as big as my father's grocery store chain . . . and I'm going to do it on my own merits."

"There's no need to live a hard life if you don't have to. Just kick back and enjoy the benefits of being a Chadwick."

"That's not my nature," Heather replied in a stilted manner. She was getting hot under the collar. Who did this man think he was, telling her what she should or shouldn't do? Gerald always understood her need to be independent and never questioned the direction she took her life. Before she lost her cool, she reminded herself that this man was just a business associate, and the only thing he needed to know or understand about her was that she could do the job she was hired to do. "Anyway, I really need to go. It's getting late, and I have a full day of work tomorrow." Laying her napkin on the table, she gathered her purse and pulled out a few pieces of literature on her company. "I realize we didn't get a lot of business discussed tonight, and I do apologize for my mother's interruption, but I'm hoping we can continue the business discussion in your office. Sometime next week, perhaps?" Heather stood up and placed her credit card on top of their meal ticket.

"I'm sorry you have to go. Things were just starting to get good." Warren made no attempt to shove her plastic back at her or open up his own wallet. He looked down at the credit card and up at Heather. Smiling like a cat after a satisfying bowl of cream, he purred. "This has been an interesting evening. I really am sorry it has to end. How about we at least go to the bar for a quick nightcap?"

The waiter showed up and nodded at the credit card, then at Warren. Warren motioned for him to take the tab and card. For a second, a flash of anger surged through Heather's petite body. *He could have at least offered to pay. I'm sure this qualifies as a school expense and then to act as if the credit card was his! What gall!* Then, she remembered her goal to secure him as a reference. *Well, to hell with that. I'll find someone else to use as a source of information and as a reference. I won't hang my career on Mr. Warren Patterson.* At that moment, Heather decided that she didn't care for this Warren Patterson man after all. In a hard voice, she replied, "Again, I have work tomorrow I need to prepare for."

The waiter returned with her credit card and a pen. He handed the credit slip to Warren. Before Warren could take the paper and pen, Heather snatched the items from the waiter, scrawled her name, and tore off her copy. Stuffing her receipt into her bag, she laid the literature next to Warren's now cold coffee cup and told him quite directly, "Have a good evening."

She turned and walked off without another word. Seething all the way to the parking lot, she cursed one particular man. "What a jerk," she murmured to the black velvet sky as she waited for the valet to bring her car around.

Within minutes, she was zooming and zigzagging through downtown, then south toward her home. With the radio turned up high and the windows rolled down, she soon forgot the terrible evening she'd had with Warren and focused instead on the clock. If she broke the speed limit, she could still catch the last few minutes of Gerald's game. Now, there was one man who was as far from a jerk as the North Pole was from the South Pole.

Warren had a hard time keeping up with Heather. She was driving way beyond the posted speed limit and added to that, the capabilities of her sports car far exceeded those of his Beamer. But, his determination made up for the lack of speed and maneuverability. Plus, he had a general idea of where she lived.

Jackpot, he kept repeating over and over again in his mind. *I've hit the jackpot.*

Ever since he was a young boy, Warren had fantasized about living a life as carefree as the rich white folks whose houses his mother and grandmother cleaned. But, by the age of twenty, he realized the rich women he came across wanted him only as a love slave, a plaything, while their husbands or boyfriends were out of town or otherwise focused on how to capture that next million. He'd had to refocus and had decided that he needed a career that would give him exposure to rich folks. His decision to become a schoolteacher was made solely on the basis of moving up from the classroom to a community relations type role where he could mix and mingle with all the community leaders and school backers, many of whom came from money. His decision to become a schoolteacher was also based on the fact that teaching was still a heavily female populated world. He never had had any trouble seducing women and getting from them whatever he needed at the time, be it money, a promotion, an invitation to a must-be-seen-at-event, or sometimes, just information.

True enough, there had been some drawbacks to his plan. Some of the women got emotionally attached, some felt used, and some just didn't realize that their usefulness had expired. Those were the women who tried to use their power to hijack him, and that's when he would have to set them straight. The departing scenes were all the same: the woman cried; he laughed; she cried some more and threatened him; he laughed and threatened to tell her husband, boyfriend, lover, father, etc. The woman would threaten legal or police action, and that's when he would physically or verbally attack the woman and threaten her life. The woman would pack her things and leave his town house, destroyed, much like the woman he'd entertained and beat before his dinner with Heather. In the aftermath, he'd always hung on to his and pinpointed his next victim.

That was how he'd gone from substitute teacher to program manager, a position only five spots from the top level, the superintendent job, in less than ten years. Every promotion had gotten him closer and closer to his dream of living the life of the rich and famous, and now his job had gotten him in touch with Heather

Chadwick. Heather Chadwick—the only child of Everett Chadwick.

He tingled with excitement. He could almost reach out and touch the reality of his dream.

When he'd first seen Heather Chadwick, he had desired her from a purely male standpoint. She was gorgeous, sexy and intelligent. But, as he attended school district meetings with her, he noticed she had that "lost look" he liked to prey upon. Not everyone could pick up on the "lost look," but he had that gift. And, it was typically present in women who seemed to have it together, externally. Subconsciously, they were usually dealing with some devil and it came out in small, easily overlooked ways like avoiding certain subjects or constantly using closed body language. They were little things but he picked up on them. In Heather's case, he'd noticed how much she smiled and how the smiles were manufactured, cookie-cutter, factory-installed smiles that probably hid some pain that the outside world didn't know about. It was a pain he hoped to understand and exploit now that he knew she was pedigreed, available for marriage and monied. And, the big, big pluses: she was young, beautiful, and sex with her would not be a problem.

Yes, Heather Chadwick, you are the one. You will make my dream come true.

He pulled into the alley behind her building and watched as she worked the control box, commanding the gate to open. As she drove her red Porsche through the gate, Warren wondered if he should shop for a Porsche tomorrow, possibly even place an order for one. After all, once they got married and he quit work, he would need a car befitting his new status, and a Porsche would be a nice choice.

He killed the motor and sat there in the safety of his car, in the darkness of the alley, watching her movements, memorizing them so he could replicate them at the proper time.

Once she passed through the gate, the brown iron gate slowly closed. By timing it, Warren determined there would be plenty of time to follow in behind her if it ever came to that. A remote control, probably inside her car, opened the triple door garage. He could dimly see the company van inside and a motorcycle. The garage door closed much quicker than the security gate, but if he was fast he could make it. Less than five minutes later, lights blinked on on the top floor of the half-a-city-block-long building. Starting his car, he decided he'd seen enough for tonight. Besides, he was getting a sexual urge that he needed to satisfy. Heather and the promise she represented had done that to him. Pulling out an alphabetical black book, he turned to the M's and lifted the receiver of his car phone. Quickly, he punched in the number as he watched the top floor of Heather's building.

"Is your husband gone?"

"Yes."

"Good. I'll be there in thirty minutes." He hung up the phone before the woman could manufacture a fake denial. That was the only thing he tired of: the games. Why women acted like they didn't want it when they wanted it as much as the man, confused him. But, he needed relief, so he would deal with the game. Anyway, it would only be a short while longer before he could throw away the black book and the games and concentrate solely on spending Chadwick money.

As he slowly circled the block to gauge the neighborhood, he smiled. *Heather Chadwick. Soon you'll be mine. And, of course, if you don't work out, Marilyn Chadwick-Wolfe would be the next best thing. Even at her age, she's still a looker.* Warren slowly nodded. Yeah, he could do the mother with no problem. *Heck, who knows. Maybe I can work them both to ensure a happy ending for me,* he thought. Warren laughed and gunned his car as he sped out of the arts district toward the affluent Manchester district.

Seven

"Gerald, you're acting like I haven't taught you a thing." Mrs. Forrester lifted the silver mesh screen off the frying pan and used a stainless steel spatula to turn over the catfish. Stepping back from the stove, she bent low to check on her corn bread in the oven. "You're going to end up hurting yourself if you don't learn to control your feelings." She sat down hard at the fifties-style chrome dinette that she and Johnny Forrester had bought when they purchased this house so many years ago. Although Gerald was a millionaire several times over and had offered to buy her a custom-built home in the suburbs of Atlanta, she had refused his offer. This three-bedroom, one bath, wood frame house, with all its good and bad memories, was not replaceable. This neighborhood, where her children had grown up, where her friends were, close to her church and job, was not replaceable.

Gerald had inherited his Hershey's-Kiss skin coloring from both his parents but his smile, that congenial smile, and those sparkling dark eyes that were almost black, he'd inherited from Dorina Forrester. She was a handsome woman, and although she'd had plenty of suitors after Johnny's death, she had elected to remain single.

Mrs. Forrester was a big woman—tall, standing at five

feet ten inches and big boned, not obese. Not much jiggled when she walked, she was as solid as a steel girder. She was what the older men referred to as healthy. If she had worn her hair in any other style except a twisted bun, one would marvel at the length—halfway down her back—and texture, thick and silky, of her coal-black hair.

Mrs. Forrester would have placed her thick legs under the table, but Gerald's long legs took all the space. Instead, she crossed her legs, turning them to the side, and leaned back in the green and white chair. She linked her hands together over her stomach. "You're courting disaster, son."

Attired in a blue and white Nike sweat suit, Gerald sat on his spine and rolled a black plastic drinking glass between his large hands.

After the final regular season game last night in Dallas, he had planned to stay in town until the playoffs began in two short weeks. However, the long, dark and lonely night and the memories of Heather and their loving moments in his house had changed his mind. This spring morning, he had awakened with the desire to surround himself with people who loved him. Two calls later—one to his coach to let him know where he'd be and one to the airline to book a seat on the next Delta flight to Atlanta—Gerald was eastbound. A few hours later, he surprised Mrs. Forrester by appearing on her doorstep. Pleased as punch to see him, she'd immediately started a meal fit for a czar.

In the short span of time in which he'd been home, a calming sense of peace, love, and contentment had settled over Gerald like new skin. Maybe here within the confines of his mother's love, he would be able to forget, at least for the next few days, the start of the playoffs in two weeks and, most importantly, the breakup with Heather. Yes, this is what the doctor ordered: a mother's loving embraces, gentle kisses, time with his four nieces and nephews, and home-cooked meals. This was his prescription for healing.

Gerald's eyes were focused on the now empty drinking vessel as he listened to his mother's gentle scolding. "Mom, I'm not . . ." He started to protest her words.

Mrs. Forrester swatted Gerald's hand. "You know darn good and well that you haven't been acting like yourself. Your behavior is atrocious. You've been arguing with referees, fighting your teammates. How many times have you been thrown out of the game? Coach called here asking me if I knew what to do to get the old Gerald back before the playoffs. I couldn't tell him a thing. You're letting your anger and hurt control you, son. That's not good."

Gerald hung his head. He knew his mom was right. Heather's betrayal was destroying him from the inside out. No matter how many times or ways he tried to put her out of his mind, something would happen to bring her back in focus. It could be something as simple as a hint of the cologne she used to wear or the girlish giggle of some female or even a TV commercial featuring a talking puppet. Everywhere, he was bombarded with images and remembrances of Heather. He couldn't seem to escape her or the pain. He couldn't believe someone had had the gall to say time heals all wounds. It had been a month without her in his life, and it still hurt like hell.

Gerald spoke slowly, the pain evident in his voice. "Basketball used to come fairly easy. I could go out on the court, execute plays for a few hours, and be totally focused on the game. A nuclear bomb could go off, and it wouldn't impact my playing the game. Now, I have to force myself to concentrate, to think about the plays, and it's become so mechanical. It makes me mad at myself, Mama . . . to think that I may be losing it."

Mrs. Forrester noticed the full-blown tension and

pain on her son's face. No mother liked to see her child troubled; every mother did whatever was in her power to ease the troubles of her children.

Dorina stood up and moved to the side of her only son. Placing an arm around his shoulders, she used her other hand to lay his head against her bosom. As she had done so many times when he was younger, she lovingly caressed his head and spoke to him in a mother's loving voice. "Baby, I know you're hurting, and I know you think life seems real harsh right now. I wish there was something I could do to ease the pain, but this is one of life's lessons that, for some reason, God wanted you to learn."

Gerald melted into the warmth of his mother's embrace. He closed his eyes and let the tension evaporate. He sighed a sigh that was as deep as a natural well. This felt good. To be held by loving arms, to feel safe, to feel peace. For the moment, the troubled waters were still—until his mind betrayed him by conjuring a picture of Heather. He squeezed his eyes tighter and almost as if connected to his eyes, his shoulders drew up, tight. Heather holding him. He remembered the scene as if it were happening now.

He'd had a really poor performance on the court. After the game, the press had eaten him alive for having an off night. His teammates were supportive, and although they had not uttered their disappointment in his leadership, Gerald could see it in their eyes, in their manner. When he'd finally made his way through the after-the-game circus and hooked up with Heather, she had always insisted he come to her home. Upon his arrival there, she had bathed him, fed him, and they had cuddled on her sofa for the remainder of the night. There had been little talk, no lovemaking, nothing but the comfort of being held by someone who loved him regardless of whether he'd had a good game or not.

Knowing he had a good woman in his corner who loved him and watched his back had fortified him and given him the strength to come back strong.

Will I ever find another woman like Heather? he wondered. *A woman who is supportive yet independent enough to maintain her own agenda, her own opinions, her own career. A woman who loves children as much as I do. A woman with a sense of humor, spontaneity, and lots of love. Will I ever get over her?* He'd thought that being with another woman would help him get over Heather. He'd been with many women since that awful day when Heather kicked him to the curb. Short women, tall women, dark, light, fat, thin, and in-between women—and for a time, when he was with those women, he could concentrate on them, but after each encounter, he felt empty, lonely, and afraid. Afraid that he'd never find another woman like Heather and afraid because deep down he knew there was only one woman for him—Heather Chadwick.

"You know what I fear, Mama?" Gerald mumbled into her heavy chest.

His mother moaned a response, continuing her motherly caresses and rocking her big baby.

"I don't know if I'm ever going to find another woman like Heather. I don't know if I'll ever open up to another woman like I did with Heather." Gerald lifted his head and stared into his mother's eyes. "Do you know what I mean?"

"Oh, but I do, son. I loved your daddy dearly." Dorina sighed. "I know exactly what you mean."

Gerald circled his arms around his mother's waist and prompted her, "How did you do it, Mama? How did you keep it together after Daddy died? Is he the reason you never remarried? I know Mr. Foster at the corner store was interested because he always asked about you whenever Linda and I went in there. The only time he smiled was when he said your name."

Mrs. Forrester focused on a spot on the wall. Her mind took her way back, to a time she hadn't thought about in years. Her hand automatically massaged her son's head, back, and shoulders as she shared with him for the first time some of her life with Johnny Forrester. "Oh, son. I can't count the number of times I comforted your daddy like this when he returned from the war. He was a complete man when he left for Vietnam. He was getting ready to open his own mechanic shop. We'd found the exact corner to put the shop on and had put the money down on it. But all that was halted when he went to war. Then when he came back, his spirit was broken." Mrs. Forrester extinguished her hold on Gerald long enough to take a seat next to him at the table. She took both his hands in hers and held them tightly. "You and Linda didn't know the hell we went through after he returned. You two were toddlers, but Donna and Theresa . . . they knew." Dorina looked at their hands clasped tightly together. Her face was drawn tight like a mask. "Your daddy used to wake up in the middle of the night, sweat pouring down his face, screaming for help. Sometimes his memories got so bad, he would get physical. One night, he tried to choke me; he thought I was the enemy. Thank God, Donna and Theresa came into the room and helped me snap him back to reality. He fought the demons of war even up to his final days before the cancer ate him up. He . . . we, our family, never did get back on track. We never did open that mechanic shop. The dreams we had died."

Dorina released a deep sigh and lowered her eyes to stare at a spot on the spic-and-span table. She spoke hesitantly, tripping through thoughts and feelings she hadn't wanted to examine in the past. But, if it would help save her child, she would face the reality of her loss. "When they lowered your daddy's casket into that ground, a big piece of me went with him. I felt hollow and drained but determined. Determined not to let the war steal my children like it stole my man. So, I focused on you kids, becoming the best mother and father I could be. Life became a mission to make you all the best you could be. I returned to my nursing duties at the VA, pressed the clothes, went grocery shopping, repaired the car, helped with homework, cut the grass, took you kids to vacation Bible school, went to basketball games, pressed the girls' hair, planned birthday parties, took you all to Sunday school." Mrs. Forrester rubbed her son's hands. "And I liked it that way. Keeping busy, throwing myself into you-all's lives meant I didn't have to deal with the pain of losing your daddy. I didn't have to deal with the angry feelings that made me think I had been robbed. Soon, it got very easy to brush aside feelings and emotions unless it had to do with you-all."

Dorina used one hand to lightly rub Gerald's head and neck. She smiled sadly. "I wish you hadn't been so young when Johnny died. I wish you'd had more of a chance to really know your father. He was a wonderful man." She blew out a breath and eased back the chair. "I guess that's why I didn't take Foster or any other man seriously. I didn't think they would measure up to your daddy, and . . . I didn't want to cheat you-all of my spare time. It was bad enough that at times I had to work two jobs or extra shifts when we were short of nurses. I sure didn't want to give the little free time I had for you-all to some man who may or may not have deserved it."

Dorina stood up, shaking off the past as easily as she took off her winter coat. Gone were the remembrances, the old haunts. She was Mrs. Forrester again. She quickly hugged Gerald to her bosom. Releasing him, she rubbed his back. "Son, I know you're hurting now, but it gets easier with time. Trust me, I know. And, unlike me, you don't have children to fill your life. But, please, don't make the mistake I did. Don't shut yourself off from thinking you can't find another good woman. There's a good woman on every corner—you just gotta open your eyes and look. That's the only way you're going to get over Heather."

Mrs. Forrester kissed the top of his head, then walked over to the stove to turn off all the controls. "Now, promise me, you'll quit tearing down your life." She turned around to face her son. With a stern look on her face, she encouraged him. "Gerald, you have to be about building up. You had goals, ambitions, dreams before you met Heather. What have you done about the college scholarships you wanted to establish for black children from single-parent homes? What progress have you made on building a rec center here in the neighborhood so the kids will have an option besides drugs and gangs? Son, you had some great ideas. You just need to take up that part of your life again. Don't be like me, going through the motions of living, and please don't think I regret giving up my life for you kids. I don't! But son, I just want you to live your life . . . fully."

Gerald smiled. He stood up and went to his mother, circling her around the waist with his long arms. "You're right, Ma. I do owe myself a good life, and I'm going to start this weekend. Although the playoffs don't start for another two weeks, Coach wants me back in Dallas on Monday, but that still gives me time to get some things rolling. Maybe Theresa'll keep my plans on track for me until after the playoffs."

"That's not a bad idea, son. That'll give Theresa something to do besides moan about how bored she is with her job at that big CPA firm downtown. You know she's always wanted to open her own accounting and management office, and to have her brother as a client would sure give her a nice start."

Gerald bent low and kissed his mother loudly on the cheek. "I love you, Ma. You're the greatest mama on earth."

"And I think I have the greatest children on earth so . . . now . . . go on. Quit hanging on me and go wash up. Lunch is ready."

Laughing, Gerald kissed his mother one more time. He headed toward the door, which led to the single bathroom in the house. An overwhelming sense of peace washed over him, allowing him to release the tension that had kept him company for weeks. This time, when he examined his pain, it didn't feel as raw, the hurt not as handicapping. This time, he felt hopeful that he would recover from Heather's rejection. He was starting to feel alive again.

"And hurry back." He heard his mother's voice follow him down the hallway. "Donna'll be dropping Darren off soon."

Mrs. Forrester fixed her child a plate, all the while humming her favorite Diana Ross and the Supremes song. When Gerald returned, he had a plate full of catfish, greens, corn bread, yams, and red Kool-Aid in a tall, frosted glass waiting for him. All the foods that would fix the body that he'd been neglecting and all the motherly love that would help patch the hole Heather had created. He ate with gusto.

As he sat back in his seat, as stuffed as a tick, the back door opened and in walked his ten-year-old nephew and his oldest sister, Donna Tucker. Darren ran to his uncle and threw his arms around his neck. Gerald returned the hug, feeling warm and serene. He kissed his nephew on the neck and held him back for an inspection. "Boy, you look just like your daddy."

Not surprisingly, Darren was tall. He towered over all the other kids in his fifth grade class and like his grandmother, he was healthy in size.

"Don't he though?" Donna stopped long enough to kiss her baby brother on the top of his nearly bald head and continued on to the spread on the stove. Donna was ebony in skin coloring, with her mother's long, dark, luxurious hair and healthy body. Her features were arranged similar to Gerald's, making her look years younger than she actually was. She, like the rest of her family, was tall, standing five feet, eight inches, which made her the shortest of the Forrester clan. She still had on her postal uniform, evidence that she had either worked extra hours over her midnight to eight shift or had had a lot of errands to run after getting off work. "Mmmmm, Mama. This smells great." Donna reached into the cabinet to get a plate. "You guys had better get going if you're going to get to the birthday party on time. Gerald, thanks for taking him for me. I sure am glad you called him when you got in. This gives me a chance to get some sleep before I have to go in again tonight."

Gerald and his mother exchanged a quick knowing glance after Donna's statement, but neither one said a word about all the long hours Donna worked to support her family while her husband seemed to drift from one job to another, barely staying long enough at any one job to get a paycheck.

"No problem. When we get back, my good-looking nephew can show me some basketball moves, huh?" Gerald playfully rubbed Darren's tightly knotted hair.

Darren's eyes lit up. He was proud that he could tell the kids at school his uncle was a world-famous basketball player. Now, when he returned to school on Monday, he could tell them he had showed his uncle some moves. "Daddy's been letting me drive the car. I can go up and back."

Gerald looked impressed. "Oh, yeah. Next comes sideways."

Darren screwed up his face. His daddy had never mentioned anything about a car going to the side.

Gerald laughed at Darren's comical expression. "I'm teasing, kid. Let's go."

Donna's voice halted their progress. "Uh, young man. Are you forgetting something?" She cut her eyes over to Mrs. Forrester, who sat at the table, smiling like she had just won the employee of the month award at the hospital.

Darren laughed and skipped to his grandmother. "Hi, Grandma." He kissed her smooth cheek and hugged her neck.

Mrs. Forester hugged him tightly and released him with a single hard spank on the bottom. "Have fun, you two."

Darren ran out the door, pulling Gerald behind him.

On the drive to The Cave, a combination arcade, amusement park, and pizza joint all rolled into one and partly situated underground, Darren chatted nonstop. Gerald appreciated the distraction his nephew provided, since it meant he could concentrate less on his broken heart and more on Darren's ten-year-old wondrous comments. He agreed with his mother. Heather would remain in his heart, mind, and soul regardless of what he did to try and forget her, but that didn't mean he would throw his life away. No, sirree, from this point on, he was going forward with his life.

They pulled into the parking lot and as they secured a parking space close to the entrance, they saw several other children with grown-up escorts and gaily wrapped birthday presents going into the white stone building.

One woman in particular caught Gerald's attention. He thought he recognized her, but his mind couldn't latch on to a name or background or anything that would give him an idea of where he'd met her or knew her from.

Darren skipped into the entrance and as soon as Gerald walked in behind Darren, a crowd of ten-year-old boys and girls surrounded him, holding papers and pens up to him for his autograph. Gerald laughed, eyeing Darren. "Looks like someone told all his friends that Uncle Gerald was going to be here. Hmmmmm?"

Darren just smiled, looking like the cat that swallowed the bird.

After the initial hoopla and excitement of having a superstar at the party wore off, the games, rides, and food grabbed the kids' attention. Darren, along with the other children, soon scattered throughout the cavernous building. Some of the children headed downstairs to ride the underground roller coaster and go through the scary house, others stayed on top to try their luck at video games, pinball, and laser tag.

Infected with the kids' excitement, Gerald dumped the birthday gift on the table with the rest of the gifts and headed for the laser-tag game. A huge smile was plastered on his handsome face.

"Gerald." A hand on his arm and a soft voice calling his name stopped him.

Gerald hid his disappointment at being curtailed from laser tag and smiled down at the pretty face of the woman holding his arm. "Hi. How are you?"

The woman he'd seen outside and thought he recognized stared up at him with a saucy smile. "You don't even recognize me," she teased. "After all we've been through." She crossed her arms over her full breasts and pouted her red lips.

"I'm sorry." Gerald wracked his brain. Why couldn't he remember her? She looked so familiar.

The woman was very pale, even lighter than Heather. But, whereas Heather had yellow undertones to prevent anyone from thinking she was white, this woman had no pigmentation. She could easily pass for white if not for her Negroid features: full lips, broad nose, and hips for days. Her collar-length hair was reddish-brown, the color of Oklahoma red soil, and she was taller than Heather, standing about five-five.

It was obvious the woman was enjoying having the upper hand. "I can't believe you've forgotten me so easily. We used to be like this." She held up a hand and crossed two fingers.

Gerald spread his hands and smiled. "I'm sorry. You got me."

Suzanne Armstrong laughed, tickled at Gerald's little boy confused expression. "Suzanne Armstrong. I used to be Suzanne Wilson. The little girl who lived around the corner from you. Remember we used to court . . ."

Halfway through her introduction, Gerald hit a hand to his forehead. He finished the sentence for her. ". . . in elementary school. Hi." He hugged Suzanne, laughing. "It's good to see you. It's been years."

"Yes, it has, and you haven't changed a bit. You still look as if we were ten years old." She lifted an eyebrow and nodded her head in the direction of the laser-tag game. "And judging by the hot trail you were beating to laser tag, it appears you still enjoy little-boy games."

Gerald pretended to be shamefaced. "Well, I do admit the game was calling my name. But, then, don't women say men are just little boys at heart?"

"I'm not going to confirm or deny that statement." Suzanne laughed.

"Come on." Gerald took her by the arm and led her to one of the picnic tables. Sitting down, he straddled the bench, facing Suzanne. "So, catch me up. What have you been doing with yourself for the past"—Gerald did a quick calculation—"twenty-five years? Where have you been?"

Suzanne laughed in her soft voice. "Whoa, Mr. NBA. One question at a time." Suzanne paused to reposition herself more comfortably on the bench. "Oh, gosh. I don't even know where to start."

"Well"—Gerald looked at his watch—"we have about two hours, so start at the time you left to go to that stuffy prep school."

"Oh, yes, that is when we got separated, isn't it?" Suzanne's eyes lit up, remembering.

Gerald clutched his heart as if it still hurt to this day. "Yes, you broke my heart on the last day of sixth grade by telling me you were leaving to go live with your grandma in Florida and wouldn't be back because you had been accepted to some class-act school down there."

Suzanne giggled and spread her hands. "Hey, I was just a kid doing what my mother told me to do. I was sad, too. I was leaving so many good friends."

"Yeah, I know it must have been hard for you. So, you went to Florida and then what?"

Suzanne crossed her legs, stretching her already nice-fitting jeans. "Well, I graduated from the 'class-act' school you mentioned. I landed a college scholarship to Florida A&M, graduated with a prelaw degree, and went to law school at Howard. Moved back here several years ago when my mother became ill, and now I'm practicing law here in Atlanta."

"Whew! You've been busy."

"Mama. Mama. Mama." A round-faced little boy, raffia in color, ran up to Suzanne, singing her title as if he were in concert. "Can I have some more money? Pleassssee."

Suzanne reached into the pocket of her denim shirt and separated a five dollar bill from the other bills. "Excuse yourself for interrupting."

"Excuse me, Mr. Forrester. You're my favorite basketball player."

"Why, thank you, Mr. . . ." Gerald held out a hand for the boy to shake.

The little boy laughed. Gerald noticed he had a soft voice like his mother. He tucked his chin in, in embarrassment. It was the act of a shy child. "Mr. Armstrong's my name. Brandon Armstrong," he proudly told Gerald. They shook hands.

"Nice to meet you, Brandon. Did you know me and your mother used to be girlfriend and boyfriend? We were about your age."

Brandon's eyes grew as large as potatoes. "You mean you could have been my father?"

Gerald shrugged his shoulders. "Who knows? Could have been, I guess." He glanced quickly at Suzanne, whose mouth had fallen open.

"Wow!" Brandon whispered and then zoomed off, no doubt to brag to the other kids about his newfound status.

"Oh, Lord." Suzanne rolled her eyes. "How could you say that? I'll hear about this for the next ten years."

Gerald laughed and couldn't resist further teasing. "I don't know why you didn't tell the boy about us. Were you trying to keep our relationship in the dark?"

"Oh, please," Suzanne gasped, in between laughter. "What relationship! We were ten, eleven, twelve, maybe. I barely remember."

Gerald seemed hurt by her admission. "You don't remember. Those were the best years of my life," Gerald pointed out dramatically.

"Negro, please."

They broke down in laughter.

LOVE EVERLASTING

After their companionable laughter settled, Gerald continued his teasing. He was having a good time. It felt good to laugh and unwind. "So, you have a son. I don't see a wedding ring, so let me get personal if I may?"

Suzanne lifted a brow and pointed an unpolished nail at Gerald. "Be careful," she warned playfully.

"You met some young brother either in college"—he wagged a finger—"no . . . knowing how determined you are, you probably put your schoolwork first, which means you fell in love after passing the bar. Got married, had a baby, and—"

Suzanne interrupted his fictional storytelling. She rocked her head back and forth as only a black woman can do. "I fell in love in college. Thank you very much." She smiled and after a slight chuckle, continued. "We got married. Went to law school. Had a baby shortly after we passed the bar exam. Then things fell apart. The demands of our careers got the best of our marriage. We became strangers. We divorced and that's that." Suzanne wiped her hands together to indicate the finale.

"Well, that's not exactly the ending I was planning but, okay . . . reality works, too." Gerald shrugged his broad shoulders.

"And what about you? Let *me* get personal, if I may. Why aren't you married? And how in the heck did you get roped into a ten-year-olds' party?"

A dark cloud passed over Gerald's face. He quickly banished it by remembering his mother's words. Putting on a brave, albeit false, front, he answered her. "Actually, I was engaged to be married. It didn't work out, so here I am—single with no children." Gerald snapped his fingers, trying to jump-start his memory. "Let me think. What do they call that . . . single income, no children . . . a SINC . . . I believe is the correct term."

"Oh, God, doesn't the terminology these days make you want to throw up?"

"Amen." Gerald chuckled.

"And, as for being here"—Gerald spread his hands to indicate their surroundings—"I actually volunteered. I was so busy with regular season that I didn't spend much time with my nieces and nephews. Since I have a few days off, I thought I would play catch-up. Darren is my older sister Donna's son. Do you remember my sisters?"

"I remember you seemed to have a lot of sisters, but the one I really remember is your little sister. Boy, she was mean and tough. What happened to her? What's she up to? Is she still threatening to kick the girls' butts if they don't cheer for you?"

Gerald knew they were both remembering the driveway scene when Linda threatened to kick Suzanne's butt. That was so many years ago, before college entrance exams and nightclubs, before the NBA draft, before taxes and bills and children and broken hearts. But based on the past and more recently on the confrontation with Heather, it was stabilizing to realize Linda had remained constant in her loyalty to Gerald.

Gerald shook his head and chuckled. *Little sister Linda. I love that girl. She's still got my back.* "Oh, yeah. She's still taking names and kicking plenty of butt. She's doing fine. Playing for the Phoenix Mercury under Cheryl Miller. Loves it. Plays as hard as I do."

"Good for her. I knew she was as talented at the game as you. Probably better, huh?" Suzanne teased with that same challenging smile on her face.

"Hey, don't start that feminist stuff with me. I just came to play laser tag with my nephew, not get into a deep discussion about who's better—men or women." Gerald held up his hands, backing off.

"All right. I'll cut you some slack this time."

Gerald wiped his brow. "Whew! Thank goodness. I do have enough sense to know not to get into a heated discussion with a lawyer." Wriggling his brows and cocking his head toward the laser-tag game, he threw down a gauntlet. "So, think you can hang with some laser tag?"

"Oh, yeah. I've been watching you eyeing that game." Suzanne stood up. "Go ahead. I'll meet you over there after I check with the hostess to make sure she doesn't need help with anything."

Gerald stood up, towering over Suzanne. "Okay, but I have to warn you first, loser buys dinner tonight." He winked.

"Why, Mr. Forrester. Are you, in your own sly, mannish way, asking me out on a date?" Suzanne's open smile brightened her pretty face.

"Pretty slick, ain't I?" Gerald flashed an open, little-boy smile that no living human being could ignore.

Suzanne saucily threw a hand on her hip. "I see right now I'm going to have to keep an eye on you. You're just as fresh now as you were years ago." Pointing a finger in his chest, Suzanne challenged. "But, I'll take the bait. So, go dust off your wallet. You're paying tonight."

"We'll see," Gerald counterchallenged.

Grinning like two hyenas, they parted company for the time being.

Eight

Nachelle munched on a carrot stick as she moved carefully toward the oversized and overstuffed easy chair in Heather's living area. Heather, who had just rinsed the last of their dinner dishes, threw the dish towel on the white ceramic tiled counter and followed Nachelle into the living area, stopping long enough to pick up her glass of wine.

"So, what do you think Nathaniel's going to do now?" Heather plopped down on the cream-colored sofa, crossing her legs under her.

"Oh, he's continuing on with the lawsuit. He's refused to sit down and talk with either Steven or Adolphus. Adolphus, of course, is blaming Steven for the lawsuit, and Steven is angry at himself for not anticipating it. I've been trying to convince him that even with a crystal ball he would not have been able to plan for this surprise. I've told him over and over that it's not his fault, but you know Steven . . . forever concerned about his family's business and its future. I'm just tired of this whole situation."

Heather shook her head sympathetically. "Yeah, I can imagine." After a slight pause, she changed the subject. Concern lined her voice. "And how are you feeling? Have those pains gone away? Have you gone to the doctor yet?"

Nachelle smiled wryly. "I was so dizzy and had such an awful headache last Friday that I went in as an emergency patient."

Heather screeched, hurt that her best friend hadn't leaned on her. "Nachelle! You didn't tell me? Why didn't you call me? I would have taken you to the doctor's office. Please tell me you didn't drive yourself."

Nachelle held up her hand in a stopping gesture. "I didn't call you because I knew you were doing your show at the school, and I know you've been concentrating on doing a superb job so they'll recommend you to other school districts. Millie drove me to Dr. Sanders's office. She checked me over, took some urine and blood and told me my blood pressure was high. She insisted I go home and rest, so I did. I have to admit, I did feel a lot better after I got some rest."

"Do you feel like Dr. Sanders is doing all she can to try and figure out why you've been so sick during this entire pregnancy?"

"Oh, yes! Dr. Sanders is great." Nachelle nodded positively. "I really like her. She's thorough and patient and since she's been through several pregnancies herself, she can relate to the various aches and pains I complain about. One thing she did remind me about is the metamorphosis one's body goes through during pregnancy." Nachelle rubbed her rounded belly and stared down at her stomach. Sometimes, when she thought about the fact that she was with child, it frightened her. She was bringing another life into the world. What a major responsibility! It was overwhelming to think about. "I have a follow-up visit scheduled for tomorrow."

"I'm driving you then," Heather defiantly stated. "What time?"

"Heather, tomorrow is Wednesday. You have the performance at the school."

"So?" Heather protested. "Vandy and Chris can handle it. We've done it before with two people."

Nachelle smiled at her friend. "Thanks, Heather, really. But Steven's due in in the morning. He can take me. As a matter of fact, he'll insist on taking me once I tell him."

"Nachelle, you haven't told Steven that you've been having trouble?" Heather asked incredulously.

Nachelle squirmed in her seat. "Yes and no. I told him I haven't been feeling well, but I haven't told him the details—you know, the headaches, the swelling, the dizziness. He thinks it's just the usual aches and groans that comes from a body adjusting itself to pregnancy."

Heather crossed her arms over her chest and gave her friend a stern look. "Let me guess who planted that misaligned thought in his head."

Nachelle smiled coyly. "He has enough to worry about. You know how hard he works, and I really think it's nothing."

"Yeah, well, I don't remember you ever going to medical school, so how could you mislead him like that? He needs to know it's more serious than just aches and groans. You'd better tell him tomorrow—or I will." Heather leaned forward, placing her elbows on her knees. "Nachelle, you're in your fifth month. You're near the end. You can't fool around at this stage. Please be careful."

"I will. I promise." Nachelle held up her hand in a pledge of honor.

"If it turns out Steven doesn't make it in tomorrow, you'd better call me. Do you understand?"

"Yes, ma'am." Nachelle joked to cover up her fear. Heather was right to use the word "if" in her statement. Lately, the only way she and Steven had been communicating was via the telephone. They hadn't been in the same town in over two weeks, and those dogged fears and feelings of resentment were dragging her down. As she progressed through this pregnancy, she felt like a single parent, which made her wonder if this was a sign of the times to come. Was it foreshadowing? Would Steven be a stranger to their child, to her? She prayed things would somehow change.

"You know, Heather, I came over here tonight to catch up on your life, but all evening all we've talked about is me and Steven and Nathaniel and the baby and my crazy, heavy-duty workload. I feel like I've been so out of touch with your life lately. Our conversations have been so short and hurried. What's going on? You said something the other day about a gift. What's that about?"

Heather smiled, staring dreamily past Nachelle, out of the open windows facing Twelfth Street. A cool summer breeze, tinged with moisture from the earlier rainstorm, billowed the sheer panels covering the windows. The early evening traffic on the busy main street nearby competed with Al Jarreau's soft crooning and body-playing coming from the CD player in one corner of Heather's living room.

Three months ago, Heather had made the decision to halt the wedding. The first month after that had been sheer hell. She'd been miserable because Gerald had become the invisible man, an elusive ghost. He hadn't returned any of her calls, she hadn't been able to catch up to him at Reunion and even though she had spent hours parked in front of his house, hoping to catch him coming or going, she had never been able to see or talk to him after that disastrous weekend. Even the calls to his mother's home in Atlanta went unreturned.

Then, one Monday morning about four weeks ago, two months after the wedding that didn't happen, she'd received a single red rose in a bud vase with a card that simply said, "Your secret love." Included with the rose and card was the latest CD by Luther Vandross titled *Your Secret Love* with the last cut, "Goin' Out Of My Head," highlighted. She recalled the feeling of elation when she'd opened the gift, the feeling of joy when she'd listened to the spotlighted song. Feelings of hope and love ballooned out of control because deep down in her soul and heart she knew the gift was from Gerald.

When a few days later, she received another gift—the latest Babyface CD with a basket of fruit—she was convinced this was Gerald's way of saying he'd just needed some time—time to think about their love and their future. She knew he was saying with his gifts that he would grant her the one-year hiatus she so desperately needed.

The gifts kept coming. One day, a simple friendship card, another day a card professing his love forever, a week later, an R. Kelly CD with his great love songs and a charcoal portrait of herself on beige paper, rolled and tied with a pink ribbon. Even though none of the gifts were signed with a personal name, Heather knew they were from Gerald. She'd been smiling and on cloud nine ever since receiving the first gift and even more so when, just yesterday, the postal person delivered the latest gift: open-date travel tickets to Niagara Falls, their thwarted honeymoon spot.

Heather roused herself from her reverie. Her expressive hazel eyes lit up bright as firecrackers, her smile overran all the wattage measurements. Leaning forward, Heather spoke in her soprano voice, her voice tinged with a dreamlike quality. "Nachelle, Gerald and I are getting back together. Isn't that great?!"

Nachelle opened her mouth, intent on congratulating Heather, when she remembered Steven's recent words. "Oh. Heather . . . I . . . You are?" Nachelle lowered her head and stared hard at Heather.

"Yes, Nachelle. We are." Heather giggled and clapped

her hands together. "I thought you'd be a little more excited than that."

Wriggling out of her chair, Nachelle made a beeline for Heather. Sitting close enough to count Heather's eyelashes, Nachelle enclosed Heather's smaller hands in hers. "How and when did this come about? Tell me everything."

Angling her body to face Nachelle, Heather squeezed Nachelle's hands. "I've been getting these gifts, and cards signed, 'Your Secret Love.' " Heather bounced up, dragging Nachelle with her into her bedroom. "Sit down. Let me show you." Heather ran to the nightstand by her bed and within seconds brought over to Nachelle two hands full of goodies.

The women rifled through the smaller, more portable gifts, with Heather explaining the whats, whens, and hows of each one.

"What's wrong, Nachelle? You don't seem excited or impressed. This is major for Gerald. You know how adamant he was about not continuing our relationship." Heather's excitement was catching, and Nachelle wanted to believe as solidly as Heather that, indeed, Gerald was the sender of the gifts, but something wasn't adding up nice and neat.

"Yeah, I know, Heather, and I'm happy for you, really I am. And these are some fabulous things. As a matter of fact, if you're not going to use that Evelyn and Crabtree gift certificate, I could sure use it."

They laughed when Heather snatched the gift certificate from Nachelle's hands. "I will have no problem using or consuming any of these wonderful items. But, I will share some of this candy with you." Heather ripped the gold lid off a box of Godiva chocolates.

"Ummmm." Both confirmed chocoholics murmured in unison as the first taste of chocolate hit their senses.

"Delicious," Nachelle declared around the chocolate

in her mouth. Surveying all the gifts on the side table, she wondered if she should keep her mouth shut. *Maybe Heather's right. Who else but Gerald would send her such elaborate, thoughtful gifts? Who else would go through the trouble of commissioning a portrait?*

"So, tell me why you're holding back? You're being too quiet, and you've got that worried look on your face." Heather knelt on the floor beside the table and the chair Nachelle occupied and stared up at her friend. "And don't try to lie to me because I know when you're not being truthful."

"I was just wondering how you're so sure Gerald sent them?" Nachelle shrugged her shoulders casually.

"Why would you say that?" Heather chuckled. It was obvious the old Heather was back. She was lighthearted, teasing, and openly expressive. "Of course, Gerald sent them. He's the only man I love, and he loves me."

"Has he called? Has he initiated any contact, other than these?" Nachelle spread her hand to indicate the gifts.

"No, he hasn't, but we both know Gerald loves to surprise and lavish gifts on the people who are important to him. But, now that the Mavs have fallen out of the playoffs, I'm sure that he'll call and soon we'll be back together." Heather's smile was so angelic, Nachelle hated to go on with her interrogation.

"Heather, you know Gerald had some problems late in the regular season and early in the playoffs, right?" Nachelle asked softly, hesitantly.

"What type of problems? What do you mean?" With a quizzical expression on her face, Heather leaned forward, placing her elbows on her knees.

"He wasn't acting like himself. He was having a really tough time on the court. When I spoke with Steven about it, he said it was Gerald's way of dealing with his feelings, his emotions. Did you watch any of the playoff games?"

"When I could. Remember, I told you I had a lot of evening meetings with Warren Patterson, the Fort Worth school administrator I was telling you about. He has a very busy calendar, and it seemed the only time we could get together was during the games." Heather sat up straight as if yanked up by a string. "What did Steven mean? What was Gerald doing?"

"During some of the final games of the regular season and some of the initial playoff games, Gerald was nothing nice. He was fighting other players, challenging the referees. He even got technicals and was thrown out of a few games. It was like someone else was in Gerald's skin. Steven said Gerald was fighting the pain of losing you."

Regret lodged in Heather's throat, making her voice shaky. "I didn't mean to hurt him, Nachelle, and I certainly didn't want his game impacted." Heather wished the floor would open up and swallow her. She hated to think her decision not to marry him this year had caused him to lose his game head.

"I know that, Heather." Nachelle reached out a comforting hand to brush Heather's short curls. "But he snapped out of it. It seemed like overnight, Gerald quit acting a fool and became the same old thriller he's always been—a strong leader, a good points man, an exhibitionist to a certain extent. I didn't understand it until Steven explained that he . . . just . . . maybe his focus had changed."

A perplexing frown settled on Heather's face. "What does that mean?"

Nachelle took a deep breath. "Heather, Gerald's been seeing some other woman. A Suzanne Armstrong. She's a lawyer in Atlanta. They've been linked together in the society pages of the *Atlanta Constitution,* and she was at all of his playoff games. There's talk that Gerald may be moving back to Atlanta permanently. Supposedly, he had lunch with that black coach for Atlanta, and who knows what'll come of that."

Heather blanched. Her already pale skin lost all coloring, and her heart plummeted to the floor. "You're saying this Suzanne is the reason for his turnaround, his new focus, as Steven put it?" Heather stood up and began beating a path around the woven rug on the pine wood floor. The same fear and pain she'd felt on the night she discovered Gerald with the beautiful dark beauty in Houston renewed itself. "That's not true. Gerald loves me. I'm sure he wants to get back together."

"Heather, how can you be so sure? Gerald is not the player-type. Yes, initially, he may have used women to try and forget you, but he wouldn't seriously date someone else while sending you gifts, sending you false, empty promises. Not Gerald."

Heather felt light-headed. "Gerald loves me and I love him."

Nachelle had reached her limit—the kid gloves were coming off. It was time Heather faced the bare truth. "If you love someone, you don't leave them standing at the altar. You marry them. You pledge your life to them. You live happily ever after."

Distraught, Heather cried out, "That's what I'm willing to do." She stopped pacing and turned a frightened face to Nachelle. Gone was the blissful state she'd been in for the past month as the realization that Gerald might not be the sender of the gifts sank in, that he might be seriously involved with another woman. That would certainly explain why he hadn't returned any of her calls over the past few weeks. Sinking her head into her hands, Heather wailed. "All I need is more time. Gerald has to understand that!"

"Honey, the only thing Gerald understands right now

is moving on with his life. He's started the process. Heather, if you don't want to lose him for good, you'd better do something and it'd better be quick."

"I'm making progress. If I could just get ahold of Gerald and tell him the therapist said I'm doing well, then maybe we could set a date for sometime next year."

"Next year! That'll be too late." Nachelle stood up and went to Heather. Grabbing her arms, she forcefully said, "Do you realize that by next year Gerald could be married to some other woman? Do you realize that he was serious about not ever seeing you again? Heather, you hurt him badly—and for you to get back in his heart, you're going to have to come back strong. I'm sorry, but telling him the counselor said it would be a year is not going to cut it."

"Gerald would never marry another woman when he's in love with me." Heather declared, more for herself than for Nachelle.

The beginning of a headache forced Nachelle backward to the chaise lounge she had recently vacated. Closing her eyes briefly, she said in a gentler, softer tone, "A year is plenty of time for Gerald to fall out of love with you and in love with Suzanne Armstrong. Everyone in Atlanta is already speculating about Gerald and Suzanne. The whole town has them paired off. It's apparent that he's *not* waiting for you." Nachelle hated to be so harsh with her words, but time for pussyfooting around had fled. She could see her friend's happy future slipping away. "Why do you need more time? Talk to me, Heather. We've never kept secrets from each other. Please don't shut me out like you did on your wedding day. Whatever this issue is, you don't have to manage it by yourself or with the help of a stranger. Let me help you."

Heather was silent, digesting Nachelle's words. *Is it possible that Gerald is moving on and not looking back? But, no it can't be. He's sent me gifts of love. Then why hasn't he returned my calls? Why didn't he come home after the playoffs?* Heather paced while the dueling went on within her. Back and forth. Back and forth. The war of emotions and logic. *Can it be that I could lose the only man I've ever opened my heart to? It's not possible, is it? He's with this Suzanne lady. So, he's been with other women. This time, it's public. But, he still loves me. How do I know that for sure?* It was driving her crazy, the debate. The conflict overwhelmed her. Suddenly, she needed to release and let go of her frustrations, her fears. She didn't want to keep the poison of her childhood stuffed in the deepness of her body and mind. She wanted peace, something she hadn't had since being in her mother's womb.

Heather looked deep into Nachelle's eyes and seeing nothing but sincerity and love, she knew she could count on her friend to help her fight the demons of her childhood, help her achieve the peace she desperately needed for survival.

Moving forward, she reclaimed the edge of the chaise lounge. Slowly, Heather used words and the support of her best friend to help her exorcise her demons.

"Gerald's the only man I've ever loved. He's so affectionate and sensitive, and he makes me feel like I'm special. I know I was attracted to him initially because he was always so supportive and never tried to stifle me, which is completely opposite of my mom. He encouraged me to make a serious commitment to my puppet company. He convinced me to ignore what everyone else wanted and do what made me happy. Then, as the months flew by, I found myself leaning on him, asking him his opinion and seeking his advice. He became so very important to me, and that's when I realized I had fallen in love with him. That's when I realized I couldn't think about a life without him in it. And that's when I got really scared."

"Scared, why?" Nachelle sat up, anxious to hear more.

"Because I wasn't sure I could be a long-term, forevermore wife for him. Then I started dueling within myself because I also didn't want to end our relationship. But, I knew eventually I was going to have to either select marriage or dissolution, and I didn't want either. I got so mixed up and didn't know what to do, so I kept stalling on the wedding date. It was working until he and Mother got together and turned up the pressure."

Puzzled, Nachelle asked, "What do you mean, you're not sure you can be his long-term wife?"

Heather scooted into a more comfortable position. "It may be easier if I start at the very beginning. My mother." Heather smiled ruefully, sadly. "Dear, darling Mother. What a one-track mind she has. I wouldn't be having this problem if I'd had Steven's parents or yours as role models. Both of y'all's parents understand what it means to keep a commitment."

Nachelle smiled, thinking about her mother and father. Married for over thirty years, Sharlet and Ray Oliver were as committed to each other's happiness now as they were when they first jumped the broom. Once they retired, selling the family insurance business in Austin and the house that Nachelle and her older brother, Vincent, had grown up in, they had seemed to build a shell around the two of them, closing out the outside world and locking in their love. Even now, neither Nachelle nor Vincent knew exactly where their parents were. They knew only to expect check-in calls from them every Wednesday and Sunday. They had become wandering nomads, traveling the United States, Canada, and Mexico in their RV—just the two of them.

A ragged sigh coming from Heather interrupted Nachelle's happy musings. Seeing the mournful look on Heather's face, Nachelle realized Heather's burden went deep, that she was greatly troubled. But, staring into her friend's face, she also discerned the desire for expression. Nachelle inched forward, close enough to Heather to rub her back in comfort, to touch her arm. "Take your time, Heather. Everything's going to be okay."

Nachelle's soothing touch and her gentle words helped Heather to remove any residues of doubt. In a low, halting tone, Heather began the painful process of opening up the scar that had governed her life. "Nachelle, I never told you this, but I've always admired the relationship you and your parents have. You tell your mom everything, and your dad would do anything for you. When I look at how you interact with them and how they relate to each other, I feel so sad. It makes me so depressed." Heather bounced up as if she had sat on a tack. Gesturing dramatically, she began pacing the room. "I mean, when we were in college and your dad would come up to the dorm and take your car to get it serviced and washed, and ask you about your boyfriends and classes and professors, and then take us all out to eat and bowl, I thought that was the neatest thing. And then your mom would come in the middle of the week to drop off a gift basket of home-baked goodies and cute home-made cards, and sometimes she would even wash your dirty clothes for you. I thought that was the ultimate. I remember I used to go to bed at night and dream about a happy childhood, dream about parents like yours. But, in the morning, I would wake up and the dream would disappear."

Nachelle made an effort to keep her face serene, although she was greatly troubled by what Heather said. "Oh, Heather. I didn't know!"

"No, of course you didn't." Heather plopped back down on the chair. Snatching a tissue from the box on the table, she twisted it around and around her finger.

She could not be still. "Then my mother would come and visit me at school. What a nightmare!"

Nachelle looked surprised. "That's so ironic, Heather, because all of us in the dorm used to eagerly wait for your mom to visit. We thought she was the most beautiful, most sophisticated and cultured woman on earth. We were so jealous of your having a mother who was so un-momish. I mean, she always wore the latest fashions and always had a good-looking man on her arm who doted on her. After her visits, we used to practice walking like her and talking like her and gesturing like her. And, as if that wasn't enough, she always left you with gobs of money and clothes—closets full of clothes, and you never even wore them. I remember that time you made me ride with you to Goodwill to drop off clothes that still had tags on them. I always hated that you were smaller than me."

Heather's voice was low. Nachelle had to strain to hear her, but there was no mistaking the tears shimmering in the hazel eyes. "Money and clothes are nothing compared to a family unit that is intact. I would have given it all up for just a conversation with my father and a mother who respected me for who I am—and not the person she wanted me to be." Swiping at the tears rolling down her cheeks, Heather continued. "The ugly truth is, my childhood and my adult life have been a lie."

Nachelle grabbed another tissue from the box and dabbed at Heather's cheeks.

Heather locked a hand around Nachelle's wrist and stopped her action. There was urgency and desperation in her movements, her words. "Nachelle, you have no idea what it's like to be a child repressed, confused, and depressed because you don't have a real daddy and you can't be yourself. I was young when I recognized three constants in my life: my mother would have a different husband every three to four years, I would never learn anything about my father, and my mother would dictate who and what I would be. Every time I thought about those things, I would get depressed. But, Mommie Dearest didn't allow depression in her house because it makes you frown and causes wrinkles. So I was required to wear a happy face and pretend everything was A-okay." Heather dropped her head into her hands. "I'm sick of having to put on my happy face—the face my mom expects to see; the face people, including myself, have grown accustomed to seeing."

Nachelle circled her arms around Heather's shoulders and rocked them. Laying her head against Heather's, she murmured, "I'm so sorry, Heather. I didn't know."

"Of course, you didn't," Heather muttered into Nachelle's neck. "That's how good an actress my mother made me to be." Heather pulled back, her large eyes glistened. "Nachelle, I don't want to be unhappy anymore. I don't want to live under my mother's shadow anymore and most of all, I'm afraid of losing Gerald because I fear I'll be like my mother—fall in love and then destroy the relationship with marriage." Heather wiped her eyes and tried to steady her breathing. "Despite any difficulties you may be having in your marriage right now, you and Steven will be together forever because that stable foundation, that good role-modeling is there. I'll never have that. My marriage will be temporary just like my mom's, and I don't want a temporary marriage to Gerald. I want to be married to him for a lifetime. Anything less would kill me."

Nachelle tried to project herself into Heather's shoes. If her mother had claimed to be in love and married multiple times and if she had witnessed all this activity at an impressionable age, would that have impacted her view of marriage? Nachelle decided that it would have. Her heart burst with new understanding, with empathy.

She understood now how the early warped introduction to love and marriage had colored her friend's view. It was as clear as ice now why Heather had left Gerald standing at the altar. And it didn't stop in Heather's love life—there was spillover into her professional life, too. Heather's background illuminated her choice of a career, entertaining children—making them laugh and ensuring they were exposed to sound principles and values. It explained why her puppet shows always featured the traditional family, and, at the core of the shows, family themes with happy endings and good role-modeling. These were the things Heather had needed growing up, and now she was doing her best to make sure other children got what she hadn't received.

Turning Heather's face to hers, Nachelle said, "Heather, you don't have to remain captive to your mother's image. Just because your mother has had a terrible string of marriages doesn't equate to your following in her footsteps."

"But, I'm my mother's daughter. I am her flesh. Why would it be any different for me?" Heather's bleak face broke Nachelle's heart.

"Because you have the strength to change the cycle. You have the willingness and the desire to rewrite the script."

"I wouldn't know how to make it different. My mother fell in love, married, then divorced—repeatedly. How can that change for me? I don't want my beautiful love for Gerald destroyed by marriage." Heather's shoulders sagged. Her voice was devoid of all energy. "I wish Gerald hadn't been so insistent upon getting married—things would have been all right, then."

"No, Heather, things wouldn't have been all right." Nachelle spoke with strength and conviction. "Gerald's a patient man, but even a patient man has his limits. With Gerald being the marrying type, he would have insisted you marry him at some point. Which is what happened."

Heather jumped up. Tilting her face to the ceiling, she declared her dilemma. "Nachelle, I'm scared. I want to marry Gerald, but my mother's influence is strong. I'm afraid our marriage won't last and the next thing you know we'll be in divorce court, the kids will be in counseling, and I'll start work on marriage number two."

Nachelle stood up and walked over to her friend. She grabbed her by the shoulders and turned Heather so they stood face-to-face. "Heather, how can you say that when you just used my parents and Steven's parents as examples of couples committing to and staying in love? Use them as your role models for your marriage to Gerald. Interview them as you would interview someone for your puppet shows." Softening her words and tone, Nachelle continued. "Being in love and being married is a blessed thing. But, like anything else, it takes work, Heather. Trust me, it is hard work." Nachelle thought about her own dilemma with Steven and realized the words were for her own benefit as well.

Heather scooted out of Nachelle's hold. Walking to the window, she leaned her head against the pane and plaintively remarked, "I don't know, Nachelle. It's such a big risk. I wonder if Gerald would maybe consider living together first."

"No, he wouldn't, and I'm not going to let you shortchange yourself with that suggestion." Nachelle spoke adamantly. With short swift strides, she was beside Heather. "You've already recognized the need, the desire to be different from your mother, and to start that ball rolling, I think the first thing you should do is have a conversation with your mother. Have you talked honestly to her about this, Heather? Have you asked her why she married so many times? Are you sure she was

LOVE EVERLASTING

in love with all the men she married? Maybe she married for other reasons. You should sit down with her, just the two of you, and share with her your true feelings. Tell her everything . . . tell her everything you just told me. Until you do that, you'll never have a chance at real happiness, either, with or without Gerald."

"You know how Mother is. She won't listen. It'll be like when I was growing up. She'll be doing a million other things while I'm trying to talk to her. Her mind won't focus on me or my words. The only time my mother doesn't shut me out is when she's treating me like her favorite china doll, which she dusts off, changes clothes, and talks to briefly once a month."

"Then it's up to you to *make* her listen. You've got to find some way to capture her complete attention. But, Heather, again, your change will not happen until you talk to your mother and select a wonderful marriage to model. You have the power to make your reality a dream, okay?"

Heather smiled timidly. "You're right. I will talk to Mom and then somehow, some way, I'll catch up to Gerald and plead insanity. Maybe then he'll take me back."

Nachelle smiled at her friend. "It's okay to plead insanity, but make sure you also tell him the exact same thing you told me. I guarantee you, Heather, if you're as up-front and honest with Gerald as you've been with me, he will be your biggest champion for change and your strongest ally." Nachelle hugged her friend. Pulling back slightly, she finished, "Of course, you know you always have me when the going gets rough. I'm just a quick car drive across town."

Nine

The friends exchanged a long, heart-to-heart hug.

Drawing back slightly, Heather said, "Thanks, Nachelle, I needed that. Even though I still have some work to do, I feel lighter, less troubled. It did help to discuss this with someone who cares."

Nachelle smiled encouragingly. "Good, I'm glad."

They hugged again quickly, and over Nachelle's shoulder, Heather spied the table loaded with gifts. Moving out of Nachelle's arms and toward the table, Heather asked, "So, you really think Gerald's not the sender?" Heather picked up one of the certificates, examining it as if it were a new species of life.

Nachelle joined her, staring down at the treasures. "I don't think so, Heather. Gerald would have contacted you by now if that were the case." A tremor of excitement and anticipation spiraled through Nachelle's body. "So, the question remains . . . who, if not Gerald?"

Heather was silent. For the past month, as the gifts rolled in, she had put her money on Gerald as the sender. Now, faced with the possibility that it might not be him, she had no idea who it might be. Shaking her head, she slowly murmured, "I don't have a clue."

Nachelle picked up one of the gift tags and flipped it open to look at the signature. "Whoever it is . . . has beautiful handwriting. Gerald sure doesn't write like this."

"Well, I thought about that when the gifts first started arriving. But, I figured Gerald had the salesclerk write the card for him so I wouldn't guess who sent it."

Shrugging her shoulders, Nachelle agreed. "Yeah, that makes sense. Hmmmm." Nachelle's analytical brain sorted through the facts. "What address was listed on the envelopes?"

"I don't know. I think they had only my name and address." Heather sighed deeply. "I can't remember, and I've thrown the envelopes away." Flinging herself down onto the chaise lounge, she remarked, "But, you know what, Nachelle, it doesn't even matter. If it's not Gerald, I don't care."

"I understand, Heather, but this person obviously has a major crush on you. I mean, this man has gone through a lot of trouble declaring his interest in you. It's only fair that he be informed that you're not interested, so he can move on."

"You're right. I didn't think about that."

Nachelle sat down beside Heather. "Of course, to let him know that, you need to know who he is." The friends had matching puzzled expressions. Nachelle continued. "Okay, Heather, so think. Who in your personal or business life has been acting secretive or has expressed an interest in you?"

Heather scrunched up her face. As she opened her mouth to answer Nachelle, the loud buzzing of the doorbell silenced her thought and words.

"You expecting someone?" Nachelle quizzed.

Heather got up and walked to the window facing the street, which ran in front of her building. "Only you, and you're already here." She looked down and scanned the parking spaces. Warren's burgundy car was parked in one of the stalls.

"Ohhhh!" Heather's surprised expression said it all. "Shoot! I forgot he was coming by to pick up that proposal for the Arlington School District."

Nachelle followed Heather through the bedroom and into the living room. "It's the guy from the school district?"

"Yes, Warren Patterson." Heather spoke into the intercom. "Be right down, Warren." Scratching her head, she began searching for her oversized, circular key ring, similar to the ones school janitors carried on their belts. "He set up a meeting for me on Thursday in Arlington to talk informally with a peer of his. He mentioned he would be by tonight to pick up the proposal so his friend could review it before the meeting. Awww. Here they are." Heather plucked the keys from the space under the sofa table. "Come on." She motioned for Nachelle to follow her downstairs and to the front where Warren stood waiting entry.

Nachelle obediently followed. "I thought you said the guy was weird?"

Even though, in her huge, cavernous building, there was no way Warren could hear them discuss him, Heather lowered her voice. "Oh, you're thinking about the first dinner meeting I had with him, when mother and Roger showed up. Well, that night he tripped me out. One minute, he was Mr. Personality, the next minute, Mr. Cold Fish. One minute, he was making references about a personal relationship, the next, he was back on business. He just seemed really wishy-washy, very hard to read and almost two-faced. It was a trip, a disaster. I didn't think he would be able to help me with other contacts, and actually I was prepared to find another contact within the school district who could assist me with obtaining leads."

Heather sorted through the numerous keys on her ring and locating the two for the wooden double front doors, she continued. "Then we had a follow-up meeting, and it went so well. It was like night and day. I found out he's really a nice guy, and he's been such a big help to me. He has turned into the biggest supporter of the Twelfth Street Puppet Company." Heather half-turned at the front door. Smiling charmingly at Nachelle, she shrugged her shoulders and said, "I just chalked that first meeting up to that awkward, initial, getting-to-know-you stage."

As she worked at unlocking the door, she continued. "I don't know how I forgot he was coming by this evening to pick up that proposal."

"You *did* do the proposal, right?"

"Yes, silly. I just forgot he was coming to pick it up. My typical MO is the mail."

Heather turned her head to Nachelle, who stood behind and to the side of her. Grinning like Chester Cheetah, she winked at her friend. "I'm on the verge of landing another big school contract, and I owe it to Warren Patterson." With a flourish, she flung open one of the wooden front doors.

"Hello, Warren. Come in. Come in."

"Thanks. How are you this evening?" Although he wore a tricolor silk sweat suit, which seemed to spotlight his dark coloring, he looked no less sophisticated than he did when wearing one of his custom-tailored suits. Gold sparkled at his neck and wrists, and his wavy black hair was brushed away from his forehead. His smile was as beguiling as any experienced salesperson's. He nodded politely to Nachelle.

Nachelle returned his smile, her eyes roamed over his face, then covertly dropped to scan the rest of his person. Her eyes opened wide when she spied the gift cradled in the palm of his right hand. *Oh, my goodness. He's the secret admirer!*

"Just fine." Heather closed and locked the door behind Warren, then moved to Nachelle's side. Seeing the amazed expression on Nachelle's face, Heather asked, "Nachelle, what is it?" Heather's eyes followed the path to where Nachelle's eyes were glued.

"Oh." Heather's breath caught in her throat. In Warren's hand was a rectangular-shaped box wrapped in plain brown paper with a dried flower arrangement on one side, along with a gift tag.

Warren looked down to where the ladies stared and extending his arm, smiled graciously. "I wish I could claim this, but unfortunately, I can't. It was sitting in front of your door."

Simultaneously, both women released their breath. Exchanging a quick glance, they knew instinctively what the other had been thinking. Nervous laughter dissipated their identical thoughts.

"I'm sorry. That was rude of me." Nachelle reined in her embarrassment and flashed a friendly smile. "Hi! I'm Nachelle DuCloux. Heather's friend."

"And business advisor and accountant and proposal, grant writer." Heather tacked on all the other functions Nachelle helped her out with in the course of running the Twelfth Street Puppet Company.

"Nice to meet you, Ms. DuCloux." They shook hands. "I'm Warren Patterson."

"Yes, Heather has told me of you. It's really great, the assistance you're providing her. I hope things go well on Thursday." Nachelle made a mental note to call Heather that evening to see how the meeting went.

Warren looked at Heather and conspiratorially winked at her. "I think they will. My counterpart seems very interested." Pleased with how well his plan was progressing, Warren's chest pumped up a bit. *So, this is Heather's friend . . . the one she talks about all the time. Obviously, Heather's mentioned my name to her. That's a good sign, as well as their reaction to the gift. I must be making quite an impression on Heather. Why, we'll be married in no time, and then I can rest on her laurels.* His-many-times-practiced, falsely tolerant smile widened.

Nachelle nodded her head approvingly.

Warren continued. "DuCloux . . . that's an uncommon name. You wouldn't by chance be related to the DuCloux Enterprises DuClouxs?"

The friends again exchanged a knowing look.

"My husband, Steven, is the CEO of DuCloux Enterprises."

Warren's genuine smile outshone the setting sun. "Well, it's a small world, isn't it? I've helped many students get summer intern positions with the Hayes Group . . . now, of course, DuCloux Enterprises." Any more good news about his future wife's connections, and he would burst with happiness. First, to discover she was one of two heirs to the Chadwick fortune and then to discover she was "in" with the DuClouxs, whose names appeared in almost every edition of *Black Enterprise*. The world would be his playing field. The bright future he had envisioned for himself was nearing reality.

Once he was successfully married to Heather, he could relax and live the life he was destined to live. And he was thankful because he was tired. Tired of having to work, tired of "playing" middle-aged women for promotions and money, tired of having to manhandle women, tired of being ignored, belittled, and subject to the whims of others. Once he got his hands on Chadwick money, he would live a life of convenience. Although he hated that his opportunity to lead his destined life depended still on a woman, he would shelve his hatred for women for the time being and make Heather Chadwick his exception, because this time next year, instead of having to work in July because of summer school and the new year-round school calendar, he would be relaxing on the sandy white beaches of Monte Carlo, being unfaithful to Heather with some Italian or European beauty. He would be pampered to the hilt.

Staring into Heather's lovely face, he admitted to himself, *Oh, yes, I'm ready for what's rightly mine: power, social position, and money. The things denied me, all because my mother was a curveous and beautiful, but poor, backwoods girl from Louisiana who didn't know how to stand up for herself or her bastard child.*

"Nachelle is not giving herself enough credit. She is the CFO of DE. She has the checkbook."

The ladies smiled, knowing full well that Steven would agree with that simple assessment.

Warren looked doubly impressed and he quickly, covertly, sized up Nachelle, wondering if she cheated on her husband. The DuCloux fortune was another pot of gold he wouldn't mind getting his hands on. "Oh, well, then, as they say, true power lies behind the throne or in this case, behind the CFO."

Polite smiles and murmurs of agreement followed his comment.

Remembering Warren still had the gift in his hands, Heather moved forward. "I'm sorry. I'll take that."

"And please excuse my reaction earlier," Nachelle said again. "It's just that Heather and I had been upstairs talking about these wonderful gifts she's been receiving and, lo and behold, you show up with one."

"Well, I'm sorry. I wasn't trying to hide the gift. I simply forgot it was in my hand. Is it your birthday?" The fine lines at the corner of Warren's intense brown eyes crinkled, the only clue that he had a hidden motive for asking his question.

"Oh, no. Just someone with a crush, I think. Quite honestly, I don't know." Heather flipped over the gift tag and found the same message that was written on the other cards, in the same beautiful handwriting; "I'm sorry, I know this is rude but I just can't wait." Her hazel eyes glowed as she ripped into the wrapping paper and then the box. Eyes opening wider, she pulled out a bottle of Dom Perignon. "Wow, Nachelle, looks like we'll be celebrating something soon."

"What does the other tag say?" The women were huddled together, oblivious to Warren's presence.

Another gift tag around the neck of the bottle read: "One day soon, I will make my presence known, and there will be a celebration of love like no other."

Heather and Nachelle looked at each other. Heather spoke her thoughts. "Are you sure it's not Gerald? This could be his grand scheme, you know—send gifts and then ignore me until he's ready to spring his big surprise on me." An idea popped into Heather's head. "Call him for me, Nachelle. Casually tell him about the gifts. See if he confesses to you. Please, please, do this for me, okay?" Heather pleaded.

"Heather, why don't you just let it play out?"

"I don't want to. I want Gerald, now." Remembering Nachelle's words upstairs, Heather decided to use them in her favor. Her excitement bubbled, making her face glow and her eyes animated. "You said I should speak with him anyway. So, set up a lunch with him and instead of you going, I'll show up and ask him myself. He won't refuse you. Please do this for me."

It was on the tip of Nachelle's tongue to agree when she remembered they were not alone.

Off to himself, as he had been for most of his life, pushed aside while the rich black folks huddled together, plotting his demise, Warren worked very hard at keeping his anger in check. But seeing Nachelle and Heather huddled together, giving credit for his gifts and time to another man, and plotting to get *that* man to confess his undying love and thoughtfulness, carried him back to this childhood where he suffered greatly at the hands of rich black folks. He expected rich white folks to ignore and belittle him, but for his own to do so, especially his own father—the richest, most socially upward black aristocrat in New Orleans, Louisiana—was a stab in the heart.

Taking deep breaths, he made himself focus on a less volatile situation. He made himself conjure an image of his grandmother's calming face and soothing hands. It worked. He could feel his anger subsiding, and he was thankful. His anger was a powerful thing and if it had gotten loose, he would have had no trouble beating both women. Until he married Heather, he couldn't afford to do that. Oh, but, after the wedding, he would beat her and good. *How dare she treat me as if I don't exist? How dare she give my credit to another man?* Well, in just a few weeks, he would be subject to this lack of respect no more. Warren could feel his anger giving way to revenge. Oh, how sweet it would be.

But, until that blessed day, he would have to take his anger out on Mary, his friend and part-part-time lover at the Arlington School District. They would meet tonight for drinks and afterward, go back to her place where he would beat her for Heather's indiscretions and then make wild, passionate love to her. Yes, it would be a good night after all.

"Please forgive our bad manners, Warren. As you can see, we get a little excited at times and forget ourselves." Nachelle apologized for the two of them.

"Oh, no problem. I understand," Warren smoothly replied and meant it. Anxious to get on with his exciting evening plans, Warren added, "Heather, I must confess that in addition to coming over to pick up the proposal, I was hoping I could get a tour of your facilities. I feel I'm becoming so intimately involved with your business, I'd like to know more about your place, if you don't mind." Warren had spent plenty of nights learning about the outside of the building. He'd been looking for a way to get inside so he could capture the layout in his photographic memory and plant some sound bugs so he could monitor her activity and conversations. He placed his hands inside the pockets of his sweatsuit and fingered the miniature bugs he'd bought on the black market. Top-quality equipment, the same stuff the CIA used.

"Of course, I don't mind. Nachelle, would you mind taking this upstairs?" Heather handed the bottle and torn gift wrappings to Nachelle. "Warren and I will be up shortly."

Nachelle headed toward the back of the building, to the stairs leading upward, while Heather and Warren headed to the left to view the lobby, theater, and offices.

Ten

The ticking of the Mickey Mouse wall clock competed with the adult classics playing on V100, which competed with Heather's private conversation with herself—all sounds that disturbed the otherwise peaceful evening.

"Okay. Nachelle said put business meals into the entertainment expenses folder and gas receipts go into the auto expense folder along with the mileage log." Heather scratched her head.

Closeted away in her private office downstairs, Heather talked herself through the monthly process she usually avoided. Despite the fact that she thought filing her business expenses was the epitome of boredom, and that she hated being cooped up in her office when she'd rather be working on a new script or preparing for this weekend's engagement at a local community center, she didn't mind tonight. The day had been good. She had received the contract with the Arlington School District! Even the monthly record keeping and filing that Nachelle made her do didn't knock the smile off her face or upset her happy mood. *My second contract. Twelfth Street Puppet is on its way!*

Heather reared back in her chair, the receipts and filing forgotten. She grinned, thinking about the success of her meeting this morning. Suddenly, she got the urge to dance in celebration, like the African-American man on the HUD first home-buying commercial. Impulsively, she kicked off her Minnie Mouse house shoes and climbed up on top of her desk, stepping all over the yet to be filed receipts and folders. Throwing her hands in the air, she excitedly swung her hips and shimmied her shoulders. Like Rocky Balboa, she made fists and pumped them high in the air.

The ringing of the telephone interrupted her celebration. Without climbing off the desk, Heather swung low and snatched the receiver off the hook.

In a singsong voice, she answered good-humoredly. "Good evening, and how are ya . . . whoever you are."

"Heather"—Nachelle's voice floated through the line—"you sound really happy."

"I am!" Heather's exuberance exploded through the line. "Guess what I'm doing?" She laughed her Tinkerbell laugh as she sat down on top of the desk, cross-legged.

Nachelle laughingly replied, "What?" The Heather she'd known for over ten years was on the other end of the line—enthusiastic, playful, and full of energy.

"Celebrating. Ask me why. Ask me why."

"Well . . ." Nachelle dragged out the word. She repositioned herself in her leather chair in her office and leaning back into the cushiony softness, offered the most logical answer. "I assume since it's Thursday and since you called me earlier today and left a cryptic message with my secretary and since you're so happy, happy, happy, I can only guess that you had a successful meeting this morning. Am I right?"

"Yes, yes, you are! I got the contract! I did it!" Heather pumped her hands in the air again.

"Congratulations! I knew you could. I'm so proud of you."

"Thank you," Heather gushed. After taking a quick breath, she said, "And, oh, Nachelle, it was so much easier than getting the Fort Worth contract. All I had to do was pitch it to this Mary woman. There wasn't a panel of folks like with the Fort Worth school district. She was so nice and friendly and helpful. She gave me on-the-spot feedback. I can't remember her last name, but I have her card." Heather's thoughts zoomed in another direction. "Hey, if I send her flowers and a card, is that tax deductible? That's not considered a bribe, is it? Oh, well, it doesn't matter. I'm going to do it anyway. I'm so excited. Let's celebrate! What are you doing tomorrow night? Is Steven going to be in town?"

Even though Heather couldn't see her, Nachelle held up a hand. "Whoa. Stop. You're going way too fast." Heather's excitement was infectious. Nachelle giggled. "Before I answer any of your questions, I want to hear everything—from beginning to end. Don't leave out anything."

"Okay. Okay." Taking a deep breath, Heather briefed Nachelle. "I arrived on time, of course, and Warren was waiting for me. We walked to Mary's office, and she let me run through my presentation. Then I did a little skit with Aretha and Marvin." Heather added conspiratorially, lowering her voice a fraction, "You know, everyone loves Aretha and Marvin. After that, I gave her a brochure, some business cards and a contract and asked her when I could check back with her on her decision." Heather hurried on. "She took my information but told me she'd already made up her mind. She said she was very impressed and thought my program would be extremely beneficial to the development of the children, and if it were up to her she would sign the contract right then. Then we tried to go to lunch. Isn't that great?" Heather squealed.

Nachelle wrinkled her brow in confusion. "I thought you said you have a signed contract?"

"I do." Heather reached over and turned down the

radio a notch. "Mary explained that since it was July, most of the legal staff and the top brass were still out for the summer break. The only reason she was available to meet me is because she heads the summer school program, as does Warren, which I didn't know until this morning. But, Mary said that as soon as the staff returned in early August, she'd have the contract waiting for them, and it would only be a matter of days after that. She even asked me if I could be prepared to start in August for the fall school year, given the short lead time. I, of course, said no problem, mon." Heather mimicked a Bahamian accent. "It's been a good day, Nachelle, and I give thanks to Warren and Mary. I took Warren out to lunch. I can count that on my taxes, right?" Heather raised one hip and scooted the receipts from under her fanny. Holding the Goofy phone against her ear, she searched through the scattered records, looking for today's receipt.

"Yes, you can deduct a business meal during which business is discussed. We'll itemize it with your other receipts." Nachelle turned the conversation back to Heather's meeting. "I'm surprised this Mary woman has the latitude and power to make this big of a decision on the fly. It took forever for the Fort Worth administrators to make a decision, and then it had to be written in the budget. So, you don't have to deal with any of that with Arlington?"

"No. But, I think a lot of it has to do with Arlington being a smaller school district—you know, less bureaucracy. And Mary is almost at the top of the ladder. She's one of the assistant superintendents, and she's the one who heads the curriculum. Plus, Warren was great! He opened the door for me. I owe him a great deal. It's hard now for me to think that at one point I thought he was weird and was prepared not to have anything to do with him."

"Yeah, first impressions can be misleading. So, why didn't Mary join you all for lunch? Considering it was for business."

"We were all set, the three of us, to go, but when I returned from the rest room, Mary said something had come up and she wouldn't be able to join us after all. I was disappointed. She seemed like such an interesting lady and so smart. I would have loved to talk with her outside of a professional setting. I can tell she loves children as much as I do. Even with that awful black eye, her eyes glowed when we talked about the development benefits my program could bring to the children."

"She had a black eye!" Nachelle squealed. "What happened?"

"Car accident. Her lip was split, but it was starting to heal over, and there was a gauze pad along the side of her temple. She looked pretty bad. I feel sorry for her having to work under those conditions. I wish I had known beforehand because I could have easily rescheduled until she felt better."

"She must really be dedicated to her students and profession to work," Nachelle said, "when it sounds like she should be home resting and recuperating."

"Speaking of resting and recuperating, young lady . . . What did your doctor say about your continued headaches?"

Nachelle squirmed in her seat. "I didn't go to the appointment. Something urgent came up here at work." When Heather tried to interrupt, Nachelle hurried on. "I had to give a verbal, tape-recorded deposition to the lawyers regarding Nathaniel's stupid claims."

"Oh . . . well, I understand that—but nothing, Nachelle, is more important than your health and the health of your child."

Nachelle sighed deeply. "You're right. I did reschedule my appointment for next week. Steven's going to take me." Hurriedly, before Heather continued her probing, Nachelle jumped onto Heather's least favorite subject. "Have you had time to talk to your mother yet . . . about your feelings and marriage?"

Heather hesitated. She was still highly uncomfortable with the whole subject and deathly afraid of talking to her mom about it. It was one thing to unload her heartache with Nachelle—a kind, understanding, compassionate, totally innocent party—but altogether a different thing to talk to her mom, the root cause of most of her problems. She was sure her mother would find a way to turn the tables, leaving Heather to believe she was being foolish and silly. Or, her mother would completely ignore her and her feelings, which was her usual MO, and proceed to lecture Heather about the need to marry a multimillionaire. "No, Nachelle. I haven't, but I promise I will."

"Heather . . ." Nachelle dragged out the word as if she were talking to a kid.

"I said, I promise." Heather crossed her heart and stuck a pledge hand in the air. "I cross my heart and hope to die." Heather quickly changed the subject. "So, what about Gerald?" Heather's heart raced as his name slid smoothly off her lips. "Is he going to meet me? I mean . . . you . . . which will really be me."

"Don't think I'm going to forget about your talk with your mother, but I can take a hint." Nachelle sighed and settled deeper into her chair. One of those blasted headaches began beating against her temple. "Gerald and I had a nice long conversation. I didn't realize how much *I* missed him until I was talking to him." She smiled despite the growing ache.

Despite Nachelle's voice in her ear, the ticking of the clock, and the muted radio, a slight, foreign sound caught Heather's attention. Swiveling her head toward the open doorway, she stared into the blackness beyond the hallway. For a few seconds, she remained frozen, listening, trying to discern the unfamiliar sound. When the sound didn't materialize again, she shrugged and focused on Nachelle's words.

". . . his mother's house. He's been in Atlanta almost one hundred percent of the time. One of his sisters . . . the CPA . . . what's her name?"

"Theresa."

"Yeah, Theresa is starting her own business, and Gerald's going to be her client. They have some great things planned, Heather, and he said he's been meaning to call to ask if DuCloux Enterprises will cosponsor the basketball camp for underprivileged kids. But, I'm digressing. You want to hear about what he's been up to personally."

"Yes. What?" The breath caught in Heather's throat. Visions of Gerald marrying this Suzanne lady floated past her eyes, making her hands sweat and her stomach dip. After the talk she and Nachelle had had several days ago, Heather had driven to the downtown library the following day and pulled back copies of the *Atlanta Constitution*. Indeed, as Steven and Nachelle had reported, Gerald and Suzanne were splattered all over the society pages of the paper in several issues. Heather had been sick. She'd cried all evening.

"Gerald will be back in Dallas, but only to talk to the Mavericks organization about a trade to the Atlanta team. He is looking for a house in the Atlanta area. Gerald was the one who actually brought up Suzanne. He said they had lived around the corner from each other when they were kids, and they'd been elementary school sweethearts. I'm sure he thought I was being nosy, but I asked him if they were dating seriously or just having fun. He said they were dating exclusively but not talking about or planning a future together . . . yet.

He said they were spending a lot of time together, getting to know each other again and spending time with her son."

"She has a child? She's been married before?" Heather's soprano voice rose higher.

"She's divorced with one child."

Heather groaned. "Gerald loves kids." She was getting more and more depressed by the second. *What a stupid fool I've been. I can't lose Gerald. I just can't!*

"But, he did ask about you. I told him you were coming to grips with some heavy-duty things, and that you regretted your decision. I know I was talking out of turn, but I thought I would help you get this thing rolling . . . and I kept it very vague."

"What did he say then?" Heather held her breath.

"Nothing. He was silent for a long time. Then, he beat me to the punch. He suggested me, him and Steven get together for lunch or dinner when he comes to town this weekend. He said he'd call me."

Heather was both elated and depressed. Happy because she would finally get a chance to talk to Gerald. It had been a little over three months since she'd last seen or talked to him, and she was pining for him something bad. Depression latched on to her and covered her like the dust that surrounded Pig Pen from the "Peanuts" cartoon. This meeting with Gerald would be crucial. She had to impress upon him her love and the need for his understanding. Somehow, she would have to find the nerve to tell him everything: her fears, her mother's influence and how it had negatively impacted her idea of marriage, her desire to be with him until eternity. She just prayed she could do it—open up to him like she never had before. *I will do it,* she vowed. *I will give him all the consideration I should have given him months ago.*

Quietly, Heather spoke. "Thank you, Nachelle.

Thank you for everything. Have I told you lately that I love you and don't know what I would do without you?"

Nachelle smiled and wiped a tear from her eyes. "Yes, but I like hearing it. I love you, too . . . and Heather, good luck with Gerald."

"Thanks, Nachelle. Bye."

Heather hung up the phone, a seriously thoughtful expression on her face, as she mentally rewound the phone conversation she'd just had with Nachelle. *Yes, this may be my only chance. I will tell Gerald everything.* Fortified that her love and need for him would force her to do what she should have done months ago, Heather slid off the desk and stared at the mess of receipts on her desk. "This can wait. I can't concentrate on this stuff right—"

Suddenly, she heard the same unfamiliar sound she'd heard earlier. Turning toward the door, Heather cocked her head and listened intently. She stood as still as a Buckingham Palace guard, a curious expression on her pretty face. Eight years in this old building had made her as familiar with its creaks and groans as she was with her own body's sounds. The sound she strained to hear now was not the usual settling noise the building made. It sounded almost like the shuffling of feet on the hardwood floors.

"Impossible. No one's here but me." Heather turned off the radio. Snatching the ring of keys off the peg board, she walked out of her office and toward the front of the building. "I'd better check and make sure I locked up earlier." Even though she didn't want to admit it, she felt a trickle of apprehension glide down her spine. She wanted to laugh at herself at how spooked she was. And, maybe, tomorrow she would, but for now, she was more concerned about finding the source of that noise and making sure the building was locked up as tight as a cork in a bottle.

Quickly, yet thoroughly, Heather crept throughout the vast space downstairs, checking for any shadows that were out of place. The lobby, the auditorium and stage, even backstage checked out. There was no sign of anything out of place. Deciding she was being silly, Heather forfeited surveillance on the conference rooms and instead flicked on the neon lights outside, double-checked the locks on the front doors, and doused the remaining inside lights. With deft fingers, she initiated the security alarm sequence and headed for the stairs at the back of the building.

Suddenly, very tired from the eventful day, she dragged her body upstairs, shimmying out of her sweatpants as she went. It was early still, only ten-thirty in the evening, and yet she felt like she had gone days without sleep. *A nice, fragrant bath and a hot glass of herbal tea will help settle me for a deep sleep,* she thought as she slipped her T-shirt over her head. *I want to make sure I look good for Gerald when he sees me this weekend. I can't afford to look tired and worn out. Suzanne looked too good in those pictures.* Thoughts of Gerald's return and their meeting zapped all memories of school contracts and spooky sounds from her mind, making her totally oblivious to the brown eyes that watched her from a hiding place beneath the stairs.

Eleven

Georgia's Restaurant, located in southside Fort Worth, was not impressive from the outside. The cement and brick building was in need of another layer of sky-blue paint, the parking lot needed to be resurfaced, and the derelicts and bums who lingered outside the club restaurant sometimes harassed the customers going in or out for spare change. Despite that, Georgia's stayed packed. People of all stations in life craved Georgia's because it had the best cajun/creole seafood dishes west of New Orleans. In the evenings, it also featured the most soulful band in the area, belting out rhythm and blues, jazz, gospel, and Motown classics. During the daytime hours, piped-in music in the same vein served as a suitable substitute.

At two o'clock on a Saturday afternoon, while other restaurants struggled to bring in customers for late lunch, Georgia's had a full house. Inside the filled-to-capacity restaurant, it was cool and dark, a great contrast to the bright sun outdoors, which warmed the earth to the mid-nineties mark.

To accommodate more hungry patrons, the staff of Georgia's had covered the small dance floor with five additional rickety wooden tables for seating parties of four or less. It was at one of these tables that Gerald and Suzanne sat waiting patiently for Nachelle and Steven.

"This place has such atmosphere!" Suzanne sparkled in a yellow silk short suit—a gift from Gerald. With her bright hair in a ponytail tied up by a matching yellow scarf, she looked like a teenager. "I wonder if Ms. Georgia would consider expanding to Atlanta."

"Not Georgia. She *loves* Fort Worth. The only other city she would consider is her hometown in Louisiana. Believe me, I've asked." Gerald smiled playfully, hiding the mixed feelings that plagued him.

He was excited about seeing Nachelle and Steven. Although he and Steven had talked a number of times in Atlanta, they had not actually seen each other, due to frantic schedules. And, Nachelle, well, he hadn't talked to her since that awful day. Not that he hadn't wanted to, but to do so would have invited Heather's name into the conversation, and he hadn't been ready for that.

When he had confirmed lunch with Nachelle yesterday, it had been his idea to meet at Georgia's, knowing full well it was located in Fort Worth and minutes from Heather's neighborhood. He had only himself to blame for his turbulent heart and wandering mind. *Where is she at this moment? I wonder if she's doing a show at the mall today? How does she look? Is she as sad and lonely as . . .* He flicked his mind's switch. He would not dwell on the past today. He was meeting good friends. He was in the company of an attractive, smart, and sensual woman. He was getting ready to stuff his belly full of good food. What else could a man want? Unbidden, the truth boomeranged through his mind: Heather Chadwick! No amount of lying to himself could drown his desire to see her, hold her, touch her despite the pain she had caused him.

"Hey, Gerald." Suzanne's feathery touch on his arm made him start.

"I'm sorry."

"Boy, you were far away. Are you okay?"

"Yeah, fine," he lied. Gerald looked at his watch. He needed to get away, back to Atlanta where he could better camouflage his feelings and squelch the memories of what might have been. "I wonder where Nachelle and Steven are? They're usually very punctual."

Gerald glanced at his watch again. Ten minutes after two. "I'm starved. Are you?" Opening a packet of Club crackers on the table, he stuffed his mouth.

Suzanne started chuckling. "You're worse than Brandon."

With his mouth full, Gerald lifted his brows in a questioning manner.

"Here"—Suzanne leaned toward him, using her napkin to brush the residual crumbs from around his mouth—"let me brush those crumbs off your face, little boy."

Driven by the need to avoid further thoughts of Heather and to appreciate the woman who sat near him, Gerald's sincere brown eyes caught Suzanne's lighter ones. His wrist captured her smaller wrist in a gentle grip. "Thank you, little mama." He closed the remaining space between them and angling his head, kissed her softly, openly on the mouth. Withdrawing slightly, he kissed her nose, her forehead, and then returned to her lips, which were parted in invitation. The kiss this time felt like a caress of naked flesh against satin. It excited, it soothed, it made them sigh in subdued ecstasy.

"Excuse me."

Gerald jerked back as if he were a marionette being manipulated by an amateur. He stared fixedly, mouth open, eyes wide. "Heather!" he softly exclaimed.

"Gerald, I want to speak to you, please." Heather's eyes flickered to Suzanne. She was even prettier in living color. The newspaper photographer hadn't picked up the light scattering of freckles running over the bridge of her nose and fanning out toward her cheeks and the bewitching coloring of her eyes—cinnamon brown. Witnessing their display of intimacy, Heather had faltered in her steps until the greater need to reach out to Gerald propelled her forward to their table. It had been painful, watching Gerald kiss another woman. Her body quivered as if the fiery steel blade of pain and heartbreak was still jammed in her heart. "Please. I promise I won't take much of your time. Please."

At one point, not too long ago, Gerald would have given Heather all the time she needed. But, that was yesterday. Today, he didn't trust himself to be alone with her for a second. Already, he could feel the natural tugging on his heartstrings. But, no! She was the one who had dumped him. She was the one who had embarrassed and humiliated him in front of his family, friends, and coworkers. She had kicked him to the curb. No! She could not get any of his time. She would not get another chance to break his heart. Making his voice as icy as possible, he boldly stated, "Whatever you've come to say, you can say it here and then move on."

Heather shrank at his coldness, his inhumanity. *I did this,* she thought dazedly. *I gutted the nice, gentlemanly Gerald and turned him into this . . . this hard, cold person.* Despite the unfriendly welcoming remarks from Gerald, Heather was determined not to give up her quest. She *knew* she could sew their lives back together if only he would listen to her for a few minutes. Squaring her shoulders, she quickly glanced at Suzanne. She would have preferred a private, two-party conversation, but Gerald had made his point very clear. She wasn't going to walk away from what might be her one and only chance to speak honestly to him.

"I . . . want . . . to apologize again for hurting you. I was stupid and . . . Look, Gerald—" Heather stepped closer to his chair. She held out a tentatively pleading hand. "Can we talk privately, just for a moment? I won't keep you. I promise."

Gerald leaned back in his chair, crossed his arms over his chest, and made his eyes as hard as a gangster's. "No," he said in a low, flat voice.

"I need to run to . . ." Suzanne scooted her chair back and started to rise from her seat.

Gerald's strong hand stopped her and guided her back down in her seat. "Sit down." His dark brown face, contorted in pain, booked no argument.

Not normally a person given to mindless obedience, Suzanne complied without saying a word. She had never witnessed Gerald being less than courteous, kind, and nice. This was a side of him that was alien to her. She sat still, quietly digesting the scene playing out in front of her.

From deep in her soul, Heather corralled all her strength and courage. Pulling out the chair nearest Gerald, she sat down and leaned toward him. This close, she could feel the tension radiating off him. The clenched tightness of his jaws was a sure sign of his closure. "Steven and Nachelle are outside. They agreed to give me a few minutes to talk with you." Taking a deep breath, she closed her eyes briefly then opened them to stare into the unyielding face of her love. "I wanted to tell you that I'm . . . I was afraid of marrying you, but I'm not anymore. With Nachelle's help and with the help of therapy, I've realized the damaging effect my mother had on me. She . . . it was her influence that warped my view of marriage. But, I'm . . ." Heather forced herself to swallow the lump that had formed in her throat and continued. "I really believe that our love can overcome anything. I need you, Gerald. Will you forgive me my past mistakes? Will you be my friend, my lover, and my husband?"

"Are you finished?" Unmoved, Gerald stared through her. His own thoughts had him imprisoned in pain.

"Did you hear what I said?"

"Yeah, I heard you. I also know you're a well-trained actress, and that you're spoiled and used to having things your way. And, because I won't give into you, you consider me a challenge. You don't want to marry me. You want to play with me." His voice was cold, hard.

Heather sucked in her breath. Her body stiffened as the harshness of his voice pelted her. For every hard word he spoke, another tear formed in her eyes. "Gerald, that's not true. I'm not acting. I want you as my husband! I want to marry you!"

"You didn't want to marry me three months ago," Gerald challenged. "What's changed since then?"

"That's not true!" Heather cried. "I wanted you then, but I was afraid. Now, I've decided not to give in to my fears. I don't want to live without you. I can't stand another long night, lying in bed, tossing and turning, plagued by the lingering smell of you on my sheets, mocked by your leftover clothes hanging in my closet and your toiletries in my bathroom cabinets. I miss your touch, I miss your voice, and more than anything else, I miss your friendship. I want you back, Gerald, and if that means I have to face and fight the fears that are hidden deep in here"—Heather pointed at her chest—"I will. But, I need you in that fight with me, Gerald. Please."

Gerald was silent. His eyes had lost some of their coldness as she touched on old memories that warmed his heart. But still, how could he be sure she wasn't saying these things because she was lonely? Was she really ready to make a total and lasting commitment? What had happened to the one-year time frame she had mentioned on the day they were to be wed? Could he rebound from another broken heart if she failed to follow through a second time? Gerald's eyes skirted the condiment jars, the fresh carnations sticking out of an old ketchup bottle, and the gold tin ashtray on the table as his mind searched his heart.

Heather lowered her voice and laid a compelling hand on his arm. "Gerald, I want us to get married. Now. Here. Just say the word and we can use Mother's connections to get married today."

The feel of her skin on his arm sent spasms of pleasure shooting through his body, bringing to mind the countless times they had made love and enjoyed each other's flesh, the innumerable times their minds and hearts had communicated without aid of words. He lowered his head into his hands, hiding his face from his companions.

"Gerald . . ." Heather paused for effect and now whispered directly in his ear. "This is the weekend we were scheduled to leave for our honeymoon, anyway."

Honeymoon . . . Gerald mentally counted the weeks. She was right. They had agreed to honeymoon during the school and basketball hiatus. Of course, this was before the Fort Worth ISD decided to go with a year-round school pilot. But, right now, if they had gotten married, they would be sitting in first class on an international plane headed across the Atlantic Ocean toward Egypt. And, why weren't they? Because Heather had destroyed all their dreams. That thought put the final stamp on his decision. He couldn't do what she asked. The risk of pain was too great! He was having one hell of a time getting over his heartbreak. He surely wouldn't be able to survive another. He needed a sure sign that she was indeed a changed woman, ready to get married and commit totally to him. She had not offered that assurance, except in words, and he already knew she didn't stand by her words.

Lifting his head, he slowly turned toward Heather and looked into her light brown eyes. He shook his head, subconsciously shaking away the memories of her touches, the dreams they had crafted. "No, Heather. It's over." His heart splintered into a million pieces . . . again.

Gerald removed his arm from her touch. He repeated softly, in a whisper, "No, Heather. It's over."

Heather stared at him with tears lining her eyes. She looked into his troubled eyes—the only outward indication that he was hurting. As if a lightning bolt had just jolted her into reality, she realized she had made a very bad mistake. Wrapped up in her own hurt and misery on their wedding day, she hadn't tried to understand his point of view, his needs. She had been so stuck on her own agenda, she had paid little attention to Gerald. Now, she saw the reality of her selfishness and it was too late. She should have told him *that day* that she feared marriage because she thought it would destroy their love. She should have told him she couldn't visualize a life without him after the destruction of their love. Instead of being completely honest, she had kept her fears bottled up and had destroyed any chance of a future for them. In the end, she had hurt them both—Gerald more so because he had believed, trusted, loved her. How could she ever forgive herself?

Studying the profile of Gerald's face one last time, Heather stood up. In a low-pitched voice, she said, "Gerald, I am sorry for hurting you. I never meant to. I hope one day you can forgive me and please know that I love you. I always will."

She backed away from the table, continuing to stare at Gerald, whose face was averted. He never looked up to see her leave.

When she could see him no more, Heather slowly turned around and exited the restaurant. The bright sunlight blinded her momentarily and before her eyes could fully adjust from the darkness to the brightness, Nachelle and Steven were upon her.

"Heather?" Nachelle asked in a worried tone.

With a watery smile and in a trembling voice, Heather said to Steven and Nachelle, "Your turn."

"Are you okay, Heather?" Steven asked in a concerned voice. The sparks created from Steven's salt-and-pepper hair mating with the hot July sun made the tears in Heather's eyes seem overwhelming.

Heather said nothing for a while. Her throat worked overtime, trying to keep the tears from breaking free. Finally, she spoke. "It's over. He said so. I'm going home." Without another word or look at her friends, Heather trudged to her car.

Nachelle waddled behind her. When she caught up to her, she huffed, "Heather, go straight home. I'm going to fake a headache and be with you shortly, okay?"

"No, no, Nachelle. Really. I just want to be alone for a while. Enjoy your lunch." Heather slid behind her steering wheel and into the leather driver's seat. She started the engine.

"Okay, then, I'll be by right after lunch."

Heather nodded her head and threw the car into gear. Slowly, she made her way out of the pothole riddled parking lot. The blaring of car horns, the curses aimed at her from other drivers, the hot tears that washed her cheeks—none of it registered. The only thing she felt was pain, a deep, hot pain that the cleansing tears couldn't begin to alleviate.

Suzanne sighed and sank deeper into the leather seat. Gerald had been quiet ever since they had parted company with Nachelle and Steven. Even during lunch he'd been subdued, which was completely out of character for him. To match his boyish good looks, Mother Nature had blessed him with a jokester's character. He usually kidded and teased her on their dates, but now, he just sat quietly behind the wheel of the car.

Suzanne had enjoyed his company over the last month. He always made her feel light and unburdened. It was refreshing compared to the heavy lifestyle she maintained: being a single parent and trying to raise a gun-free, drug-free, gang-free son; caring for her dying mother; and managing a demanding workload at the office. Gerald had given her the opportunity to escape those demands, if only for short passages of time, and she was thankful for those escapes. However, although she enjoyed his company, she always suspected a secret hidden beneath his charming exterior. Some hurt or pain that peeked out of its hiding place during discussions about male-female relationships, but never quite exposing itself. But, today, she had learned why Gerald had kept her at arms' distance. She now knew why sometimes he seemed so out of reach. He was still in love with Heather. Suzanne was glad she had maintained that shield around her own heart.

"So, that was the woman who broke your heart." Suzanne couldn't hold her peace any longer. She turned in her seat to face him. Expecting a response, she wondered what was going through his head.

Gerald glanced at her. Without saying a thing, he pulled the car over onto the shoulder of highway I-30. It was amazing to him that three months ago, he and Steven had been heading down this same highway toward his house in Dallas after the woman he loved had verbally slapped him in the face and kicked him in the heart. He sat still for some minutes, thinking about the past and what he should say to Suzanne.

Twisting his long body in the seat to face her, he took her hand. "I'm sorry, Suzanne. I should have told you about me and Heather. I know I told you I wasn't involved with anyone and I'm not, but I didn't tell you the reason why. You're a smart attorney. You've probably figured everything out by now." The little-boy crooked grin on his face endeared him to Suzanne forever.

What a stupid fool Heather is, thought Suzanne.

"I'm sorry I wasn't totally honest." Gerald leaned his head back against the headrest and closed his eyes. "It . . . this has been too painful to deal with." Gerald's voice dropped to an all-time low. "I still love her. It was very hard to push her away today when all I really wanted to do was hold her and never let her go. I hope you can understand this was nothing personal against you."

"Gerald, you don't have to apologize for anything. I'm very sorry she hurt you. Believe me, I understand what it's like to love someone yet make the difficult decision to call it quits. It's a decision made more difficult with the addition of a child."

Gerald opened his eyes. He lifted Suzanne's hands to his mouth and lightly kissed her knuckles. The smile he bestowed on her communicated his thanks and appreciation more than any words could have.

"I don't want to get all in your business, but since you kinda put me there, I'm going to say this. And all I want you to do is just think about it. Is what she did to you so bad that you're willing to forgo the fulfillment of your love for her?" Suzanne paused to let her question sink in. "The only reason I'm asking is because this woman shamelessly begged for your love, begged for you to marry her in a crowded restaurant and . . .

in front of a woman she had just seen you kissing. In my book, that's a desperate woman who knows she's messed up and wants a second chance and is willing to acquire that second chance at any cost. Just think about that."

Gerald sighed raggedly, "She left me at the altar. She put me off for years and then left me looking like a fool. She threw my love back in my face."

"I'm sorry, Gerald, but, I think she realizes her mistake. I know you haven't asked for my advice, but I think you at least owe it to yourself to question her. You need to find out what was going on in her head when she stood you up. There has got to be a damn good reason why a single black woman in her thirties with her biological clock ticking away, would jilt a tall, dark, and handsome millionaire, AIDS-free, single, black male. You know y'all ain't so easy to find. Sister *must* have had some serious problems."

Gerald didn't say anything. His mind was whirling, thinking about Suzanne's comments.

Suzanne leaned over and kissed Gerald's forehead. "So, is this the part where we agree to be friends?"

Despite his pain, Gerald laughed. "That depends. Are you going to up and move to Florida on me, *friend*?"

They laughed away the heavy atmosphere in the car.

"No, I'm not. I'm in Atlanta to stay . . . at least until my mom gets better or worse."

"Good." Gerald started the car with a smile on his face.

With an exaggerated sigh, Suzanne teased, "Thank goodness that's settled. I'm glad to know you're not gay."

"Gay?" Gerald yelled. He almost swerved off the road again.

"Well, you've never tried to get me in your bed, so I

figured you were either gay or in love with someone else. Now I know."

The friends looked at each other and howled in joyous laughter.

Twelve

Marilyn huffed and puffed, muttering under her breath, as she ascended the stairs to Heather's private domain. "She could at least return my calls. She knows I worry about her. Why she has no respect for me, I don't know."

An hour ago, when her flight from D.C. landed, she had tried to call Heather. No answer. Then, as she drove from the Fort Worth home in which she and Everett Chadwick had shared their brief life together, to her only child's home, she had called her daughter's line incessantly. Still no answer. She knew Heather was ignoring her, but Marilyn was determined to spend the day with her daughter, discussing Heather's future. If that meant she had to sit and wait all night for Heather to show up, she would do so.

"Heather acts like a child," Marilyn muttered. "She doesn't realize her biological clock is ticking. We need to make some decisions about her future. I want grandchildren, and I need to know someone is going to be around to take care of her when I've passed on." Before inserting the key Heather had given her years ago, Marilyn paused at the outer door to catch her breath. *The girl's no closer to getting married to Gerald than I am*, she fumed. *This is not what I had planned for her life. Imag-*

ine . . . a Chadwick preferring work to a happy marriage and children. I don't know what my daughter is thinking of.

The door swung open quietly. Marilyn slipped inside the moody domain. *If Mohammed won't come to the mountain, then the mountain will come to Mohammed. And how surprised Mohammed will be.* Marilyn placed her handbag on the bright yellow kitchen counter and headed for the refrigerator. The one thing she didn't miss about home was the 100-plus degree temperatures in the summer. D.C. got hot but nothing like Texas. Placing the ice-cold Diet Coke bottle to her chest, Marilyn held it there for several seconds, being careful not to wet her silk tangerine-orange dress. Sufficiently cooled, Marilyn opened the bottle and poured the contents into a frosted glass.

Where could she be? She glanced at her watch . . . 2:00 P.M. *She must be doing one of those performances that barely pays the rent.* Marilyn sighed and rolled her eyes heavenward. *This is not the life I had planned for her.* Marilyn headed for a chair in the living room to kick off her shoes and rest. *Hopefully, she'll at least have something good to read while I'm waiting for her.*

"I didn't hear you come in."

Marilyn spun around at the sound of the man's voice. At first, she thought it was Gerald. His voice slightly resembled Gerald's in tone. He was tall and dark and posed against the doorjamb leading to Heather's bedroom. He seemed quite comfortable in her house. As he moved closer to the living room, Marilyn saw that that's where the resemblance ended. "Who are you?" she asked in her cultured voice with just the right amount of haughtiness.

"I'm your son-in-law. Didn't Heather tell you?"

Marilyn's eyebrows lifted to almost meet her hairline. "Excuse me, young man. Repeat that please," she demanded.

LOVE EVERLASTING

Warren slid his hands in the pockets of his slacks and strolled lazily into the room.

"Hello, Mother. How's Washington, D.C., these days?" Warren slowly sank down onto the couch and eyed his mother-in-law with great interest. He patted the couch.

"Who are you?" Marilyn ignored his invitation. "Why are you calling me mother, and what do you mean you're my son-in-law?"

Warren's anger flared. He was aware of the tactics of rich folks. To claim they didn't know you was their way of saying you were beneath them. Well, this time it wouldn't work. He extinguished his anger, knowing this time he was in control. For once, in dealing with rich folks, he was superior—he was the master manipulator. Marilyn represented an opportunity for him to get back at the rich and give it to them as harshly as they had given it to him.

"Heather should be back within the hour. She went to Georgia's to say good-bye forever to Gerald Forrester. You remember him, right?"

"Of course, I remember Gerald!" she replied incredulously. "He's the man my daughter is going to marry—not you!" Marilyn paused, studying Warren, trying to figure out if she had ever met him before. As the wife of a powerful man, she met many people every day. Names and faces zipped in and out of her memory like a speeding car whizzing past billboards. And, she was ashamed to say, as she got older, her memory worsened. She decided she hadn't met him, didn't know who he was. "How do you know so much about my daughter's business? Are you one of her employees? If so, you shouldn't be up here. Your place is downstairs."

Warren, again, had to control his anger. Her comment sent him into a tailspin of childhood memories. Times when he was forced, due to his supposed lack of breeding, to use the back door. Periods of his life when he had to walk behind rich folks or give up his prime seat at the movie house for some rich black man and his date. Rich folks had reminded him time and time again, he wasn't good enough. That he would never be able to claim his heritage.

With his fists clenched, Warren spat out between tight jaws, "I am where I belong. If you don't want to get hurt, you'd better remember that."

"How dare you threaten me! I am Marilyn Chadwick-Wolfe. Wife of Roger Wolfe. Widow of Everett Chadwick." Marilyn's posture, already ironing board straight, straightened even more. Her chest poked out and her chin lifted degrees. "I'm not going to stand here and dally with you. If you are one of my daughter's employees, consider yourself fired." Marilyn set the half-empty glass of soda on the coffee table and pointed a finger toward the doorway. "Leave now, or I will be forced to call the police."

Warren lazily picked up the phone receiver and held it out toward Marilyn. "Call them. I don't mind" His voice had lowered dramatically, threateningly.

"Didn't you hear me? Don't you know who Roger Wolfe is?" she sputtered. "Haven't you heard of Everett Chadwick . . . a great African-American businessman who made millions? He was born, raised, and operated his stores here in Fort Worth."

Warren replaced the phone receiver and sat up on the edge of the couch. In his silkiest voice, he explained, "Mother, I know that. Why do you think I'm marrying into the family?" Warren stood up. He was growing tired of Marilyn's exposé. In an agreeable voice, he said, "Look, Mother, I know Heather would want us to get along. Why don't we start over, hmmmm?" Warren closed the space between them. The smile on his face did not reach his eyes—eyes that were dark, piercing, and filled with hate.

He held out a hand. "I'm Warren Patterson, your son-in-law."

Good manners made Marilyn stretch out her hand automatically—but, when she realized what she was doing, she snatched it back. "Mr. Patterson, I'm sure there must be a big misunderstanding. My daughter, Heather, is not married to you." Marilyn continued sarcastically. "I don't know why or how you latched on to the idea that you're part of my family—but, trust me, you're not. Heather is a single woman engaged to and in love with Gerald Forrester. She wouldn't marry you!" Marilyn moved around Warren, heading for the phone. "Now, if you just hold on one minute, I'll call the police, and they can pick you up and take you back where you belong."

In an instant, Warren's anger exploded. "How dare you tell me I don't belong here? How dare you belittle me!"

Before she could react, the back of Warren's knuckles connected with Marilyn's cheekbone. She flew backward, landing on the floor by the couch. With one arm twisted under her, her head bounced once, then twice, against the hardwood floor, momentarily knocking her out. After a few seconds, her lashes fluttered open. She moaned.

As soon as she landed, Warren bent over her, yelling at her, with a finger pointing in her dazed face. "I'm so sick of you rich, black folks acting like you're gold and I'm trash. I should have been admired! I should have had my pick of schools, women, clothes, cars, professions! But, no, bastard children of rich black men don't get that privilege." For every atrocity Warren suffered as a child, he kicked Marilyn in her side, her head, her back. "All we get is hand-me-down love from the beautiful silly women cajoled into bed by the rich man. We get bloated stomachs, patched clothes, ridicule, and pain. Dogs of the rich are treated better than their bastard children." Winded, Warren stood up straight, heaving, trying to recapture his breath, regain his control. "Rich bitch," he hatefully spat at her.

Marilyn, near the point of passing out, cried as the explosions of pain continued to wrack her body. She moaned and winced at any movement. Never, never before had she felt so much pain. She prayed he was through with his assault. She prayed for help. She prayed that she would pass out, and soon. She prayed he didn't kill her.

Leaning over her, Warren roughly pushed Marilyn over onto her back and felt for a pulse. He laughed. "I guess it wouldn't do for me to kill my mother-in-law on our first formal meeting."

Heather had forgotten! But, as soon as she spied her back parking lot, she remembered. For the next two nights, a church group would be her downstairs company. They had rented the theater for a play they were producing, and the multitude of cars in the normally bare lot was a testament to that fact.

Heather groaned, staring at the clock in the car. Less than four hours to showtime for the group. *Of all weekends, why this one? Why this weekend? I just want to be left alone.* The tragic meeting with Gerald rested heavily around her like a San Francisco fog. Her head, muddled with thoughts of Gerald, and her feelings, in a stewpot of confusion and pain, combined to make her less than personable. She was not in the mood for company or business. She laid her head against the steering wheel, trying to determine her next move. *Maybe I can slip upstairs undetected.* She banished the thought as soon as it formed. It was her responsibility to welcome and settle any group who rented her facilities. She at least needed to check and make sure they had everything under control, and that they knew how to work all the controls, lights, mics, curtains, etcetera. *At least I had enough sense to get the paperwork, payment, and keys out of the way earlier this week. Hopefully this won't take long.* Steeling herself to meet the group, she slowly navigated through the various assortment of cars and found a parking space near the side fence.

Internally, she gave herself a pep talk and quoted positive phrases, hoping the right mental attitude would help her make it through the following minutes. She was so intent on fortifying herself that she almost missed the champagne-colored 300E Mercédes-Benz. *Is that Mom's car?* Heather frowned. A groan followed the frown. "Not today! Not now, please, Lord, let it be someone who has a car like hers." She wasn't up to speaking with Marilyn today. Shaken from the episode with Gerald, with bruised feelings and raw and exposed nerves, she was not interested in her mom's lectures about marriage, children, and her old maid status. *If indeed it is Mom, she'll have to go. I'm going to put my foot down and throw her out. I need the peace and solitude my home offers.*

Heather found the back entry unlocked. She slipped inside the garage. A few steps more, she opened the back door, the entryway leading to the inside rooms. She heard the ruckus immediately. It was a signal for her to straighten her spine and say a few last words of encouragement. Forcing herself to forget the scene at the restaurant, she headed toward the noise. At the center of the Y in the hallway, she saw a small group of gregarious people clustered together, chatting animatedly. Faking a smile, she walked toward them with her hand outstretched. *Start with the easy stuff first,* she coaxed herself.

"Hello and welcome. I'm Heather Chadwick, owner

of the Twelfth Street Puppet Company. I'm glad to have you all here."

Heather managed to hang on to her smile until she made the rounds, ensuring the people assigned to work the lobby, concessions, and ticket booth knew what to do. When she arrived at the backstage area, she ran into the director she had been working with the past months. Heather quickly discovered the gods were smiling on her, for the director informed her they had several thespians in the group who were well versed in the inner workings of a theater. The long, drawn-out lesson in mic handling, lighting, and set work, that she had anticipated and dreaded, was suddenly a non-issue. Heather was off the hook and in less than ninety minutes, she was headed upstairs to her private haven.

With heavy feet matching her heavy heart, she trudged upstairs, way out of sorts. At the door to her suite of rooms, Heather dug in her jeans pockets for her keys. Her arm accidentally brushed against the door. It creaked open slightly. Frowning, Heather pushed the door open and slipped inside. She studied the locks for a second and seeing nothing out of the ordinary, shrugged her shoulders. *I must have forgotten to lock it in my rush to get to Gerald,* she thought. *Figures, since I completely forgot about the church group, too.*

Just thinking Gerald's name caused Heather's control to crumble. Barely in the foyer of her home, the tears and cries of anguish came hard and heavy. The pain, the remembrances of Gerald's hard, cold face and harsh words telling her it was over, beat her down to the floor. Even the banging of her fist against the hard grain of the wood floor couldn't compete with the pain in her heart. For a long time, she grieved for the loss of Gerald and for the loss of their love.

Many, many minutes later, the tears slowed. Heather pulled herself up and on unsteady legs walked to the bright, cheery yellow kitchen. At the sink, Heather threw water on her now red face, totally oblivious to her mother's purse lying on the counter. As the tap water flowed forcefully down the half-dollar-sized drain, she stared unblinkingly into the hole, watching the water disappear to reappear eventually in the sewer. She likened her future without Gerald to the water. It was just as bleak. Laying her head on the cool ceramic counter she thought she would never get over loving him. She thought her life force had been snuffed out. With a wretched cry, she shut off the faucet and headed blindly for her bedroom, her haven within her haven. Curled into a tight ball in the middle of her bed, she pressed a fist against her mouth and cried herself to sleep.

"Heather. Heather. Wake up." Nachelle's insistent voice reached through to Heather's conscious mind. Nachelle shook Heather's shoulder again. "Heather, wake up."

Heather opened her hazel eyes and rolled onto her side. "I'm awake," she replied, feeling as if a wad of cotton had been stuffed in her mouth.

"Here, drink this. It'll help you feel better." Nachelle handed Heather a cup of steaming Quiet Time tea.

Heather struggled to a sitting position and took a deep sip of the hot drink. "Thanks, Nachelle." Heather spoke dryly, trying to shake herself back to reality. "How long have I been sleep? What time is it?"

"Don't worry about the time. The important thing is that you got some sleep. You needed that to reenergize your mind and body." Nachelle smoothed Heather's hair off her forehead. "Now, how are you feeling?"

"Like crap. Why did you wake me? Everything is coming back in vivid color." Heather placed the hot tea on the night table and returned to the fetal position.

"I'm sorry, Heather. Do you feel like talking about it?"

"No. I mean . . ." Heather lifted her head. Accompanied with a deep sigh, she scooted on her spine to a semiupright position against the headboard. Her voice was low and shaky, lined with tears. "There's nothing to talk about. He said he doesn't want to see me ever again. He said it's over."

"Heather, I'm so sorry. I prayed it would turn out differently. But, I . . ." Nachelle stopped, unsure of how to proceed. She didn't want to give Heather any wrong ideas. She knew her friend's tendency to ignore facts and run instead with her imagination. But, at one point, after the luncheon, as they stood in the foyer waiting for Suzanne to return from the ladies' rest room, she could have sworn Gerald was on the verge of telling her something. He'd even gone so far as to say "Heather," but Suzanne's return clammed him up. Before she shared this tidbit with Heather, she needed to talk to Gerald.

"What, Nachelle?" Heather lifted her eyes, searching her friend's eyes for any encouraging sign.

"I was afraid that was the outcome. Gerald was really bummed out at lunch. I could tell he was trying really hard to be sociable and fun . . . you know, be his old self, but the sadness of 21having to tell you that was still evident. Actually, we had a relatively sober, stilted luncheon. We mostly talked about the basketball camp and other community projects. I could tell Gerald was having a hard time concentrating."

Heather drew her legs into her body as if shielding herself from further heartache. "He was so cold, Nachelle, so cruel. It was almost like he was another person."

"Yeah, I understand what you mean. He was very . . . un-Gerald-like."

Heather rolled off the bed. "I don't know what else to do," she said dejectedly. "Do you think I've lost him for good?" Heather paced the room, speaking in disjointed phrases. "I mean, I know what he said but, do you think . . . What else can I do, Nachelle? I can't live without him."

Nachelle dropped her head to study the weave pattern on Heather's comforter. "I don't know, Heather. I need some time to think about it." She shrugged her shoulders. "I just don't know."

Stopping on a dime, Heather stared at her friend. Her eyes were filled with sadness. "In the meantime, I still have to get through the days and even worse, the nights." They shared a meaningful look.

The tears, ever present beneath a thin layer of self-control, threatened to erupt. Heather's throat worked convulsively.

Sensing Heather's internal battle for control, Nachelle said the first non-Gerald related thing to cross her mind. "Where's your mother?"

"What?" Heather asked, looking lost and confused.

"Your mother. Where is she? I saw her car downstairs when Steven dropped me off."

Heather moved slowly to the bed. Shaking her head, she spoke in low tones. "I don't know. I haven't seen her." Managing a wry smile, Heather said, "Probably downstairs running the church group's production if I know my mom."

"Oh, well, then, if you haven't seen her, it must not be her car."

Heather lay back, staring up at the ceiling. "That's what I assumed. Otherwise, she would have been in my face, and I'm so glad she isn't. I wouldn't be able to handle Mom right now."

Nachelle jumped off the bed and clapped her hands. "My wonderful husband gave me the afternoon off.

Isn't that grand of him, considering it's a Saturday." She chuckled. "So, I thought we could do something fun, like go to the zoo or see a movie or bowl or maybe even go to Six Flags. Whatever you want to do." Nachelle grabbed Heather's arm and rousted her from the bed. "What do you want to do? I'm not going to let you sit around here and mope."

"All right, I'm up." Heather straightened her clothes and followed Nachelle to the living room. Not that she had a choice. Nachelle had a death grip on her wrist.

"I'm going to check the paper and see if there's some kind of festival going on this weekend. Didn't I see the paper on your counter? Why do you take the paper when you don't read it?" Nachelle babbled on happily, trying to lighten the mood.

Like her lifeless puppets downstairs, Heather mutely and blindly followed Nachelle's machinations. At the kitchen counter, she leaned her head into her hands and stared down at the countertop. Drably, she said, "This hurts even worse than last time. At least last time I had some hope that Gerald would change his mind. Now . . . Oh, Nachelle if you had seen the look on his face." With no preamble, silent tears trailed down Heather's cheek.

"Oh, Heather, come on, now." Nachelle hugged her shoulders, speaking cooingly. "We'll figure out something." Nachelle looked around for Kleenex. Opening the purse lying on the counter, she pulled out almost all of the contents before she found a small package of tissues. "Here, wipe your face. I promise, Heather, it's not over yet. Hang on to that thought, okay?"

With a turned-down smile, Heather nodded.

As Nachelle started stuffing the contents back into the tangerine-orange purse, she spied Mrs. Wolfe's driver's license. "Heather, why do you have your mother's driver's license?"

"I don't." Heather looked up at Nachelle, then down at the evidence in Nachelle's hands. "Where'd you get that?"

"From your purse." Nachelle held up the purse.

"That's not my purse. I would never carry something that bright." She paused as her mind clicked. "But, Mom would."

The friends looked at each other and a split second later, Heather took possession of the purse. The review of only a few items confirmed the fact. "This is Mom's purse. How did it get here?"

"And, she wasn't here when you came in?"

"No, at least, I didn't see her. She could have been out on the patio, in which case she wouldn't have heard me come in." As Heather spoke, she cut a direct path to the rooftop patio. "Not that I'm anxious to see or talk to her right now, but I would like to know if she's around."

Nachelle sat down on one of the kitchen stools to wait for Heather's return. She didn't wait long.

"No sign of her. I'm going to check the guest bedroom."

Seconds passed while Heather scouted the extra bedroom and bath. "Not there, either," she proclaimed as she joined Nachelle at the bar. "Where do you think she would be without her purse?" Without waiting for a response, she remarked, "I know my mom, and there is no way she would go anywhere without being fully coordinated." Heather waved the purse in the air. "She must have left this purse one previous time she was here."

"If that's so, wouldn't she have called you or come by to pick it up? In addition to her license, she has credit cards and cash in here."

"Oh, Mother has several purses with credit cards and cash. She believes in the Boy Scout motto. Trust me,

"That is an odd question. Why do you ask?" The lawyer training, instilled in him almost since birth, kicked in.

Nachelle tapped Heather on the shoulder. Gesturing with the keys in her hand, she whispered, "I'm going downstairs to see if these keys work on that car. I'll be back."

Heather nodded, then repositioned the mouthpiece to her mouth. "Well, Mom's purse is here on my counter, and I was wondering if this is the purse of the day."

"Your mother's purse is there, but you haven't seen or talked to her?"

"Right. But, I'm not sure if this is an old purse or not."

"I see. And no one's at her home?"

"I don't know. I thought for sure she would be in D.C. so I didn't even try here."

"Hold on. I'm going to call the house and see if we can solve this little mystery." There was an imperceptible click as he used his conference line feature. Less than a minute later, he was back on the line. "Heather?"

"Yes, I'm here."

"Your mother isn't at home. However she did make it to Fort Worth. According to the housekeeper, Marilyn made a few calls, then left in her car. The housekeeper hasn't seen her since she left earlier in the afternoon."

"Did Mom tell Mamie where she was going?" The lines in Heather's forehead deepened. She turned around to check the time on the kitchen clock. *Five-thirty. So that puts Mom in Fort Worth for about five to six hours.* "Did Mamie happen to say what Mom was wearing? The purse on my counter is orange."

"She didn't tell Mamie anything. And, I didn't ask about clothes. Ummmmm, I know when she left here this morning she was wearing a . . ." There was a lengthy pause as Roger searched his brain for the minute detail. His keen mind backpedaled through the day. His intense courtroom training supervised by his father, focused on key, barely revealed facts and details. His ability to target on those facts and exploit them led to his brilliant career as a criminal attorney, which led to an even more sparkling career in politics. ". . . a long, white dress that buttoned down the front. It was very tailored, of course. You know your mother. But, all that really doesn't matter since your mother is known to change clothes as frequently as the wind blows."

Indeed! Heather thought.

"Don't worry, Heather, I'm sure your mother probably met a friend or went shopping and lost track of time. Tell you what . . ." During the pause that followed his last remark, Heather heard him shuffling papers. "If you haven't heard from her by nightfall, call me back. My calendar is booked until midnight, but I can always catch a red-eye. So call me, okay?"

"Okay, Roger, and sorry for bothering you with such a small thing."

"When it comes to your mother, nothing is small and nothing's a bother. I love her very much. So, when she comes flouncing through your door, tell her I said she's in trouble with her congressman. She knows she's supposed to check in with me. She's getting hardheaded in her old age."

Heather hung up the phone, smiling. Her mother was lucky to have a man who really cared about her. *You had that once yourself and threw it away because of your captivity to fear.* The thought was there before she could anticipate it. Heather laid her face into her hands. "Yeah, I miss him so much. Wherever you are, Gerald, I love you, and I'm not afraid of a loving future with you anymore."

"Who are you talking to?" Nachelle returned, out of breath.

"Myself."

Taking a deep breath, Nachelle leaned against the counter. "It's her car. The car keys worked on the lock and started the engine." The women looked at each other.

Still struggling to catch her breath, Nachelle suggested, "I'm sure there's a reasonable explanation. What did Roger say?"

Quickly, Heather informed Nachelle of her conversation with Roger.

Nachelle, the voice of reason, outlined a plan of action. "Well, I'm still sure there's a reason for this oddity. I know you already looked, but maybe we should check around here one more time. I'll take upstairs and you take down."

"And, if she's not here?" Heather's imagination had her on a cliff of concern, tottering toward the edge.

"Then, we sit and wait until she shows up. I bet you anything she'll show up with an armload of clothes for you, which I'm sure you will promptly take to Goodwill."

Sharing a smile full of fond memories, the ladies split up.

Ten minutes later, they reconvened in Heather's kitchen, neither one successful in their attempt to locate Marilyn.

"Okay, so what did you say we do now?" Heather asked her best friend, trying not to succumb to her feeling of concern. For now, she could live with the explanation Roger and Nachelle seemed to agree on for her mother's disappearance. After all, who better than Heather knew her mother was the world's greatest shopaholic. She was sure her mother would come flying through the door any minute now with garments out the wazoo, apologizing profusely for her very lengthy delay in seeing her only child. Then, like Nachelle prophesied, she would start throwing clothes at her, which in due time would be sent to charity. Heather sighed. *Yup, I can visualize the whole thing. Kiss, kiss, apology, apology, cold drink, fashion show, talk about my life, then whisk, she'll be gone. Dear Mom, one day she'll realize that the only thing we have in common is Everett Chadwick.*

As soon as she thought it, Heather realized that truth applied to her and Gerald's situation as well. Yes, her mother might be second to Elizabeth Taylor in marriages, but Heather was nothing like her mother. Even though she had begged Gerald to marry her several hours ago, she had still felt that moment of doubt, a dead weight of fear that threatened to clog the words. But, knowing Gerald had moved on without her, could possibly marry another woman, had been too unbearable to consider, so she had begged and pleaded. The lightbulb went on, shining bright on her future. *I'm not like my mother. I'm free of the influence of my mother's lifestyle. I do have a choice.* Heather felt a heaviness she had carried all her life lift, and even at six o'clock in the evening, with the sun's rays dimming in brilliance, she had never felt more warm, more full of life, more free. *I'm ready to make a lifelong commitment to Gerald. I want to marry him and we will live happily ever after.*

Heather felt like kicking up her heels. Instead, she grabbed Nachelle by the arms. "Look at me. Do I look different?"

Nachelle frowned. "What?" she asked, puzzled, rearing back her neck.

"Do I look different?" Heather repeated.

Nachelle stared into her friend's face. "Noooo. I've seen you wear that big, goofy grin before. But, you *are* acting weird. Is this some sort of delayed reaction to the news that we can't find your mother?"

"Nope." Heather's grin stretched from ear to ear. "I just realized I *want* to marry Gerald. I really do!"

"Okay." Nachelle's bemused look spoke of her confusion. "That's good." Shrugging her shoulders, she decided not to try and figure out Heather's thought processes. Instead, she opened a kitchen drawer and took out a set of playing cards. "Do you want to play Crazy Eights or Go Fish until your mother shows up with clothes for the entire neighborhood?"

"Go Fish." Heather smiled, leading the way into the living room. "And you can start calling me Mrs. Heather Forrester." She snagged a pillow off the sofa and dropped it on the floor by the coffee table. Sitting cross-legged on the pillow, she accepted the deck from Nachelle and began dealing. The concern that had been building within her for her mother's whereabouts took a backseat to her newfound knowledge.

"Oh, yuck, Heather! What is this?" Nachelle jumped up from her seat.

"Awwwww." Heather screwed up her nose as if a foul smell permeated the place. "What is that?"

"It's wet." Cautiously, Nachelle put her hand to the wet stain on the sofa. Bringing the hand to her nose, she sniffed. "Smells like . . ." She repeated the action, got no clue, then dunked her head toward the stained cushion. "It smells like Coke, Heather."

Heather had crawled from her side of the coffee table to where Nachelle was standing. On her knees, she hovered over the darker spot on the couch. She sniffed long and deep. "It is. But, I didn't do it. I don't even drink—" Heather's eyes grew as large as dessert plates.

"What, Heather? What?" Nachelle asked. Her eyes opened as wide as Heather's.

"Whenever I go shopping, I always buy Kool-Aid for me and Gerald, iced tea for you, and Diet Coke in a bottle for Mom. She's the only one who drinks Coke."

"So, your mother is here. Or, was. She must have left in a hurry in order for her not to clean up her spill."

"Or remember her purse . . ."

"Or . . ." Nachelle stopped. "She must have left with a friend, but I wonder what was the big rush?"

Heather shrugged. "I wish I knew." She looked at the stain and followed the tiny droplets until she found the glass lying by the side of the sofa. Droplets of wetness surrounded the glass.

Nachelle returned from the kitchen with several paper towels and a dishcloth in hand.

Heather wrestled with the evidence that was contrary to her mother's manners. "Nachelle, something's not right. Mom is a neat freak. Even in a big hurry, Mom would never have left the glass on the floor. She would have cleaned up the spill, and she certainly wouldn't have forgotten her purse. No matter the emergency situation, under no circumstance, would my mom leave without being completely together. You know how big she is on matching ensembles. Something is just not right. I can feel it." Even though she told herself not to give in to her imaginings, a cold strand of fear and panic pierced Heather's heart. Concern for Marilyn took first place over her and Gerald's estrangement.

Thirteen

Warren sat in his favorite chair with a half-filled glass of Scotch and water in one hand and a bag of pretzels between his legs. The TV, facing him in the oak entertainment stand, flickered images at him. Although he stared at the thirty-two-inch screen, the scenes and commercials didn't register. His mind's eye held him captive, thinking, concentrating on the woman tied up and gagged in his bedroom on the upper level of his town house.

Glancing at his watch, Warren noted he was running out of time. *Two and a half hours before my date,* he thought. *How do I hide Mother so I can bring Terri back here and have sex with her?* He sat up straight and leaned over so that his head hung over his gaped knees. The glass, cupped between his hands, served as a new focal point. "What to do with Mother?" he repeated. Warren mentally walked through every room and closet in his one-bedroom, two bath minihouse. The thought of Marilyn's soiled body touching his expensive furnishings, purchased by the multitude of women who owed him, made him want to snap Marilyn's neck.

"It's her fault I'm in this predicament." His hands clutched the glass harder and harder. *If only she hadn't been so rude, so high-handed and almighty,* he thought, *acting like every rich person I've ever met, including my father.*

All I wanted to do was sit and talk. She angered me. She made me beat her.

Warren tilted his head back and downed the rest of his drink. *She's given me no choice but to leave her in the garage until tomorrow morning.*

With his decision made and his anger on low burn, Warren stood. His long legs quickly covered the distance from the living room to the kitchen where he rinsed his glass and placed it in the automatic dishwasher. Using a yellow potato chip clip, he closed the pretzel bag and set the bag on the second shelf of the food pantry with his other snacks. A wipe down of all the counters completed his chore. With the kitchen neat and tidy once again, he headed for his bedroom, stopping in the living room long enough to power off the TV and fluff the cushions on the chair he'd been sitting in.

The upper level of his town house was loft style. Doors were scarce, windows and mirrors were generous, allowing a person to feel like he was in a wide open prairie. Warren stopped at the top of the stairs long enough to survey his domain below. Satisfied everything was in order, he turned immediately to the left and glared at Marilyn's battered body lying in the middle of his bed.

Warren leaned over the bed, speaking directly into Marilyn's ear. "You're not so strong after all, *Mrs. Chadwick-Wolfe*. I've known women I can beat one day who come back the next day for round two," he rebuked. "Here you are—" he reached out and pushed her shoulder, forcing her onto her back—"knocked out, as if I beat you like a man." He examined her closely, looking for signs of consciousness. Her breathing was very faint, a pulse thumped sluggishly at her neck, and there was some rapid eye movement beneath her closed lids. That was good enough for him. "Wake up, dear Mother. It's time to take a short trip."

LOVE EVERLASTING

Slowly, Marilyn's eyes opened—not all the way since they were swollen, discolored and hurting. The pain in her head and body seemed to redouble its presence with her eyes open so she closed them again. A moan slid around her silk scarf that he had stuffed in her mouth. She wondered when the nightmare would stop. She wondered when Roger would come get her. She wondered why her.

"Are you ignoring me?" Warren angrily retorted. He yanked on her arm, trying to shake a response from her. Marilyn winced, and her groan became more pronounced.

"Yes, dear, I know it hurts," he said in a false sugary-sweet empathetic voice, ". . . but, you'll feel better once you learn how to keep your mouth shut and quit looking down your nose at people. I may not be a Chadwick but I am *somebody!*" Warren stuck out his chest, pointing a thumb to it. "I am the first son of a great and powerful rich man. I should inherit his kingdom but because my mother was only his whore, he won't even acknowledge me." Warren paused to swallow the bitterness. "But, I'm over that," he said in a less boisterous tone. Switching to a cajoling tone, he continued. "Your inheritance will be a fine substitute, dear Mother. Marriage to your daughter will ease all the suffering I've endured at the hands of people like you."

Marilyn's eyes crept open at the mention of her daughter. Although her head hurt like nobody's business, she shook it. Tears welled in her brown eyes and slid onto her smooth brown cheek.

"Oh, Mother? Are you trying to tell me something?" Warren mocked. "Let's see what Mother has to say." Like a great magician, he snatched the scarf out of Marilyn's mouth with a dramatic hand movement. Quickly, he followed up with a hand to her throat, squeezing it like bread dough. Putting his face in hers, he threatened, "Scream and I'll kill you right now. I've done it before. I'll do it again."

More tears fell in response to his threat.

Patting her head like an obedient puppy, he said, "Now, dear, what did you want to tell me, and it'd better be nice." Warren's voice was nice and soothing yet hard and cruel.

Marilyn's throat worked convulsively for several seconds before she could get a sound out. When she spoke, her voice peaked and ebbed, in strained tones. Warren had to bend low to hear her. "Please . . . don't . . . not . . . daughter."

"Oh, you don't think I'm good enough for your daughter?" Warren's brown eyes clouded in anger. His hand trembled from emotions suppressed since childhood as he whacked her aside the head.

Marilyn winced, cried, and fought to retain her hold on consciousness.

"I'm better than she is," Warren boasted. "My father has way more money than Everett Chadwick. I'm doing you a favor by marrying that immature spoiled bitch. Whoever heard of a grown woman playing with puppets as a business." In his disgust, Warren stomped away from the bed where Marilyn lay curled in a ball, crying, hurting. The closet doors slid open soundlessly. "I think black linen slacks and a lightly starched collarless white shirt will do nicely for dinner tonight." Warren grabbed the pieces of clothes and spun around. Hanging them to his body, he spoke. "What do you think, Mother?" He laughed mercilessly. "Oh, never mind, your eyes are swollen shut. You can't see." He laughed again, a cold humorless laugh. "Don't worry. I have a wall of mirrors so I can see how handsome I am when I go out to slay the women. And, don't worry. Once I marry Heather, I promise to be discreet about my whoring. But, as you know, every rich man has to have diversions, and I'll be no different."

Warren hung the clothes on a clothes hook inside the closet, then walked toward Marilyn. "First things first. I'm putting you away so you won't interrupt my plans for the evening. Now, be a good girl. Open wide."

Before Marilyn could part her lips and teeth, Warren forcefully stuffed the scarf back in her mouth. Her body jerked.

"Don't you dare vomit on my bed cover. It's bad enough that I have to strip the bed to rid myself and my company of your blood. I knew I should have thrown your butt on the floor. Next time, I will."

Warren lifted Marilyn and slung her over his shoulder as if she were a sack of potatoes. "You'd better hope and pray my grandmother's homemade laundry aids get those stains out of my bedsheets, or I'm going to have to beat you again."

Descending the stairs as if she weighed no more than an infant, Warren whistled a little ditty. Midway through the living room, he remembered his Sunday plans. "Oh, by the way, Mother. Heather will be joining us tomorrow. I'm going to pick her up and bring her here so you two can decide if you both want to live or die. As you probably figured out, the decision to live depends on your daughter agreeing to marry me. But, you're a smart lady. You must be, in order to figure out how to get all those rich men to marry you and then walk away with more money than you'll ever be able to spend. Yes, yes, Mother. I admire you. But, what was I saying?" Warren's thoughts backtracked for several seconds as he lightly tromped through the hallway leading to the garage. "Oh, yes, since you're so smart, I'm sure you will properly guide Heather. I know she can be a little stubborn and hardheaded and I know she confides in Nachelle DuCloux more than you, probably because you're so self-centered, but the little bit of influence you do have had better be put to use tomorrow. Comprehend?"

Unceremoniously, Warren dumped Marilyn onto the hot cement floor of the garage. She slumped against the wall, trying to breathe, forcing herself not to give in to the blackness marching toward her mind. Every movement caused a new series of black and white shooting stars to explode behind her eyes. Every movement made it harder and harder for her to keep her mind straight. But, she couldn't succumb. She had to think, to stay focused on coming up with a plan for escaping and keeping her baby safe. Yet, the darkness seemed like such a relief, and it was coming closer and closer— coming to claim her.

After a few minutes of finagling, Warren unlocked the storage closet in the garage and with a few quick maneuvers, stuffed Marilyn's one-hundred-twenty-pound body in it. He locked the door and rapped lightly. "See you in the morning, dear Mother."

Alone, hurt, and in pain, Marilyn cried until the blackness overtook her.

Heather, Nachelle, Steven, and Buddy Abbott, a retired Secret Service agent, now full-time investigator for politicians who wanted a lid on certain confidential situations, situations that needed to be kept hush-hush from the police, the media, etcetera, sat at Heather's dining room table.

Hand-painted Disney coffee mugs sat in front of each person. Lukewarm coffee matched their lukewarm hope. At almost two o'clock in the morning, it was way past time for Marilyn to have checked in with Heather or Roger or Mamie, her housekeeper.

Earlier in the evening, after cleaning the sofa and

this is no big deal to her. And, since she and Roger have a driver in D.C., she probably isn't worried about her license." Heather looked at her friend's skeptical face. She sighed. "Okay, I can see you're not going to let this rest. I will call Roger, and I bet he'll tell us she's out shopping somewhere."

Nachelle smiled. "Well, I won't bet you on that, but it will make me feel better knowing you've talked with Roger." Nachelle watched as Heather picked up the butter-yellow phone and dialed long distance. "The only reason I'm pushing is because of the car downstairs . . . and now, this purse. What if this is the purse she's currently using and what if that's really her car. Maybe she got sick and had to be rushed to the hospital?"

Heather scoffed. "A worry wart with an imagination. Maybe you should be the one working in the creative arts field."

"I would just feel a lot better knowing, that's all."

"Didn't the doctor tell you stressing out is not good for the baby? So, you should—" Roger's tenor greeting interrupted her lecture. "Roger, hello. I didn't expect you to answer."

"I *am* on my way out for an appointment, but I'm never too busy to talk to my favorite daughter. How are you doing?"

"I'm okay," Heather lied as Gerald's image and earlier conversation skipped through her mind. Making herself sound chipper, she asked, "Roger, I don't want to keep you. I was just calling to see if Mom's there."

"Your mother flew into DFW this morning. You haven't seen her yet?" Roger's voice escalated on the last few words. "She was coming specifically to see you."

"This may be a strange question, but what was she wearing this morning when she left D.C.?" Heather's brows drew together.

floor, Heather and Nachelle had agreed to wait until all the stores closed before calling Roger. As they watched the clock, waiting for the magic hour to strike, they had called all the local hospitals and police stations. They had been relieved to know Marilyn had not checked in as either a patient or as a law breaker. Calls to her mother's friends who lived in the area had been equally unproductive. Finally, when nine-thirty came, Heather made two calls: one to Marilyn's Fort Worth home where she was told by a sleepy Mamie that Marilyn had not returned at any time throughout the day and second to Roger who wasn't immediately available but had returned her call an hour later.

It was Roger who had called Buddy Abbott and by twelve-thirty, the large man was leaning on Heather's doorbell.

By then, more than enough time had passed for Heather's creative imagination to conjure up all sorts of happenings concerning Marilyn.

"I know it seems like I've been asking you the same questions over and over again young lady, but the mind is funny. As it has a chance to cool down, so to speak, it remembers other details that seem small at first but are actually the things that make or break a case." His West Texas accent was soothing and confident, and it lulled Heather into thinking that maybe she hadn't given Buddy enough up-front credit.

When Buddy Abbott first showed up at her door, Heather thought immediately of Chief Gillespie of *In the Heat of the Night*, but only if Chief Gillespie was six inches taller and had a tiny bit more hair. They both had the same bulging stomach, and she wondered how he had gotten that stomach, with the rest of his body, into the small Cessna he'd flown from Amarillo to the Alliance airport outside of Fort Worth. Like the TV chief of police, his external appearance didn't exactly fit the summa cum laude model. He just seemed like a plain ole simple country boy.

But, it hadn't taken long for Buddy to negate all assumptions Heather had built about him. He walked in and wasted no time asking for coffee, which Steven had had to go purchase at a local 7-Eleven, and then shooting off questions. By the time Steven returned with the coffee, Heather had walked through the afternoon and evening events, chronologically, three times, and still Buddy had questions. If nothing else, Buddy Abbott was extremely thorough.

"I've told you everything. I don't remember anything else. Her car is outside, she spilled Diet Coke and didn't clean it up, and her purse is on the counter, right where we found it."

"Think hard . . . the living room and the kitchen. Seems most of the action happened in those two rooms." Buddy's blue eyes alternated between piercing and comforting. "Most women know if something isn't quite right. Why, my missus can practically sense when I put the potholder on the stove instead of on the hook by the stove."

Heather closed her eyes and tilted her head back. She expelled a deep breath. "I don't know. I just—" Simultaneously, she sat up straight and opened her eyes wide. "Wait. Now that you mention it. Nachelle, you remember . . . before I started shuffling the deck, I took a pillow off the sofa. Before I could throw the pillow on the floor I had to straighten the rug with my shoe. A piece of the rug was scrunched up. I know it was lying flat when I left for my afternoon appointment because I ran the vacuum this morning."

"That's good, Heather. Good. Now, think harder. And you, too, Nachelle. Think about anything that wasn't quite right."

Heather snapped her fingers. "The sofa was askew.

Slightly. Not much, you know, as if someone bumped against it. I remember straightening it after we cleaned up the spill."

"Good. Good." Buddy's almost-bald head bounced up and down. "What else? Did you by chance check the windows and doors at any time. Anything to report there?"

"No, no, except when I returned home this afternoon . . ." Heather shook her head to dispel the image of Gerald and Suzanne at the restaurant. *Gerald. What's he doing now? Are they together?* Forcing herself to concentrate on the present situation, she detailed her return home from the restaurant. "The door was unlocked. I didn't need my key to get in."

"The door stood wide open," Buddy asked, as more statement than question.

"No. I bumped against it and it swung open. Not all the way but enough that I could see it was unlocked and a little bit open."

"Uh-huh." Buddy said in a disquieting manner.

Heather screwed up her face in a question. "What do you mean by that? What are you thinking?"

"You said you had a group of people here for some play?" It was obvious by the inflection Buddy put on the word "play" that he thought little of the arts.

"Yes."

Steven caught on quick. "You're thinking someone from the group snuck up here, broke in, and was attempting to steal when Marilyn scared them."

"That's total speculation, son," Buddy answered. "I won't know anything until I walk through this entire place."

"But, if that's the case, where's Marilyn?" Nachelle asked. "What did the thief do with her?" She rubbed her temples, trying to rid herself of her headache. A few hours earlier, she had started feeling really bad and the last time she went to the rest room, she could have sworn she had blood in her urine. It worried her but not nearly as much as Marilyn's situation.

Both men shook their heads.

Buddy stood up. "I'ma mosey on downstairs and check out the place. Why don't you folks at least go lie down for a bit. Big as this place is, I'ma be roaming for a while." He turned his eyes on Nachelle, speaking specifically to her. "Especially you, young lady, you look like you're going to be sick any moment."

Nachelle had tried to hide the fact that her headaches, dizziness, and nausea had returned. Either she looked just that bad, or Buddy was a darn better detective than she had given him credit for.

Heather stood as well. "He's right, Nachelle. Why don't you guys go on home. I'll call if anything changes."

"Are you sure?" Nachelle queried, struggling to stand.

Steven didn't say anything, but for Nachelle to give in so quickly meant she *must* be tired. He stared at her and noticed what the others saw. Bags under her eyes, peaked under her beautiful dark skin and grayish as well. Her eyes were unnaturally bright, her smile strained. She had had an eventful day. *Time to go home and put my wife and child to bed,* he thought affectionately.

Following Buddy, Steven put a hand on Nachelle's back, guiding her to the front door. Heather trailed behind.

"I'll need all your keys, ma'am."

Heather handed Buddy one set of keys. "The rest are downstairs. I'll show you."

They split at the bottom of the stairs. Steven and Nachelle headed toward the back to the garage and the parking lot.

Nachelle shouted at Heather's and Buddy's backs as

they made their way to the front of the building where Heather's office was located. "Don't forget to call as soon as you hear something, Heather."

"I won't. I promise." She blew the couple a kiss. "And, thank you guys. I appreciate *everything*."

Instinctively, Steven and Nachelle knew Heather also referred to the failed restaurant reconciliation with Gerald in her thanks.

They waved and disappeared in the darkness.

Heather turned around and led Buddy to her office.

Buddy spoke as he followed Heather's shorter, slimmer figure. "Mr. Wolfe'll be arriving shortly. You may need to fill him in if you can't find me. I'ma be outside in the neighborhood, too."

To punctuate his prediction, the buzzer sounded. "Humph. Speak of the devil."

Heather made a mad dash inside her office to snag the keys off the wall hook. Then, using that same set, she let in a very rumpled and tired Roger Wolfe. Without planning to, she rushed into his arms and exploded with tears.

Roger held her close, comforting her. "Hush. Hush. Now, child. Everything's going to be all right. I promise."

Fourteen

The telephone rang once, then twice. On the third ring, Gerald stirred. He peeked through one eye and registered the time on the clock and the noise at the same time. Four fifty-seven in the morning. Who could possibly be calling? *After fumbling with the telephone receiver for several seconds, he managed to get the speaking device to his ear before the next ring.*

His deep voice, made deeper with sleep, formed a semblance of a greeting. "Mmmmm?"

"Gerald, Mom's missing. She's gone. I can't find her."

The voice sounded far far away as if a bale of cotton had been placed over the mouthpiece. Gerald struggled to an upright position. The struggle was made more difficult by the deep, peace-filled sleep that kept sucking at him, trying to pull him back. "Linda? That you?" *Gerald was having difficulty making out the voice and the words.*

"I can't find my mom. And, I didn't get to say what I should have." *A soft hiccuping cry punctuated the end of the declaration.*

"Heather?" *The fog in Gerald's mind started clearing, recognition slowly crept in.* "Heather, baby, is that you? What's that?"

"Mom's gone." *The caller whimpered tenderly for several seconds, then there was nothing.*

Five, blaring offensive beeps startled Gerald. "If you would like to make a call, please hang up and dial again. Recording

3098." *The voice of the mechanized operator alerted Gerald that the other line had disconnected.*

Weird, *he thought as he replaced the receiver. Sleep reclaimed Gerald before he had a chance to determine if the conversation was real or imaginary.*

Heather rolled over onto her side with her eyes closed and her mind slowly awakening. One eye squinted open to check the time. With the suddenness of having cold water thrown on her, she sat up straight, rechecked the time, then scrambled from beneath the tangled covers.

"Seven o'clock. Roger let me oversleep," she exclaimed in her heavy morning voice. After Roger's arrival last night (or was it early this morning, she didn't know anymore, the days had blended together to make one long day), he had convinced her to get some sleep. Heather had agreed with two conditions: that he wake her after two hours of sleep and that he wake her immediately upon the discovery of any further developments. The politician had agreed to her conditions. *I should have known better,* she thought.

With her short hair tousled in spikes all over her head and wearing only a Minnie Mouse sleepshirt and panties, Heather made quick work of washing her face and teeth. Ignoring the bags under her eyes, which proclaimed the meager, disturbing sleep she'd had, she rushed out of the bathroom and grabbed her house robe lying on the floor. Slipping it on, she stumbled into the living area, bumping into furniture as she went. Exhaustion and sleep still had a mighty hold on her.

"You let me sleep too late," Heather accused Roger as she advanced upon him and Buddy sitting at her dining room table.

"There's nothing to report. Go back to bed." Roger

spoke in a fatherly tone that should have eliminated any further discussions. But, Heather was driven by concern and fear for her mom, plus she was stubborn and hardheaded to boot.

"Tell me what I missed!" Heather stood at the table with her hands on her hips, her lips poked out defiantly.

Roger recognized that Marilyn-like stance and knew he could either capitulate now or later, but either way he was going to lose. He gave in now. He was too edgy to debate with Heather.

Standing, he folded the young lady in his arms and held her tenderly like a newborn. He needed the human contact as much as Heather. And, in that touch, they were bound together by the mutual love of one woman: Marilyn Chadwick-Wolfe. Each held the other, praying the same thought—that Marilyn would return to them soon, unharmed.

Ending the hug, Roger escorted Heather to a chair. He left her long enough to pour a big mug of coffee for her. Setting the mug down in front of her, he moved the sugar and creamer near her.

"It's been a long night." He eased into the chair he had vacated earlier and with his elbows on the table, ran both hands over his lowered head. Despite the long hours of vigilance he'd maintained, he looked handsome in his wrinkled white shirt and khaki twill pants. His early morning beard, so like Steven's in its salt-and-pepper coloring, added to his dark brown good looks.

Staring at him, Heather realized she had never before really paid Roger any mind other than to acknowledge him as her mother's current husband. She assumed, like the men before him, that he wouldn't be around long, so why bother getting to know him. But, this was their third year of marriage, the longest of any of Marilyn's marriages, and it seemed to be solid still. It occurred to her that Roger appeared to be truly in love with Marilyn. She wondered if her mother reciprocated his feelings.

Roger expelled a long breath. In a tired, watered-down voice, he filled Heather in on the latest events. "While I made calls to Marilyn's friends, to verify they knew nothing of her whereabouts, Buddy did what he's good at—detecting and investigating. His all-night, all-morning expedition uncovered several facts that may or may not be related to Marilyn's disappearance. He found evidence that the locks on your downstairs front and back doors had been tampered with. Apparently, it appears someone used a clay or putty mixture of some sort to get a pattern of your locks and keys. They then used that pattern to have keys made. Buddy was able to lift some pretty clean fingerprints, and he's already sent them, plus a sample of the clay mixture to a friend of his for processing." Roger paused. His focus shifted from Heather to the tangle of devices in front of Buddy. "And, he found those things in front of him."

Heather followed Roger's gaze.

At the opposite end of the table from Roger, Buddy sat quietly, but sipped long and noisily from his cup of hot, steaming coffee. Unlike Roger, Heather couldn't tell by his appearance that he had spent the whole night up. He looked the same as he did when he first walked through her door about seven hours ago.

In front of Buddy sat a turkey platter full of black and silver discs, some the size of a button, others the size of a quarter. Also, in the platter were wires and slim, silver, bent devices that resembled hook rug needles.

The retired lawman spoke without looking up. "Your house was bugged, little lady." With a miniature tweezer he turned a button-sized black disc over and over, studying it as if it held the formula for worldwide peace. "A damn good, professional job, too."

"Bugged! Like in the movies, bugged?" Heather's gaze shifted between the two men, looking for confirmation that what she heard and repeated was true. Heather was nearing hysteria. This was something out of a movie, not something that happened in real life. Not her life anyway. What was going on? First her mother . . . Now the bugs . . .

"Yes, ma'am." Buddy quit studying long enough to take a noisy slurp of coffee. "Mmmmm. Good coffee."

"Who put them in my house and why? Who did this?" Heather demanded to know. Her hands trembled, her heart raced. She was on the verge of freaking out.

Behind her head, Roger motioned for Buddy to shut up. Like any protective father, he didn't want Heather any more upset and frightened than she already was. Her mother was missing, her house was bugged, and there was a very strong suspicion the two events were related.

Roger's heart sank when he thought about Buddy's reputation. He knew Buddy got off on this sort of chase. The lawman lived for the adventure of finding clues, tracking down the culprit, and bringing the "bad" person to justice. That's why he had called Buddy in. He knew that with Buddy on the job, there would be no lengthy delays in finding the wrongdoer, there would be no mistakes, and there would be very little publicity. But, bringing Buddy in on a case also meant dealing with Buddy's flaw—his intensity. As Buddy got closer and closer to solving a case, his focus shifted solely to the case and he tended to ignore the emotional ups and downs of the family involved. Always, when a case neared climax, Buddy forgot he was dealing with human beings with feelings that needed to be carefully handled. The omission of this aspect of case handling often led to his simply stating facts that were sometimes devastating to the family.

And, that delivery of news was what terrified Roger. He hadn't said so to Heather yet, but Buddy had confessed to him that whoever had planted the bugs had gone through a lot of time and expense. Based on that evidence, the person was after something big—perhaps money, a lot of money. Buddy had even said the word Roger had shuddered to hear: kidnaping.

Roger was scared and he felt helpless. He hated that his fear drew mental pictures of his wife being manhandled by some crazed, money-hungry maniac, or worse, being tortured by some demonic citizen who opposed his politics. He hoped he sufficiently hid his fear from Heather, but he could feel the emotion rising up, threatening to drive him out of control. The thought of never seeing his wife again, of never again holding her or dancing with her or teasing her about her stuffy ways made him want to quit living. Life without Marilyn would be empty and pointless. *Get a grip, Roger. Not every kidnaping ends in death,* he thought. *Don't give in to the fear. Stay focused on the facts and on helping Heather, for soon, she would have to know, but please God, not now.*

Roger's silent plea must have filtered from his brain, through the airwaves, and into Buddy's head for Buddy surprised Roger with his comments to Heather. "Won't know anything more till we find the culprit. Need your help for that. Make a list of everyone who's been in here. Start six months back. And, I mean everybody, including repairmen, friends, family, florists, anything or anybody walking on two legs. Indicate how long they stayed for each visit and what kind of vehicle they drove, if you know that." Buddy pushed a piece of paper and pen toward her. For the first time since she entered the living room, he looked at her for longer than a second. "Our finding the answer to this dilemma depends on that list."

"But, where were they? They . . . I mean . . . I live

here. I would have noticed!" Heather struggled to concentrate on what Buddy and Roger said, although her active, creative imagination already developed scenes and acts. And, she didn't like the plays going on in her head.

"These little thangs"—Buddy lifted one toward Heather—"they were all over the place. In phones, over the doorway, furniture. I found other devices in your locks, in sockets, light fixtures, ever'where. You wouldn't see them if you didn't know to look for 'em, and whoever planted 'em knew what they was doing and knew where to shop." Buddy's eyes pinned her to her chair. "These are the best the black market has to offer." Buddy started placing the electronic devices in a Zip-Loc bag. "Start writing. Faster we get the list, faster we can solve this puzzle."

Heather closed her eyes for a second. Taking a deep breath, she asked the question: "You think these bugs have something to do with Mom's disappearance?"

Roger winced. "Honey . . ." He wasn't going to give Buddy a chance to respond. "Buddy won't know anything else until he takes them to be analyzed. The longer you detain him with questions, the more confusion we deal with. Please, baby, just concentrate on the list. Be thorough." He almost added, "Your mother's life may depend on it," but he bit his tongue.

Heather took one long look at Roger's pinched face and strained expression and knew he thought as she did. There was a connection. Her bones were telling her the two incidents were connected. It was too coincidental. Heather wanted to lie down somewhere and cry, but Roger and Buddy's words sank in. She started writing fast and furiously.

"I'ma run these beauts over to my buddy's for a thorough review. I'ma also check on the fingerprints to see if my friend at the Bureau's come up with a match.

Somehow, this puzzle's gonna be solved today or my name ain't Buddy Abbott."

The door closed behind Buddy with a solid thud. They could hear his cowboy boots first loud, then softer, then nothing as he descended the stairs.

Roger stood up and walking over to Heather, kissed the top of her head. "I'm going to shower and dress. I'll be out shortly to help you, Heather."

Heather ignored him. She wrote as if her mother's life depended on it.

With the room finally quiet and devoid of all distractions, Heather was able to concentrate on her assignment. She was able to backtrack through the last few weeks, but after that her memory faded. After a quick trip into her bedroom to write down the names of the companies who delivered her "secret lover" gifts, she headed downstairs to her office to confer with her daily planner calendar.

She had been writing for fifteen minutes when she happened to look up and saw Warren standing in the doorway.

Startled, she shrieked.

Warren walked into the room.

Placing a hand over her heart, Heather stared at him furiously. "You scared me. I thought I was going to die."

Warren closed the gap between them. "You just might."

Heather didn't see the navy cloth until too late. Warren was fast and smooth. He grasped her head and smothered her mouth and nose with the navy cloth filled with an obnoxious sleeping agent. She didn't struggle—she didn't get a chance to. The potion worked quick.

Buddy was miles away and Roger had just stepped out of the shower when Warren, carrying Heather like a groom carries his bride over the threshold, walked out of the front door of the Twelfth Street Puppet Company. Not bothering to relock the door, he carried Heather across the street and through the alley beyond Malcolm and Ali's building, where a white van with the insignia for a produce delivery company was parked. All the while that he walked, Warren had his head bowed toward Heather's as if they were kissing.

At the van, he used one hand to open the sliding side door and unceremoniously tossed Heather's body inside. Within minutes, he was on the main thoroughfare heading home to reunite his wife-to-be and his mother-in-law-to-be.

Fifteen

The bright sunlight streaming through the separation of drapery panels warmed Gerald's face. He moaned and rolled over onto his side, flinging his arm over what should have been Heather's warm body. Instead, his long arm hit the mattress and his eyes popped open wide.

Unlike Heather, he was a "toast" person, the type of person, who, unlike a "muffin" person, could bounce out of bed and start his day as soon as his eyes opened. And, he did just that. Springing his long body out of the custom-made bed, he whistled as he headed for the shower. He was at the bathroom door with his hand on the knob when the memory of the early morning telephone call hit him, stopping him on a dime.

Cocking his head like a spaniel, he thought, *Did Heather call me this morning or did I imagine that?* His mind recalled as much of the brief, sketchy conversation as it could. *Naw . . .* He shook his head. *I must have been dreaming and . . . wishing.* Gerald pushed open the door, whistling and reviewing the day's agenda in his head. With the flick of a wrist, he turned on the cold water in the shower. *I'm tripping. One look at her yesterday at lunch, one conversation with her about her turnabout desire to marry me, one look into those beautiful hazel eyes, and I'm ready to conjure up any reason to see her.* Gerald shook his head. *Forget it. I have other things to be concerned with today.*

Gerald tried to flip his mind to another station, but it refused to budge off the Heather Chadwick channel. *I wonder if she really meant those words she spoke at the restaurant. Is she really ready to take our relationship to the next level? Is Suzanne on target when she said Heather had problems that I didn't know about?* The questions kept churning in his mind as he re-reviewed the lunch conversation between he and Heather and the postlunch conversation between he and Suzanne.

Just when he thought his head would explode from uncertainty, the dream image of the early morning call resurfaced. *Was that call real? Was that Heather's way of reaching out to me? To show me she'd changed? I remember she said something about her mother missing. What was that about?* Was the predawn call real or imaginary? The question continued to plague him throughout his cold, then hot, then lukewarm shower. With droplets of water trailing down his hard, long, dark body, he stepped out of the shower and wrapped a towel around his tight waist. Swiping a hand across his steamy mirror, he stared at his reflection. "There's only one way to get this off your mind, Gerald. Call them."

In his bedroom, he opened his nightstand drawer and pulled out a four-by-six, black address/phone book. Picking up the handset, he held the book open to the D's and dialed. Two rings sounded in his ear.

"Hello." The female voice sounded strained.

"Hello, Nachelle. I'm sorry to call so early in the morning. Did I wake you?"

"Gerald, hello. No, of course, you didn't wake us. How are you doing?" Nachelle's voice brightened a bit when she recognized the voice.

"I'm great. And you? Did you get rid of that headache you had yesterday?" Gerald looked at the white cube clock on his nightstand: nine-ten. If the call really did happen, had it been only four hours ago?

"No, unfortunately not." Nachelle thought about the events that happened after the luncheon: Marilyn's disappearance, Roger and Buddy's arrival, Heather's wrecked emotional state. It amazed her to think all that activity happened in less than a twenty-four-hour period. *Come to think of it . . .* She turned her head toward the clock. *I should have heard from Heather by now. As soon as I finish with Gerald, I'll give her a call.* She turned her tired, weak body over to face the clock, and her body signaled its disappointment with that action. Her light-headedness increased, as did her dizziness. Putting a hand over her mouth, she fought down the nausea and concentrated on Gerald's words.

"I'm sorry to hear that, but listen, I have a weird question to ask you." He paused, not quite sure how to voice his concerns about what could have been his imagination playing tricks with him. "Is everything okay with Heather?"

Nachelle frowned, thinking about the broadness of Gerald's question. "What specifically are you referring to? I mean, when I left her this morning, she was doing as well as could be expected."

"What do you mean, as well as can be expected? That sounds like something bad happened?" Gerald's heart rate accelerated.

Nachelle put a trembling hand to her forehead. "Oh, Gerald. Heather's going through a lot right now. I know she would appreciate your being there for her." Nachelle sighed deeply.

"Nachelle, I *think* I spoke to Heather this morning, but I'm not sure. I thought maybe I was dreaming, but now it sounds like it was real. What happened?" Gerald spoke as fast as a New Yorker.

"Gerald, Marilyn's missing. No one's seen her since yesterday morning." The pain in Nachelle's head increased with every word. If she could have put her hands on a machete, she would cut her head off. The pain was that bad. "As you can imagine, Heather's quite upset."

"Oh, God, it was real. She really did call me, and she did mention her mother was missing. I thought it might have been a dream."

"No, it's real. And, actually, Gerald . . . hold on"—Nachelle stretched out her hand to move the phone closer to her—"let me see if I can get Heather on the line. She should have called by now to give us an update."

As quickly as her swelling fingers would let her, she clicked the phone to three-way and dialed the number.

The first ring wasn't even a quarter of the way complete before Roger breathlessly picked up. "Heather?"

"No, Roger, it's Gerald and Nachelle. Where's Heather?" Nachelle spoke for both of them.

Roger released a deep sigh. His voice was ragged when he spoke. "I don't know. Both she and Marilyn are gone . . . missing."

Gerald didn't even hang up the phone. He dropped his towel and without bothering to dry off, threw on a sweat suit and raced out of the house.

Nachelle's voice escalated. Puzzled, upset, and quickly running out of breath, she demanded answers. "What do you mean, she's gone? I don't understand. Both you and Buddy are there!" The room spun faster, and the monochrome stars burst behind her closed eyes. Still, she tried to focus on Roger's words.

"Buddy left for the lab to follow up on the evidence he found. I was upstairs in the shower. When I came out and went looking for her, she was gone. We know she was downstairs because we found a list she was making for Buddy in her office, along with a dark towel that Buddy sent to the lab. She's gone, and Buddy thinks the same person who nabbed Marilyn has Heather. But, it doesn't make sense! The person didn't leave a ransom note."

Nachelle's eyes opened wide. "Ransom note! What are you saying? Are you . . . they were kidnaped?"

"Buddy thinks so, yes." Roger spoke quietly as if saying it out loud would make the situation worse.

"Oh, my God, no, Roger, no," Nachelle cried. "He can't be right. Surely Buddy is wrong!"

"I wish he was, Nachelle, but I saw the evidence." Roger, a husband and father first, wanted to ignore Buddy's evidence but as a lawyer by training, he couldn't ignore the obvious. "Heather's house was bugged from top to bottom. Their cars and personal effects are here. Both ladies are missing." Roger spoke as if he would crack any second. "The only thing missing is a ransom note. Buddy thinks it'll show up sometime today."

Nachelle leaned her head back against the headboard. She couldn't believe it. First Marilyn, then Heather. This was movie material, not real life—or, at least not the lives of the people she knew. "I can't believe it. I can't believe it." She needed help. The pain, the tears wouldn't let her focus. "Steven! Steven!" She closed her eyes against the onslaught of physical pain, no less potent than her emotional distress. "Steven!"

The shower in the master bathroom continued running. "Roger, Steven and I will be right there. Gerald? Gerald? Gerald . . . are you there?"

Silence met her query.

"He's probably on the way there, Roger. Tell him we'll be there shortly." As she was about to hang up, she said, "Roger . . . all will be fine." Nachelle was sure he needed as much assurance as she did.

They quickly disconnected. The water in the bathroom had stopped running, and now she could hear Steven humming to himself. No doubt he was looking in the mirror, smoothing his salt-and-pepper hair.

"Steven!" she called. Bracing herself she swung her legs over the side of the bed. As she sat up, she felt a gush of liquid trickle down her legs, wetting her gown and the sheets. Looking down, she saw thin bloody liquid. "Steven!" A few seconds later, she passed out.

Gerald made it to Fort Worth in twenty minutes—a usual forty-five minute drive. Until today, he had no idea his Pathfinder could actually go one hundred and fifty miles per hour. Pulling up to the gate of Heather's back parking lot, he quickly punched in the code, not even realizing he still remembered it. As soon as the gate opened wide enough for his truck to squeeze through, he zoomed into the lot while pressing the door opener to the garage. Again, he didn't stop to wonder why he still had Heather's garage door opener in his car. He knew why. It was simple. He loved her, and those simple things represented a continued bond of their love.

Taking the stairs three at a time, Gerald had every intention of bursting through the door. But, as soon as he hit the top step, he spied Roger in the open doorway, looking haggard and shrunken.

Gerald pulled up just short of knocking Roger down. "How are you, sir?" Gerald panted, asking out of politeness. What he really wanted to know was if anything new had developed within the past twenty minutes. During the short drive, he had used every diversion, from the radio to the billboards to counting highway markers, to keep his mind off Heather's disappearance. None of the tricks had worked. Sweat had covered his palms like a new skin, and his heartbeats far exceeded the recommended guidelines posted on charts in gyms. All this in response to the news that his woman, his love, was missing. He was deathly afraid and angry. Angry that as soon as he'd made the decision to talk to Heather about their relationship, she had been snatched from him.

Roger shrugged his shoulders as an answer and backed out of Gerald's way.

Gerald brushed past the congressman and began his own personal search for Heather. It wasn't that he didn't believe Roger, he just wanted to verify for himself that Heather had indeed vanished.

Roger followed him from room to room. "She's not here. Neither woman is here." Roger's voice was on edge. The tears were near.

"I know that, sir. I don't doubt you. I just need to see for myself." Whether Roger minded or not, Gerald didn't care. He continued with his search.

Roger remained in the living area, near the telephone, while Gerald went on a searching spree downstairs. After a thorough review of every room, every cranny, every crack, Gerald returned to where Roger stood, as silent and still as a corpse.

"Please, sir, I have to know everything. Start with yesterday's news about Marilyn's disappearance. Don't leave a thing out." Gerald hoped he could hear over the wild thumping of his heart.

Thirty minutes and several cups of coffee later, Gerald knew as much as Roger. He knew things that Roger had not even shared with Heather.

"This is all we have. This list." Roger handed a legal-sized sheet of paper to Gerald. "Do you recognize any of the names on this list?"

Gerald scanned the paper. "Some, not all. Nachelle may be able to help with the ones we don't know. They're on the way, right?"

Roger nodded, rubbing his hands over his distressed face.

Gerald stared into Roger's tight face. His heart went out to him. Gerald had no doubt that if he'd been involved in this drama as long as Roger, he, too, would look like warmed-over death. Gerald could imagine Roger's feelings of fear, helplessness, regret, and rage at the unknown assailant. Gerald felt them, too. Especially regret. All the times he and Heather had fought, all the times they were separated, all the stupid arguments, came washing over him in mocking torment. What he wouldn't give to get those times back and use them to build happy memories. Now, he was faced with the awful possibility that he might never see his lovely Heather again. It scared him to think about it, so he turned his mind instead to more productive work.

"What's this notation? 'Deliveryman from Godiva's from "Your Secret Love" '? There are several of those notes. What's this about?" Gerald asked tersely.

"I was hoping you would know. I thought maybe you were sending gifts and flowers to her." Roger sank down onto the sofa as if his legs could no longer hold him. The guilt he felt at letting someone steal his daughter from under his nose was punishing him like the Turks punish their criminals: harshly, swiftly, cruelly. "I figured the two of you were getting back together."

"I'd like to say it was me, but I'd be lying." The selective words "two" and "together" suddenly generated a thought in Gerald's head. *Oh, God! I left Suzanne at the house alone. I'll bet she's still asleep or starting to wake up in the guest bedroom.* As he picked up the phone to call her, he remembered she had caught a late evening flight to Atlanta the night before. He whispered a prayer of thanks.

After the eventful lunch yesterday and the discussion afterward, they had agreed that Gerald needed some time alone to seriously think about his life with or without Heather. If nothing else, this morning's predicament pointed out the obvious. He was very much in love with Heather and regardless of what she'd done in the past, he wanted a life with her. Nothing or no one could change that except Heather, herself.

Rubbing his nearly bald head, he again focused on the list. "Heather has two lines here. I'll take the list of obvious people: family, friends, employees, et cetera. Senator, you call the companies and delivery people. I'm sure when you explain to them that you're a congressman and someone has been pestering your daughter with expensive gifts, and you want to know who purchased the gifts, they'll be more than cooperative. That way we'll know for sure the name of everyone who's had contact with Heather." Gerald shrugged his powerful shoulders. "Who knows—maybe this secret lover might lead us to a conclusion."

As Gerald's fingers punched in numbers, he put his jealousy on ice. Once they discovered who this secret lover was, he'd make it clear to the jerk that Heather had room in her life for only one man—and that one man was Gerald. But, for now, he needed all his energy focused on finding his woman.

Sixteen

Heather's coming-to was slow and uneasy. Moaning, she put a hand to her forehead and with her eyes closed, rolled over onto her back on the sofa. "Ohhhhh."

"Good timing." Warren stood over her, looking down into her face. "I just got back from eating breakfast." Sitting on the edge of the coffee table, he dangled his hands between his denim-clad legs and smiled. "Open your eyes. It's time to talk."

Heather simply groaned again and turned her head away from the noise that was filtering through her brain.

Growing impatient quickly, Warren shook Heather's shoulders. "We're on a schedule today. Now, get your butt up."

With her neck snapping from the jerking action, Heather closed her eyes tighter. Instinctively, she brought up her hands, trying to break the hold Warren had on her shoulders. "Stop that. Let go of me."

Warren obeyed her command only to start slapping her lightly about the face. "Wake up, sleepyhead. Wake up!" That action got him the reaction he'd been looking for. Heather opened her eyes and brought up her hands to protect her face.

"Quit! Stop!" she croaked. Her throat was slightly irritated from the sleeping agent he'd used, and her eyes watered. Slowly, her light eyes focused on her captor. "What do you think you're doing?"

"I'm trying to get your attention. We have things to do, *dear*. There's no time for you to lounge around in your sleep clothes." Warren sat back down on the coffee table and leaned toward her.

Heather looked at him with hardened eyes. "That's not what I meant. Why did you put that nasty stuff over my face? Why did you bring me here? What do you want? I have to get back home. I'm dealing with an emergency there." Heather eased up, pulling her sleepshirt down past her hips. Swinging her legs over the edge of the sofa, she made a move to stand up.

Warren pushed her back down, easy enough to do considering the effects of the agent hadn't completely worn off. Her wobbly legs crumpled, and soon she was back where she started. "Darling Heather. So full of questions."

Growing angrier by the minute, Heather stared him straight in the eyes. "I don't know what you want, but I told you I have something very important going on. I'm going home."

Before she could make a move upward, Warren put heavy hands on her shoulders, stapling her in place. "And, I told *you* we have a tight schedule today. I don't want any mouth from you."

For the first time since waking from her unsolicited sleep, Heather observed Warren's face. She noticed his usual straightforward attractive face looked different. Maybe it was the slant of his brows or the wild look in his eyes or the tight line of his lips, but something was sinister looking. Heather inched away from him, pressing her back into the sofa.

"Our flight for Mexico leaves in a few hours, and we still have to get you and your mother presentable. You can't—"

"Mom." Heather latched on to that one word. The rest of his sentence flew in and out of her consciousness. Desperately, she leaned forward and grabbed his hands. "You know where my mom is?"

Warren looked at her wide-open, anxious eyes and laughed. "Yes, silly. Of course I do. She's in the garage. I'll let you speak to her momentarily but first—"

"But, first nothing!" Heather bounced up and looked around the living area of Warren's home. Although she had visited him there before, she had not paid close attention to the layout. She decided the garage must be behind her down the hallway past the kitchen. "I've been worried sick about my mom. I'm going to see her." She took a full step before she was yanked backward and flung back on the couch.

With an evil, twisted look on his face, Warren towered over her. He thrust his face into hers and grabbed her around the throat, squeezing. "Don't make me beat you. Not yet." He smiled sickeningly. "You don't want our children to look at our wedding pictures and ask why you're wearing sunglasses, do you?"

Heather clawed at his hand, trying to loosen his grip so she could breathe. Her legs kicked, propelling her upward toward the arm of the couch.

His release was sudden, and she wasted not a second replacing his hand with her own. She caressed her aching throat. "You're crazy," she rasped. Heather knew then Warren was not sane. Until that moment, she had been too angry, disoriented, and concerned with her mother's whereabouts to consider the danger *she* might be in. Her heartbeats accelerated. *Be calm, Heather,* she told herself. *Try not to upset him any more than he already is. Play along with him until you can get to Marilyn and a phone.*

Warren almost spat in her face. "And you're a whore!

Who was that man in your shower this morning? Don't lie to me." He pointed a long finger in her face.

Absurdly, Heather thought that with his long, thin fingers, well-manicured nails, and elegant hands, he would make a stunning piano player. His continued yelling disintegrated the thought.

"I saw him when I picked you up. I went upstairs first to get you. You weren't there, but a man was in your shower." He slapped Heather. Her head snapped backward from the blow. She felt the metallic taste of blood in her mouth. "How dare you sleep with another man when you're about to marry me. This is our wedding day, for God's sake! Tonight will be our first night together as husband and wife, and you've ruined it by whoring around with another man."

With tears streaming down her cheeks, Heather sobbed. "I wasn't being . . . unfaithful. I . . . that was Roger. He was cleaning up, that's all."

With an ugly snarl on his face Warren said, "You're having an affair with your mother's husband?"

"No. No. God, no," Heather lamented. "He—" Heather snapped her mouth shut. She didn't dare tell this crazy man that Buddy and Roger were on to him. That they had been up all night at her house, uncovering all Warren's dirty clues. That they had his prints and bugs and soon, she prayed to God, the man himself. Better to keep that information to herself.

"That's right. Just shut up. There's no excuse for that sort of behavior," he yelled self-righteously. His hard eyes racked her from head to toe. "I expect you to drop the affair after we're married. It's acceptable for a man to have extramarital affairs, but as my wife, if I so much as smell a man's cologne on you—either Roger's or that basketball player you were trying to give credit for my gifts—I'll beat you for a month."

Heather's eyes widened. "You . . . you sent the gifts? You're my secret love?"

Warren threw his hands in the air. Heather cowered and curled up in the corner of the sofa. She ducked her head and used her forearms as shields. The blows didn't come.

Warren laughed at her. "You silly girl. I wouldn't hit you without provocation." He sat back down on the edge of the coffee table. Heather lowered her arms but kept a steady, wary eye on him. "Yes, I'm your secret love. Not Gerald Forrester. We had to have some type of courting period, some way for me to show you how much I care for you. I came up with the idea and used money from my other women to pay for the gifts." Warren spoke as if they were having a conversation about the hot Texas summer. "Of course, you're going to pay me back every cent I spent. I could have bought another Neiman-Marcus suit with that money. Instead, I had to spend it on you."

"Yes, yes, of course, I'll give you the money," Heather was quick to agree. Anything to keep him from getting angry again. Anything to keep him as "pleasant" as he was now. *Think, Heather, think,* she scolded herself. *I've got to come up with a plan to get me and Mom out of here. I can't wait for Roger and Buddy. This man is crazy.* To give herself time to come up with a feasible plan, she timidly asked the million dollar question: "Why me?"

"I selected you because you have what I'm due: money and power. Except you're not using your power, silly child." He playfully tagged her on the leg and laughed. Raising one slender finger in the air, he continued. "But, your mother . . . Now there's a woman who *knows* how to throw a name around." There was a gleam of admiration in his eyes. "That Marilyn . . . Boy, I bet she can hang with the best of the *best* power brokers. What a woman! I can't believe you're her child.

You're nothing like her. But, by the time I'm through with you, you'll have more appreciation for the Chadwick name."

God forbid, she thought, shuddering. Suddenly an idea popped into her head. *I need to slip into an acting role. Surely with an undergraduate and graduate degree in Theater, I should be able to make Warren think I'm on his side. That I'm his best friend, lover, and confidante. I've got to make him think I'm his willing cohort.* Heather knew this would be her hardest acting job ever. For her mother's sake and her own, she had to try.

Mentally making the transition, Heather masked her fear and changed her body language and tone of voice from terrified and confused to confident and friendly, from adversary to friend. "I understand and agree Warren." Heather spoke calmly, affably. She sat up and situated herself primly on the edge of the sofa with her knees together, one arm casually crossed her knees, the other raised with one hand tucked under her chin.

Warren moved from the table to sit beside Heather on the couch. He didn't even pay her any mind. He was off in his own world, speaking as if he was giving a lecture. "Actually, for the longest time I couldn't decide if I wanted to marry you or Marilyn. Although your mother is fine, she's beyond her childbearing years. And, I want children. I think I'd be a good father." Warren stroked his chin as if considering the idea anew. There was a pleased smile on his face.

"Warren, if it's power and money you want, you can *have* my fortune. You don't need to marry me. I'll have the attorney draw up papers, and you'll be a millionaire in a few days. Just think, you wouldn't have the baggage of a wife or mother-in-law. You'll be a free, rich man. The world will lay down at your feet." Heather smiled brightly at him.

"Yes, I thought about that. It is appealing since physically, you're not exactly my type." He threw her a look of disdain. "But, the drawback with that plan is it doesn't give me true power. True power comes with the name. Just saying I'm married to a Chadwick will make people tremble. Just saying I'm the late Everett Chadwick's son-in-law will open doors to country clubs, private receptions, the political arena, places I've been excluded from previously." His eyes grew dark, his smile became a grimace.

Heather could see from his changed expression that he was thinking of something very painful and heavy. "Tell me what you're thinking?" she cautiously asked. *If I can get inside his head, maybe I can develop a way to get me and Mom out of here. Perhaps I can catch him unawares or find out something to use to my benefit.*

"I'm thinking about my bastard father who laughed at me when I tried to enter his home. I'm thinking of my bastard sisters and brothers who poked fun at me and told me I'd never be more than an errand boy. None of them cared that half of my blood was their blood." Warren popped off the couch and with angry strides paced around the living room. His hands gestured wildly, and his face grew more and more distorted with pain, anger, hurt. "I should have been a spoiled, rich boy. I should have lived gloriously. I should have had people bow to my every wish. Instead, I lived with my old grandmama and my stupid, trifling mother in a shack with a scarcity of food, clothes, and utilities. It was my mother's fault! We could have all lived good if that bitch had gone to her sugar-daddy, whore-partner and demanded he acknowledge me. She refused to take care of me, so I took care of her. They'll never find her body." Warren's chest rose and fell rapidly. He had stopped pacing, and his hands were clenched into a tight fist by his side. His eyes stared off through the patio window into the past. For a split second, a look of remorse landed on his face. "I did feel sorry for Grandmama, though. For some reason, she really loved her daughter." The look was gone, replaced by a matter-of-fact expression and a shrug of a shoulder. "But, she got over it in time."

Heather's friendly smile and demeanor slipped. Her attempt at acting her way through this nightmare halted. *He killed his mother!* she screamed in her head. *He killed his* own *mother simply because she wouldn't do what he wanted. What possible hope do Mom and I have?* Heather completely lost her stage presence, dropped her characterization. She trembled from head to toe, quaked on the inside and tried to make herself as invisible as possible. Closing her eyes, she held her breath and prayed as quickly and urgently as she could.

Give him a new focus, Heather. Get him off that subject. That's the only way to stay alive. Trying not to focus on the fear that consumed her, Heather steered the conversation away from his torrid past. In a tremulous voice, she said the first thing her mind latched on to. "Earlier you said we're getting married today. That we're flying to Mexico." She cleared her voice, trying to sound more confident, less frightened. "I don't have a thing to wear and—"

Warren approached her rapidly. Heather almost lost control of her bladder. She closed her eyes and waited for the blow that would kill her.

As diverse as a chameleon, Warren's mood had changed. He knelt in front of her and gently took her trembling hands in his. He kissed her knuckles and smiled brilliantly. "I've taken care of everything." Warren laughed. "I scare myself sometimes. I'm so smart. See"—Warren lowered his voice conspiratorially—"I helped myself to copies of your keys and for the past month, I've been coming and going. On one of my trips, I packed a bag for you for our trip. You were sound asleep just a few feet away." Warren raised his eyes heavenward trying to remember. "Actually, I lost count of the number of times I stood over you, watching you sleep. But, I used the time to plan our life together."

Heather closed her eyes to prevent him from seeing the fear he inspired, to prevent him from witnessing her thoughts. Her mind overflowed with the information he shared. Like a movie in reverse, Heather viewed all the times she had willingly allowed Warren into her home. She remembered one particular night when she thought she'd heard noises, the day they had met with Mary at the Arlington School District. But, that was only one of several memories that bombarded her. She had given him a tour of her facilities. He had attended a performance in the auditorium. They had met at her home at various times to work on her pitch to the other school districts. *How did I ever believe he was my friend? He was simply using me to wreck my life. And now he's admitted to killing his own mother. If he'd do something that evil to the person who gave him life, there's no limit to what he'd do to me or Mom.* Heather cried inside, *I want my mom. I want my mom.*

Elaborating on his plans for their life together, Warren explained, "I had to borrow money from your office lockbox to finance the trip and wedding, but I'm sure you'll agree it will be worth it. Our flight to Mexico leaves this afternoon, and we're to be wed on a cliffside villa by a local priest tonight. Marilyn is going with us to act as our witness. At first, I thought she could fly back home after the wedding so we could enjoy our honeymoon—just the two of us. But, then, I realized I have some things to learn from watching Marilyn interact with people, so she's going to stay and be my private instructor. I broke into her home last night. It was harder than breaking into yours, but I managed. She also has a packed bag upstairs. Since I don't have experience in packing for women, I hope I got everything but if not, we can always shop in Mexico." Warren dropped her hands and raised up from the floor. He settled on the sofa next to her and turned to face her. Placing an arm along the back of the sofa he continued describing his plans. "We'll be on our honeymoon for two weeks. According to your planner, you have performances scheduled, so you'll have to call them and reschedule. Since I've already resigned from the school district, I can start my life of luxury as soon as we get to Mexico." He snapped his fingers. "Oh, don't forget, we need to add me to your bank accounts, will, insurance, et cetera, but we've plenty of time to take care of that." Warren almost danced a jig thinking about the achievement of his goals. "I think I covered everything. Do you have any questions?"

Heather shook her head. She was too stunned to talk. The only thought revolving around her head was developing an escape plan, getting herself and Marilyn away from this lunatic as soon as possible.

"Good, then, I'll go get Marilyn so you two can talk." Warren stood and walked to where a telephone sat on a side table. Heather, who stiffened automatically every time he moved, was paralyzed with fear. This was way too overwhelming. "You ladies need to decide if you're going to live or die. Either go along with me and live"— Warren violently pulled the cord out of the wall jack— "or buck me and die . . . like my dear mama." He yanked the other end of the line out of the telephone base.

Approaching Heather, he wrapped the plastic cord around his hand. Her fear suddenly unraveled, her legs instinctively moved. Unfortunately, she hadn't moved fast enough. Warren caught her by the collar of her sleepshirt and yanked her backward. For a second, she floated in the air before she finally landed halfway on the sofa and half on the floor. Warren straddled her and socked her in the head like he would hit a man in a barroom brawl. "That's for making me talk about the past and this"—he punched her again—"this is quiet insurance. While I'm gone to get dear Marilyn, don't you dare scream, go to the window, or try to call attention to yourself. If you do, I'll kill you right here in front of your mother. Remember, I really need only one of you."

Heather reeled from the blows. Her ears rang, her vision blurred, and her whole body ached, especially her head. She didn't know how much time had passed before she heard Warren returning. On wobbly legs, she eased up, intent on presenting a brave face to her mom. But, as soon as she caught sight of Marilyn thrown across Warren's shoulder, she almost lost her precarious balance. Covering her mouth with her hands and with her eyes open wide, she silently begged, *Please don't let her be dead. Don't let him have hurt her. Please let her be knocked out with that sleeping stuff.*

None too gently, Warren threw Marilyn's inert body on the sofa.

Heather cried immediately upon seeing her mother up close. Falling by Marilyn's side, Heather gathered her half-conscious mother in her arms and rocked her gently, kissing her dry, ashy face. Cuts, bruises, and dried blood covered her arms, legs, neck, face, and chest. Marilyn's day suit was torn to near shreds, however, enough of it existed to confirm for Heather that the material and color matched the purse on her counter.

Oblivious to Warren standing nearby, Heather laid Marilyn down and stretched her out on the sofa into a more comfortable position. Occasionally, Marilyn moaned; her eyes would bat open, making contact with Heather. As she checked her mother's battered body for broken bones, Heather's tears fell harder and faster. It was obvious Warren had worked her mother over very well. Slowly, her fear transformed to anger. She was angry that Warren had so selfishly intruded on their lives, angry that he had beat Marilyn to a bloody mess, angry that he existed. She exploded and verbally charged him. "What kind of animal are you? What did you do to her, you beast!"

"The same thing I'm going to do to you if you don't talk to me like you got some sense."

Marilyn weakly called Heather's name, drawing Heather's attention away from the source of her anger.

"Go get me a washcloth, some water, and peroxide," Heather angrily demanded. Her hands trembled in anger. "And, get me a glass of water and crackers."

With her back to Warren, she didn't see the right hook. She felt it when it connected with the back of her head. Falling to the floor with her head on the ground, Heather cried out. Although her hair was short, Warren managed to get a piece of it and yanked her head back. Spewing his hot breath all over her face, he spoke harshly. "I give the orders. Don't you forget it."

At his full six-foot height, Warren took deep gulps of air and straightened his shirt. "Now ask nicely and I'll see what I can do."

Heather stammered and cried through the request. "May . . . I . . . have . . . towel and water."

"Of course, dear. I'll be right back," he said, his voice sickly sweet.

Warren was gone for less than five minutes but returned with all the items Heather had originally requested. "We don't need to call attention to ourselves at the airport, so try to clean her up as much as possible. I can't have her looking like a fiend when we board the plane."

Marshaling much constraint, Heather clamped her mouth on the heated words that rose from her throat. Her own pain was forgotten in the anger that consumed her.

"I'm going upstairs to finish packing my own bag. When I'm through loading the car with our luggage, I'll be back to get your answer. I'm sure you understand the 'quiet' rules by now, right? Or do I need to give you a refresher lesson?"

On her knees by the couch, Heather stared at the floor. She thought about throwing the water in Warren's face and then kicking him in the balls. On the verge of acting out her thought, she felt Marilyn's hand fall on her shoulder. "No," the bruised woman croaked to her daughter.

For the first time since reaching womanhood, Heather obeyed her mother. Her mother didn't look good and to challenge Warren, who was unpredictable, quick and strong, could mean further injury to her mother. Heather turned her head to look at him. In a deathly tight voice, she hissed, "I understand your rules."

Heather's eyes shot sparks of hate at him as she boldly watched his ascent up the stairs. She didn't turn back to her mother until she heard him tromping about. "I'll get that bastard," she promised between clenched teeth.

Heather lifted Marilyn's head and held the glass to her lips. Marilyn drank thirstily despite her split, bloodied lips. "Here, Mom. Try and eat this if you can." Heather handed Marilyn a cracker. As Heather dipped the washcloth in the bowl of peroxide and water, whispering, she filled Marilyn in on the work Buddy and Roger had been doing. Just hearing that news seemed to bring a little color to Marilyn's complexion.

In a crackling voice, Marilyn asked, "How is Roger doing?" A tear rolled down her cheek.

Heather saw no reason to sugarcoat the truth. "He's very upset. He's barely holding it together."

More tears fell onto Marilyn's brown cheeks.

"But, don't worry, Mom." Heather was quick to reassure her. "You and Roger will grow old together. He and Buddy will find us and save us from that hideous fiend upstairs." After a slight pause, Heather asked, "I hate to ask you to relive the nightmare, Mom, but I have to know everything that bastard did to you."

After another drink of water, Marilyn filled in some of the missing data for Heather. Marilyn told her of "running into" Warren at Heather's place, of being locked in the closet in the garage all night, of being kicked and punched and learning of his sick plans. Heather cried throughout the diatribe and again pledged to herself that she would make Warren pay for all the pain and suffering he'd caused her family. For every kick and punch he had administered to Marilyn, herself, and anyone else, she would give it to him double.

As Heather continued to clean her mother's body, she felt the need to speak reassuring words—for her mother's benefit and her own. "I'm sure Buddy's evidence and keen investigative skills will turn up Warren's name soon. We won't be here long, Mom, and we certainly aren't going to Mexico."

Marilyn grasped Heather's hand, stilling her daughter's movement and forcing her hazel eyes to lock with Marilyn's dark brown ones. "If they aren't here soon, Heather, please, baby, promise me you won't do anything to aggravate Warren. He's already killed someone, and I believe he would have no qualms killing again. Please, Heather, I've already lost your father. I don't want to lose you. I love you. You and Roger are all I have."

Heather's eyes bucked. "Mom, I've never heard you say you love me. The only words that usually come out of your mouth concerning me have to do with how much I'm screwing up. You usually just boss me around or tell me I'm making the wrong decision."

Marilyn closed her eyes to the truth of Heather's words. "I know, dear . . . I know I will never win Mother of the Year. But, I hope one day, Heather, you can forgive me for being an imperfect mother."

Heather was too shocked to say anything.

Facing an uncertain future, Marilyn wanted to make sure Heather understood her decisions, her motivation and feelings. "Roger, bless his heart, helped me realize that your life is not mine. Thanks to his insight, I know now that I hold on too tight and am too bossy. I'm sorry, baby. I did what I thought was right."

Taking a deep, painful breath, Marilyn continued. "Heather, I've wanted only the best for you. I didn't want you to grow up poor and underprivileged like I did. I didn't want you to endure the shame of having to go to the welfare office every month for your rations or having to shop at Goodwill for your back-to-school wardrobe or having to use food stamps at the grocery store with everyone in line looking at you as if you were a slug or having to buy Christmas presents at the pawnshop. I made up my mind at an early age that I would not live my entire life like that. I also pledged that any child of mine would never know the inside of a county office and would not suffer any of the degradations I suffered."

Struggling to sit up, Marilyn allowed Heather to place pillows behind her head. Settled again, she continued. "The only way I knew how to break the cycle of welfare was to marry a man with money and quickly have a baby. I know. I know," Marilyn said, addressing the horrified look on Heather's face. "But, in those days, the options for a woman were more limited than nowadays." Heather reluctantly agreed. "So, as soon as I graduated from high school, I took a clerk job and babysat for the women on the block. With the money I earned, I bought fashion catalogs and fabric and became an expert at sewing the styles I saw on the glossy pages. I became an expert with hair, nails, makeup, white people's vocabulary, and weight control. Whenever I stepped out of my house, I looked like a million dollars. A year after graduating from high school, I got the ideal job for meeting well-to-do men. I was one of the first African-American airline stewardesses for American. And, baby, I was good at it . . . so good that they soon allowed me to work first class."

"Mom . . ." Heather breathed. Her eyes were wide with wonder. She was so engrossed in her mom's story, she almost forgot they were in hostile territory. Almost. "I never knew you worked, that you can sew, that you were on welfare."

"That's the way I wanted it. I didn't want anyone to know I was once a welfare recipient. I fooled them all, honey, including your father." Marilyn's eyes adopted that faraway look as she remembered her first meeting with Everett Chadwick. "I'll never forget. I was working a flight from Detroit to DFW. It was a late flight with very few first-class passengers, but he was one of them, and he kept staring at me. I don't know if I ever told you but every time I look at you, I'm looking at Everett all over again." Marilyn caressed her daughter's face. Love reflected in her eyes. She smiled. "Halfway through the flight, I got tired of him staring at me so I walked over to him and told him that if he continued to stare at me, he was going to have to take me out on a date. He grabbed my hand, kissed it, and asked me if I was free after the flight landed. A year later, we were married and a year after that, little Heather was born." Sadly, Marilyn finished her story. "The irony of the situation is I had the things I had grown up wishing for—money, a secure future, a child who would know nothing but luxury, and the extra icing being a man who loved me—but in the end, I lost the man who had become more important to me than breathing. A wet street, a cold night, a long work day—conditions that lured Everett into the car accident that snuffed out all my dreams." Too many years had passed by for Marilyn to shed a tear, but not enough that her eyes didn't mist. "Oh, Heather, there are so many things I wish I could do over."

"Mom, I've judged you too harshly. I never knew." Heather buried her head in her mother's neck. "Why didn't you tell me this earlier?"

"I guess I was too determined to make you my project instead of my daughter." Marilyn caressed the short hairs at Heather's nape. "After Everett left us, I had only you. That's when I started to strangle you, to try and separate you from the person you really are. I was determined to mold you into the image I'd developed for you so you wouldn't endure the hardships I dealt with growing up. Also, I wanted to keep a tight hold on the only other person I would have gladly given my life for. I mistakenly thought that if I directed your life, I could keep you forever by my side."

Marilyn paused. "So, as soon as you reached school age, I enrolled you in ballet, social etiquette classes, Jack and Jill, put you in the right schools and church and made sure you looked like a princess every day of the week. I wanted to shape you for *your* Everett Chadwick. I'm not going to lie to you, Heather. I *love* the socialite role and I tried to make you love it, too, but, the older you got, the more you developed your own personality, and that's when we started bumping heads." She lifted Heather's head so she could look into her eyes. "Remember the day you came to me and demanded to take acting and voice lessons. I almost fell over dead. When I told you no, I thought that was the end of it—and when I found out you had enrolled anyway, I was furious. I pulled you out of those classes because it was not what I had planned for you. You probably don't remember, but it was shortly after that that you started pulling away, and that scared me so I kept pushing you harder and faster into the affluent social role. Then, you went off to college and that's when I knew I had lost on two counts. I had failed to make you into the image I had designed for you. And, because of my single focus, I had killed any chance of us having a robust mother-daughter relationship. I had lost you."

"Mom, please, don't go on. It's over and done with. Time has moved on." Heather washed her mother's tears.

"I know that, honey, but for the time we have left, I want to make it right."

"It's all right, Mom. Everything is all right."

"No, I want you to know it took Roger's patience and understanding to help me understand my role in your life. I remember Roger and I had this long, in-depth conversation the night you were to marry Gerald. He couldn't understand why I was acting hysterically. I tried to explain that marrying a millionaire was right in line with my plans for your life. In a very direct manner, he explained that a parent's role is to guide, support, and love, not rule. He told me to lighten up and get out of your business. He made me promise not to interfere with your decisions. I promised him I wouldn't, but when you're used to stripes, it's hard to change to plaids. Do you understand? I want you to understand."

"Mom, it's clear to me. I understand and forgive you. I love you too, Mom."

"You do? Sometimes I think you hate me." Marilyn's eyes searched Heather's for truth.

"No, Mom, I don't hate you. Don't be silly. You're my mother." Heather paused. "I must admit, there are times when I don't return your calls or don't want to see you, but that's because I don't want to hear any negative comments and *not* because I don't care for you. I'm a grown woman, and I don't want to be treated like a child."

"I know, dear. From now on, I will treat you like the woman you are." Marilyn kissed her only child's forehead. "Have I told you that I love you?"

The women exchanged a loving smile.

"Mom, there is one other thing. You mentioned it earlier." Heather paused, thinking how best to share with Marilyn her feelings about marriage. "I do want to tell you the reason I jilted Gerald."

Marilyn encouraged Heather to proceed.

Timidly, she said, "I thought it was natural for a man and woman to fall in love, get married, and then divorce. I didn't want to follow that pattern with Gerald. I wanted to keep our relationship out of the marriage arena so I could have him in my life forever."

"But, honey, why . . . Where did you get that crazy idea?"

Heather spoke softly. "From you and the many marriages and divorces you've had."

Marilyn was stunned into silence.

Heather continued. "I know it sounds crazy now, but growing up I thought my life would repeat the same pattern as yours. I mean, since you're my mother and I'm your daughter and history usually repeats itself, right? Months ago when I was supposed to make my lifelong commitment to Gerald, I freaked out because

I knew marriage would destroy my love for him, and that we'd end up divorced. I just couldn't fathom a life without Gerald. He means so much to me."

"Oh, honey, I'm so sorry. I had no idea my actions had impacted you so greatly. I didn't love all those men. Of course, I didn't find that out until after I'd married and divorced them. In retrospect, I learned I was trying to mask the pain of losing Everett, and I was preparing myself emotionally to lose you once you grew up and started your own life. I'm sorry I screwed up your life with my screwed-up life."

"Mom, you didn't screw up my life. You just made it a little different is all." Heather couldn't resist teasing her mom, who had a thin sense of humor. "Anyway, now I know differently. Now, I know my marital life is my own, and it's up to me and Gerald to make it work. If . . ." Heather thought about the negativism of that word. "No, as soon as we get out of here, I mean to pursue Gerald with all I've got. I'm going to marry that man and love him for the rest of my life."

Marilyn was openly crying now. "Heather, I'm happy for you. I know you and Gerald will forever be hopelessly in love."

Warren's loud arrival with three suitcases in tow ended the private moments. "Oh, it can't be that painful. I haven't hit you since yesterday."

Heather wiped her nose on her sleeveless arm. Her intense anger and hate for the man instantly renewed itself. It was on the tip of her tongue to tell him to shut up and get the hell out of their lives when she caught her mother's silently beseeching eyes.

Putting down the suitcases, he threw several articles of clothing at Heather. "I'm taking these to the car. Put those clothes on. I'll be back shortly and then we can go." Warren clapped his hands. "Chop-chop."

Warren made it to the foyer with the bags when the

ringing of the telephone stopped him. "Oh, who can this be," he asked rhetorically. He raced to the kitchen but didn't pick up the phone immediately. With a punishing finger pointed at the women, he said, "Don't say a thing. Be as quiet as mice or one of you will die."

"Hello." After a slight pause he nodded. "Yes, this is Warren Patterson." Another pause. "Yes, I know Heather Chadwick. We work together on a special program for the school district. Who are you?"

"Gerald Forrester, *the* basketball player. Hey, I enjoy watching you play."

Heather's head popped up. *Gerald! I really did call him this morning. It wasn't a dream. And, he came. He's coming to rescue us. Gerald found us!*

"I'm sorry. Heather has never mentioned your name, and I don't feel comfortable giving you any more info—"

Heather couldn't restrain herself. She shouted at the top of her lungs. "Gerald, I'm here. Help—"

Warren reacted quickly. He threw the cordless phone through the air. Heather ducked, and it landed with a soft thud on the carpeted floor. She scrambled for it, aware that Warren would be on her in a few seconds. She snatched up the phone. "Gerald, come quick. Mexico, airport. He's taking—" Everything faded to black.

Seventeen

Gerald was momentarily paralyzed, rooted in place, surprised and happy he'd found the women but frightened by Heather's words and obvious fear.

Roger edged him out of his inactivity. Shaking Gerald's arm, he frantically demanded, "What is it, Gerald? Is it the girls? Tell me they were there!"

His heart dislodged from his throat and with round eyes, he instructed, "Let's go." Gerald slammed down the phone and ran to the front door. "That creep's got them." The men flew down the stairs.

They were near the end of the long hall leading toward the garage and back parking lot when the rear door opened and Buddy came barreling through.

"We got him," Buddy yelled, running toward them, shaking a thin piece of white paper. "The lab made a match." Buddy's white face was red, and his eyes glazed with exuberance.

"We just spoke to him and Heather," Roger explained as he whizzed past Buddy, following Gerald's long-legged stride.

"Oh, shit! I hope they didn't scare the punk." Buddy did an amazingly quick about-face for a big man and after banging through the garage door, threw his body in the backseat of Gerald's truck seconds before Gerald peeled off.

Buddy read from his wrinkled paper. "The address is 121 Pecan Tree Road. Do you know where that is?" Buddy screamed at Gerald.

"Got it," Gerald tersely replied.

Heading the car in the appropriate direction, Gerald pressed the accelerator until it touched the floor.

"I have a PI on the way to Warren Patterson's house. Hopefully he's already there," Buddy explained, trying to put the men's minds at ease.

"I pray so," Roger faintly answered.

Although Warren lived a good thirty-minute drive across town, Gerald got them there in ten minutes by violating every traffic law written in the books.

The neighborhood Warren lived in was straight from the pages of a glossy magazine. As they drove slowly down Pecan Tree Road, they noticed all of the lawns were manicured and green. The paint was fresh on the houses, and even the toys scattered on the lush lawns seemed to be perfectly placed.

The town house development Warren lived in sat at the end of the street. It was a small housing unit with only four separate homes. A red and white brick exterior greeted visitors, and green pine shrubbery added a year-round Christmas appearance.

A half block from the town homes, Buddy slid down in the backseat. "I know you've got a decent tint on these windows, but he may be able to make out the number of bodies even if he can't see the faces."

Roger and Gerald heard Buddy check his gun for bullets. "Slow down, go past the house, and make a U-turn in the street."

They heard him take the safety off his gun. "When you drive past the house, look and see if there are any signs of movement. A curtain shifting, a blind being lowered, anything that signals someone might be at the front of the house. Tell me if that's the case."

Warren's town house was easy enough to spot. Lucky for them, the landlord had painted the large, white block-style numbers of each house on each front door. Warren's unit was the second one.

Slowly, Gerald drove past Warren's home.

"Anything?" Buddy gruffly asked.

"Nothing," both men replied. Buddy refrained from saying his favorite curse word. He wasn't about to tell the men that that wasn't a good sign. Already, they were on edge. He could sense that, plus their fear and their desire for Warren's blood.

"I'ma get out at the end of the block. After I do, park parallel in front of his neighbor's house on the opposite side of the street. After you park, sit still for a few seconds but pretend you're looking for something or doing something. Don't get out of the car until you see me come through that front door. Am I clear?"

Although anxious to charge the house and beat the crap out of Warren Patterson, Gerald deferred to the lawman's experience and training.

Buddy tucked the gun in his belt. "All right then. See you soon."

The car lifted a bit once Buddy removed his bulk from the backseat. Gerald kept his eyes glued straight ahead as did Roger. Slowly, Gerald made the U-turn and headed back up the street.

Buddy hadn't taken twenty steps toward the housing unit and Gerald hadn't finished parking when the door of Warren's home opened.

"I'll be damned," Roger whispered. Like a hawk, his eyes had been trained to observe the slightest movement from the house. In the next second, he was out of the car, running to his wife, who lay in the arms of some thin, white man.

Buddy, who had started to veer toward the backyard, witnessed Roger's run across the street. He pivoted and headed toward the front of the house. His keen eyes quickly assessed the situation.

The PI Buddy had called in for assistance held Marilyn. As Roger took the last steps toward the PI, the detective explained, "She's unconscious, but she's starting to come around."

Roger took Marilyn in his arms, gingerly. He closed his eyes, hugging her close. Tears of joy and thankfulness trailed down his face. "Oh, baby. Thank God you're alive." He rocked her, proclaiming his heartfelt sentiments. "Sweetheart, I've never been more frightened. I thought I had lost you forever. I love you so much. I love you." Roger smothered her with kisses, holding her close to him.

Semiconscious, Marilyn snuggled in his arms. She savored his love and gave thanks that her life had been spared. And, in that short space of time, she recalled that the horror continued for her daughter.

Marilyn's eyes found and latched on to Gerald's. Speaking in a crackly, pained voice, she urged him, "Go get my baby. He's got Heather. He's gone to get her car. It's faster and you won't be expecting him in it. He's taking her to Mexico."

Before Marilyn finished talking, Gerald and Buddy ran to Gerald's truck. The PI threw his car keys and location of his car to Roger, then joined Gerald and Buddy.

A squeal of tires signaled their departure.

On the obstacle-course, high-speed drive to Heather's house, the PI called a friend of his on the force. In brief concise phrases, the PI recapped the situation and ran down Warren's vitals and statistics as if he knew him personally. Minutes later, the Border Patrol offices started receiving teletypes and faxes at their offices, alerting them of the situation. Locally, the man-wanted information put the local police on notice.

LOVE EVERLASTING 259

While the PI carried out his tasks, Gerald drove the distance to Heather's home as if Lucifer chased him.

Heather slowly shook off the hold unconsciousness had on her. Her eyelids fluttered open and slowly her blurred vision cleared. She tried to raise her head to determine her location, only the pain in her head was so paralyzing, she couldn't. Tears slid down her cheeks. She closed her eyes and whimpered softly.

After lying still for several minutes, her focus moved from her bodily pain to the rocking movement beneath her. *Am I in his car?* she thought wildly. *Surely not. It's too light in here.* Opening her eyes, she noted the tan interior, the two seats that were almost on top of her and the jumble of feminine articles on the floor behind the driver's seat. With wonderment, she thought, *I'm in my car. He put me in the back of my own car!*

Fast on the heels of that thought came, *Mom? Where is Mom? Is she in the front seat?* Again, she attempted to raise or turn her head. A thousand stars exploded behind her closed eyes. She gave up. More tears slid down her cheeks as she remembered Warren saying he needed only one of them. She wondered if her mother had been the one he sacrificed. She perished the thought.

Forcing herself to move her concentration off her pain, she squeezed her eyes tight and listened for sounds of labored breathing. But, the only sound that infiltrated her mind was the high-pitched girlish laugh of a woman and Warren's deeper voice.

"Come on," Warren begged in a singsong voice. "Give me your telephone number. We were meant to be together."

The unknown woman giggled again and said, "I bet you do this every Sunday. Drive around in that fancy car and pick up women. And, as handsome as you are,

I'll bet you're successful at it, too. Now, tell me that ain't so?" the woman flirted back.

"You'd be the only one who mattered," Warren responded glibly.

Heather cried harder. *If he's flirting, that means Mom is not in the front seat.* Suddenly, Heather's anger erupted. Her mother might be lying dead somewhere, and this crazy man was flirting with some bimbo. She balled her hand into a fist, aided by the wish to beat the stuffings out of Warren. *Don't lose it, Heather. Think! Don't act, think. You need a plan.*

The car eased forward and jerked a bit as Warren crudely shifted gears. Heather winced at the sound of her protesting gears.

"Thanks, but I think I'll keep the man I've got. See you!" the woman shouted at Warren as the light changed.

"Bitch! I didn't want you anyway," Warren tossed rudely at the tail end of her car. In a few seconds, he managed to change gears, and soon they were speeding on.

The action of the car lurching forward caused a can, which had been housed under the driver's seat, to roll toward and touch Heather's fist. That acted like a cattle prod, producing a crude plan of action. *I got it,* Heather thought. *I'm going to beat him with this can while he's killing my transmission.* Not having the luxury to think the plan over thoroughly, Heather put action to her thought.

Moving slowly so as not to make any noise and alert Warren or wake the pain in her head, Heather reached out her hand. The can felt cool to her touch as she caressed the length of it. For once, she was glad she had ignored both Gerald and Nachelle's comments about "living in her car." She was thankful she didn't keep her car as clean as they kept theirs, for then she wouldn't have the hairspray can as a wonderfully effective weapon.

The car stopped again. *Not now. I need to attack while the car's moving. He won't be able to defend himself and change gears at the same time.* Impatiently, Heather waited. The seconds seemed like hours, yet Heather's busy mind, in that short time period, hopped from one subject to another. She wondered about her mom, she wondered if Gerald had shown up at Warren's house, she wondered if the pain would ever cease in her head, she wondered if the light—and she felt comfortable it was a traffic light, for in her neighborhood there were only traffic signals, not stop signs—would ever change, she wondered if they were even in her neighborhood, she wondered if she could hurt Warren enough to stop him. A million thoughts zoomed through her mind, so many that she almost missed the movement of the car. The liquid in the can sloshing gently reminded her.

This is it, she thought. She waited for the telltale sound of the grinding gears. It came and he lurched forward. Unfortunately, Warren was a quick study. The second protest of gear changing didn't come. They sailed smoothly forward. *Soon, he'll have to switch to third and when he does, he's history.* Heather had driven her car so long, she knew instinctively when the time would come to change gears. Warren was getting closer to that time, the thirty to thirty-five miles per hour range. Another five seconds, and he'd be right where she wanted him.

One thousand one, one thousand two, one thousand three, one thousand four, one thousand five. Closing her hand around the can, she lifted it, then her body, and although the pain was deadly, she managed to rise on her knees while swinging the can in the direction of Warren's head.

Warren's reflexes were quick, or maybe it was her

image in the rearview mirror that alerted him, or maybe it was the languidness of her limbs slowing her down or the pain in her head—but whatever the cause, he ducked his head in time to avoid the first blow.

Out of her peripheral vision, Heather could see Marilyn was not in the passenger seat. Knowing her mother was dead made the job of continuing her attack effortless. Her hand raised and lowered repeatedly and on the subsequent blows, she connected and hit him so hard the blue cap of the hairspray can flew in the corner of the car.

"Stop it, you crazy . . . Ouch!"

Driven by rage, Heather assaulted Warren, giving no thought to the possible danger to herself.

Warren fought her off as best he could, but he was at a distinct disadvantage. The struggle continued until the last thing either one of them remembered was the Buick Regal that pulled into the stream of traffic in front of them.

Eighteen

Gerald and Buddy spotted the accident, a mere six blocks from Heather's home, at the same time.

"No! No!" Gerald screamed, recognizing the car at once. Stepping hard on the brakes, he brought his truck to a fishtail halt in the middle of the road across the median from the wrecked car. Slamming the truck into park, Gerald hopped out and sprinted across the street. Buddy followed at a slower, less reckless pace. The PI stayed behind and called for emergency help.

"Gerald. Stop. It could be too severe," Buddy called out, wasting his breath and time.

An eyewitness, a young Hispanic teenager with large brown eyes and long, straight hair, spoke quickly to anyone who cared to listen. "I saw it. I saw the whole thing. He hit the blue car. His flipped over. They're dead. I know they're dead," she repeated her report, crying and gesturing dramatically at the same time.

The driver of the Buick, a middle-aged African-American man, in white painter's dickies, competed with the young Hispanic girl. He paced back and forth severely upset. "I didn't know he was going to change lanes so quickly. One minute he was in his lane, the next in mine. Then I looked around, and he had flipped over. I'm sorry. I didn't know."

Gerald approached the car with fear clogging his

lungs, making it difficult to breathe. *Oh, God, please let her be okay. Let her be fine.* Heather's red sports car lay bottom side up with the wheels still spinning. The passenger side of the car was crushed in. One view of the damage and the severity of the accident registered, but his woman was in that car—and Gerald was not about to give up hope. It was hope that propelled him forward.

"Heather. Heather!" Gerald bent low, looking through the driver's window, which was now partially missing. He came face to face with Warren, whose eyes were closed, and blood streamed down his face. Looking past Warren, he spotted Heather's inert body. She was squeezed in the middle of the two front seats, her head bent at an awkward angle against the stick shift. Because of the smoke from the accident, and the angle of her body, Gerald couldn't determine if she was breathing. He couldn't miss the blood, however.

"I've got to get her out!" he yelled to no one in particular. "Heather. Heather!"

Gerald moved with agility and strength, trying to move Warren so he could get to Heather. When that attempt failed, he sprang to his feet and moved behind the car. He wrestled with the hatchback. It wouldn't budge. Frantically, he moved around to the front of the car, but because the car lay forward on its hood, he was unable to see the windshield. Moving back around to the driver's side, he used his elbow and the adrenaline pumping through his body to break the glass, then pulled Warren's limp body out of the car through the window. He tossed his body aside, not caring that it still had breath in it.

Heather's body was harder to reach. The driver's seat was in the way, cocked at a weird angle. "Heather. Heather, I need for you to help me." Gerald scooted his long body partially through the window, unconcerned that he had glass in his hair and cuts and scratches. "Slide forward a little bit, baby. Can you do that for me, honey? Just a little. I'll get you from there."

Heather batted her eyes.

"Heather. Heather. Come to me," Gerald demanded in a forceful voice.

Heather opened her eyes and focused on Gerald. "Gerald," she whispered. Coming to as if waking from a dream, she opened and closed her eyes a few more times then spoke again. "Gerald. Oh, Gerald. You did come." She cried happy tears. "You did come. You came for me." She stretched forward, intent on crawling into the arms of her love, unaware that she was wedged between the seats.

"Heather, don't force it. If you can't move, don't force it. Help is on the way." Gerald stretched out his long arm. Their hands connected, clung together. "Stay still or you might hurt yourself more." He matched her tear for tear, thankful she was still living.

The loving touch acted as the final push. Heather wriggled and strained and navigated her way out of the tight spot. Her victory cry carried her forth. "Gerald, you came. You came for me." Uncaring of the glass that littered the ceiling, she inched her way to his welcoming arms. "Gerald, you came," she repeated over and over. Nothing, except death, would have kept her from him.

The second she cleared the driver's window, Gerald grabbed her carefully, pulling her the rest of the way from the dismembered car.

With a fierce hold on her, Gerald held her in his arms on the ground, gently rocking her. Tears slid down his handsome face.

"Gerald," she whispered, looking up at him. His trembling lips crushed hers in response to the soft plea. Their tears mixed.

"Better get her to the nearest hospital before shock

sets in," Buddy's gruff voice instructed. "I'll wait for help and give them a report. I wanna make sure they lock this creature up."

Three pairs of eyes locked on Warren's busted body, lying on the ground, bleeding profusely and moaning.

Gerald set Heather away from him long enough to stand up. In one swift movement, he lifted her into his strong, capable arms. In minutes, they were headed to John Peter Smith.

Nineteen

John Peter Smith was known worldwide for its emergency room responsiveness and trauma handling.

The supervising nurse of the emergency room stood at the admissions desk, shaking her head over the number of husbands carrying in their wives for emergency treatment.

Around ten o'clock in the morning, local businessman Steven DuCloux and his wife, Nachelle, had arrived. She had been in the midst of a miscarriage, and although the team of doctors and nurses had worked hard to try and save the baby, they had not been successful. They had, however, saved the mother, and now she rested comfortably in one of the private rooms upstairs. After a short stay, the doctors felt sure she would be released under sound medical advice to get more rest and reduce the amount of stress in her life.

A couple of hours later, Senator Roger Wolfe and his wife, Marilyn, had rushed through the same doors with Marilyn suffering from a severe beating, resulting in a fractured rib, a badly sprained arm, and many cuts, bruises, and scratches. Whoever had beat her didn't know they had been dealing with a tough cookie. The X-rays showed no broken bones or internal bleeding. The emergency room doctor had prescribed a few days of rest, lots of liquid for her dehydration, and loads of painkillers for the pain. In a few days, the doctor promised she'd be up to mini-marathon shopping sprees.

Thirty minutes after Mrs. Wolfe had been admitted, Gerald Forrester, last year's NBA MVP, carried his girlfriend into the emergency area. Gerald had quickly explained that she had been in a serious car accident, and because she suffered from early symptoms of shock, they had immediately rushed her into examination room one. After a quick yet thorough exam, the doctor treated her severe cuts and put a splint on her fractured arm. The results of her X-rays indicated she, too, had been protected by a caring angel, for no internal bleeding or broken bones existed.

As the diligent nurse completed the writing of her reports, she tsk'ed tsk'ed and wondered if a full moon had been in the sky the previous night. Her thoughts were interrupted by the opening of the door for exam room one. The doctor who had attended to Heather Chadwick walked toward her, writing his notes on the chart.

Inside exam room one, the door closed softly, shutting the lovers in and the cruel world out.

Gerald went to Heather, who lay on the exam table, and bent low to kiss her forehead, being careful to avoid her dressings.

Heather grasped his hands, holding them tightly. "Gerald, I didn't think you would come. I'm so glad you did. I love you."

Gerald sat his lanky, yet muscular body on the edge of the table and gathered Heather to him. She cried into his chest.

"Heather, look into my eyes." She did so. "Tell me if you honestly think I would have turned my back on you. Do you?"

Heather saw the love reflected in his eyes. She felt a burst of happiness flood her entire body. Tears shimmered in her eyes. "Gerald, I wasn't sure. You seemed so set on your decision to end our relationship. You were kissing Suzanne at the restaurant. You looked so happy."

"I do enjoy Suzanne's company, but she and I both know that as long as you reside in my heart, there can be nothing serious between me and her or any other woman. I love you, Heather. You're the owner of my heart." He kissed the tip of her nose.

"I'm so happy." Heather smiled, lighting up her eyes. She kissed his chin.

"You know what would make me happier?" Gerald asked her with a twinkle of devilment in his eyes.

Heather's smile turned wicked. "A romp in the hay?" She lifted her brows, wriggling them in a dastardly fashion. "You know it's been a while."

Gerald laughed at his precocious girlfriend. "Yes, but that's not exactly what I was thinking about." Although his mouth said one thing, his hands said another, for they caressed her thighs and her back, desperate to feel her flesh.

Heather lifted his T-shirt, sprinkling light kisses on his hairless chest. "Okay, I give up. What?"

It flashed through his mind to take her right then and there, but there truly was something more important on his mind. Gerald's face grew gravely serious. He captured her face between his large hands. Their eyes locked. "If you agreed to be my wife. Marry me, Heather."

Gerald saw the answer before Heather could mask her pain. His heart sank, and the balloon of happiness that had been enlarging inside him popped, leaving an aching vacuum of pain and disappointment. *She still doesn't want to go the last mile*, he thought dismally. *She doesn't want to marry me*. His hands fell by his side. He scooted off the table and took a step back. To hide his pain, he stared at the yellowing linoleum on the floor.

Demurely, she murmured, "No, Gerald, I can't." Her eyes shifted to the floor as she thought about the long talk she'd had with her mom and the clearing of her marital fears. Yet this was not the time or place to explain all her history to Gerald. She wouldn't agree to marry him until she'd sat down with him and explained her past actions. He was a one-in-a-million man who deserved to know the whole truth before he asked for her hand in marriage—again. She wanted them to fully bury the past before planning for the future.

Heather opened her mouth to speak some of her pain. Before she could say a word, the door opened.

A gaggle of noise severed the tender moment.

"Here you are!" Nachelle exclaimed from a wheelchair. Steven pushed her into the room. "The cashier told Steven you and Marilyn were both here. I guess she knew what she was talking about. This is a big day for them with all these celebrities running around." Nachelle smiled at Gerald.

He returned the smile, although the pain in his heart prevented it from reaching his eyes.

"Nachelle!" Heather exclaimed. She slipped off the exam table and, in spite of her injuries, ran to her friend and hugged the stuffing out of her. Nachelle returned the tight hug. "What are you doing in a wheelchair? And, Mom's here! She's not dead?" Heather pulled out of her arms, searching Nachelle's face for truth.

"No, silly. She's as alive as you are. Marilyn and Roger will be here shortly. They're just down the hallway, waiting for the doctor to officially release her."

Heather cried, "Oh, I'm so glad. I thought Warren had killed her." She trembled with excitement. This ordeal had initiated a real relationship between mother and daughter. She was glad she would have a chance to develop it. She really did love her mom.

Steven angled around the wheelchair and hugged

Heather. Pulling back, his curiosity got the best of him. "Heather, what happened? We got bits and pieces from Marilyn but not the whole story."

Heather rolled her eyes. "The guy was nuts! A real, certifiable lunatic!" The stress of the last few days rolled off her and she smiled tentatively. Holding out a hand toward Gerald, she started her story from the time they had left her—early Sunday morning—to the present. Gerald stood with his arms wrapped around her, supporting her during the telling of the tale, and presenting data that Warren and Buddy had filled him in on.

Nachelle and Steven's eyes nearly popped out of their heads as they listened to the conclusion.

"Heather, you could have been killed!" Nachelle exclaimed. "The car accident could have been worse than what it was."

"I know, Nachelle. But, everything turned out for the best and besides, my prince came to my rescue. He wouldn't have let me die." Her eyes threw much love up at Gerald.

His heart contracted, and he knew then that even if she didn't want to marry him, he couldn't walk away from her. He'd tried it before, and every day had been a gray day. If nothing else, this matter with Warren proved he'd go through anything with or for Heather. He would just have to be content having Heather as she was and without a permanent attachment. He loved her too much to leave her world.

Heather babbled on. "So, what happened to you? What are you doing here?"

With a sad expression on her face, Nachelle looked at her husband. "We lost the baby, Heather. I had a miscarriage."

"Oh, no, Nachelle. No," Heather cried out.

"Yes." Nachelle and Steven held hands. He bent low

to kiss his wife on the cheek, forehead, the top of her head.

"On one hand, it's a major loss for us, but on the other hand, it helped us define some priorities for our life together." Nachelle never broke contact with her husband's eyes. Mutual love and respect flowed between the young couple.

Steven's deep-timbered voice filled the room. "We've made some really tough decisions and commitments in the last few hours."

Nachelle made an attempt to get out of the chair. Steven's hand on her shoulder forced her to abandon her try. She quirked a smile up at Steven, who lifted a threatening brow. Nachelle knew from now on he was going to make her follow doctor's orders. He was going to be watching her every move.

Nachelle sighed. Tears gathered in the corners of her eyes. "Heather, you and I have been together so long. I don't quite know how to tell you this. Steven and I have decided we don't want to be away from each other as much as we have been. We didn't realize what a big strain a long-distance, commuter marriage and 'other priorities' had put on our relationship. So, we've decided to escalate the merger of our Fort Worth and Atlanta offices. Instead of headquartering the offices here, we've decided to keep them in Atlanta." Squeezing her husband's hand, she finished, "I'm moving to Atlanta to be with my husband. I'll continue to work at DuCloux Enterprises, and I'll still lead the merger. But I'll do it from my office down the hallway from my husband where we'll conquer the world together and, if not the world, at least Nathaniel." Nachelle smiled at Steven but when her eyes shifted to Heather, her smile weakened and the tears rolled. "I'm going to miss you, Heather. I love you."

Heather went to her friend and hugged her fiercely.

She knew, of course, of the marital difficulties Nachelle had been battling, and if this move would help save her best friend's marriage, then she was one hundred percent for it. Still, she couldn't help feel a giant sense of loss. She and Nachelle had been inseparable for over ten years, and now Nachelle was leaving town. Heather would no longer be able to pop over and raid Nachelle's closet and refrigerator. She would no longer be able to count on Nachelle's last-minute help at the puppet shows. She would no longer have a friend right up the street that she could run to with her problems, her good news, and her dreams. Who would sit with her and watch Gerald play basketball on TV during those away games when she wasn't able to join him? Who would she go to the movies with? Who would put up with her foolish jokes and antics? Heather cried a gulf of tears, holding on tight to her best friend.

"I'm just a two-hour plane ride away," Nachelle joked, remembering she and Heather used to end almost every conversation with the phrase, "I'm just a phone call away."

Heather caught on to the phrase and despite the hollowness she felt inside, she chuckled. Pulling slightly away, Heather caressed her friend's face. "Nachelle, I just want you to be happy. You deserve it. I'm going to miss you though. I love you, too."

The two friends hugged for a long time.

"Hey, hey, hey." An exuberant Roger pushed open the door for a very sore Marilyn.

"Heather!" Marilyn exclaimed, rushing toward her daughter.

"Mom!" Heather met her. They wrapped each other in their arms. Rocking slowly from side to side, they murmured words of love and forgiveness.

Marilyn leaned back, wiping the tears from her only daughter's eyes. "I thought I had lost you. I'm so glad I didn't. I love you, baby. I love you so much. You're my only baby." Mother and daughter shared a special, knowing smile, remembering the bond that had started in the womb, that had been severed and recently reconnected just hours ago. Heather and Marilyn recognized the promise of a beautiful, fulfilling mother-daughter relationship. Their hearts burst with joy. Their smiles were heavenly.

Marilyn gathered Heather again to her bosom, holding her so tightly Heather winced, but she loved it. She couldn't remember ever getting a real hug from her mom. Heather smiled and held on as if her life counted on that connection.

When the surges of relief and happiness descended a decimal, Marilyn released Heather to hug Gerald. But she never lost contact with her daughter. She kept hold of her hand. "Gerald, thank you for saving my baby. Thank you so much. Thank you! Thank you!" She kept repeating the phrase, then put her arms around both Heather and Gerald, holding them close, alternating her kisses between the two of them.

When her emotional bank account was empty, Marilyn pulled back, wiping her eyes. "What an exciting last few days we've had. What say we accompany Nachelle back up to her room so she can get some rest?" The old-new Marilyn was back. A woman in charge. "Then, we'll go home and change out of these tired hospital scrubs and into some real clothes. We'll be back to see you soon, Nachelle." Marilyn bent low to hug and kiss Nachelle. "If you're good, we might even sneak in a New York style cheesecake with fudge topping."

Nachelle and Heather licked their lips.

All three of the men started a mild protest. "I think . . ."

The younger two men deferred to Roger. "I was going

to say, I think maybe we should come back tomorrow instead, honey. All three of you women have had a tough weekend. I think more rest is in order."

"My words exactly," Steven commented. Gerald nodded his head in agreement.

The three women looked at each other and shrugged their shoulders, let the men win this time.

Quickly, everyone completed a final round of hugs and kisses. As Steven maneuvered the wheelchair around to lead the pack from the room, the door opened again.

Buddy entered the now crowded room with a Texas-sized grin on his face. "Hey, that cute redhead out there told me I could find the whole kit and caboodle in here." Buddy removed his gray Stetson. He looked at Nachelle in the wheelchair. Opening his mouth to ask the obvious, he thought better of it, remembering his manners. Instead, he focused on his reason for coming. "Mrs. Wolfe, I'm glad you're safe and sound. Young Ms. Chadwick, your monster is behind bars. He'll be there for a long, long time."

"How long?" Gerald asked, concern etched in his voice.

"Oh, let's just say forever. After he serves his time here for kidnaping, he's off to 'Nawlins to stand trial for the murder of his mama. Those folks down there support the death sentence. I b'lieve the Bible calls it 'an eye for an eye.' "

A collective sigh of relief flooded the room.

Buddy smiled. "Just wanted to stop by and tell y'all that. I'm outta here." Buddy reached into the breast pocket of his coat jacket and pulled out a long Cuban cigar. "Senator, I want to thank you for this adventure. You'll be getting my bill." Buddy winked and nodded. The door swished closed behind him.

The group turned to Roger and smiled.

A young, freckled-faced doctor walked in. "My, my, I believe two of my patients are here—one of whom shouldn't be out of her bed and the other I haven't officially released yet." All smiles dropped, and the floor suddenly became very interesting.

Duly chastised, Steven said to the group, "Point well taken, doc. Good-bye, everyone. We'll see you tomorrow."

Nachelle waved her goodbyes.

"If the rest of you will leave for a moment, I'll finish up with Heather, and then you all can have her." The doctor looked at Marilyn and Roger.

"But, I'm her mother!" Marilyn protested.

Neither the doctor nor Roger were impressed. Roger grabbed Marilyn's arm. "Okay, okay. I'm leaving," she said. "Just let me kiss my baby one last time."

Marilyn did so. "Roger and I will be at the house." She cut her eyes at Roger. "I don't believe I'll be allowed out again today, so we'll see you tomorrow." She pecked Gerald's cheek and hugged him tight.

Roger kissed Heather and shook Gerald's hand. Without another word, but with a shared loving look between mother and daughter, they left.

"Here you go, young lady. Take three of these a day or as needed for the pain. Sign here and then you're free to go."

Heather murmured her thanks to the doctor and signed the paper he held out. With her official signature, he left.

Her Minnie Mouse sleepshirt had outlived its usefulness. The hospital had—for a price that was tacked on to her bill—agreed to give her a pair of hospital scrubs to go home in.

Gerald helped her into her new clothes. "You ready to go home?" he asked with a smile of contentment.

He still had the woman, and in the end wasn't that all that mattered?

"Only if you're coming with me?" she asked him, looking boldly in his eyes. Wrapping her good arm around his waist, she smiled up at him. "You know, that wasn't such a bad idea you guys had after all. We have a lot of catching up to do."

"Oh, no, young lady." Gerald kissed the top of her head and wriggled out of her arm. "You need rest, sleep, food, liquids, drugs, and more rest. We'll have plenty of time later for *that!*" But, even as he said it, he knew Heather would get her way. She always did—for at times, she could be very convincing.

Twenty

The Church of All Saints in Fort Worth was filled to capacity. This was the day the family and guests of Gerald Forrester and Heather Chadwick had waited for—the long awaited union between the young couple.

As with the last planned wedding in April, the church was decorated in white silk ribbons and white taper candles. The altar was dressed in a gauzy white fabric, which lent an air of evening elegance to the affair.

At five minutes to six, silence descended as the double doors at the back of the church opened with a flourish. Heather's maternal grandmother, escorted by Steven DuCloux, walked in. Both looked handsome, her grandmother in a pale pink ankle-length dress decorated with silver and pink pearls, designed exclusively for her, Steven looked like a movie star in his black tuxedo.

Following their entrance, the Forrester girls—Donna, Theresa, and Linda—entered, taking their seats on the second row from the front on the groom's side. Mrs. Forrester entered next escorted by her oldest grandson, Darren. She, too, had been outfitted in a cotton candy-colored gown created especially for her for the wedding. The subdued portrait collar framed her glorious face, and the translucent pearls at her wrists and feet twinkled with approval.

Marilyn's entry completed the family train. Escorted by Roger, they looked and acted like a couple in love. Marilyn seemed to float in a double-layer chiffon dress that seemed to wrap around her without a specific beginning or end.

As she watched her mother "take the walk," Heather smiled broadly. It had taken some persuasion but after a lot of playful threats, temper tantrums, and whining, Heather had convinced Marilyn to design and sew all of the mother's Mary Kay-pink gowns for the wedding. Once she got into the job, Marilyn had attacked it with zeal and gusto. With only two weeks' notice, Heather acknowledged she had done a superb job.

The doors shut again, and Heather moved to the center of the double doors. She could hear the rustling of the guests as they stood up on cue. Chris, one of her employees and a fantastic piano player, started the wedding march as the doors were thrown open for Heather's unescorted entrance. She took one, two, steps into the sanctuary. Although she saw no groom standing down front, by the minister, she maintained her smile, sure that Nachelle would come through for her. Floating on air, happier than she had ever been in her life, Heather smiled at her guests and nodded at faces she recognized.

She and the music stopped at the same time in front of the confused minister.

His eyes darted around, finally landing on Heather. He leaned forward. "Where's the groom?" he asked.

"What time do you have?" Heather whispered back.

"Six-ten." A sweat bead popped out and rolled down the preacher's dark face.

Heather wanted to laugh at his expression. She could just imagine him thinking, *Oh, no, not again, except this time it's the groom standing the bride up.*

With a big grin on her face, she responded. "He's coming. My girlfriend went to get him. He doesn't exactly know we're getting married today." Heather explained as if her explanation were the most logical in the world.

The preacher's face grew more perplexed. "What do you mean, he doesn't know?"

Heather turned toward Chris and signaled for him to play something, anything. Chris complied, playing a series of love ballads.

"A few weeks ago, he asked me to marry him. I told him no because we hadn't talked about the reason I stood him up last time. Then, I got to thinking that the only way he would know for sure that I really loved him and wanted to be his wife was if I planned a wedding, showed up first and asked him to marry me in front of all these people. That way he would know I really meant it. Don't you think that's a good idea? I mean, considering I've told him no two times now." Heather smiled and nodded at the preacher, sure that her words made sense.

Fourteen days ago, when she'd told Marilyn and Nachelle of her scheme, they had gone along with it and didn't seem to think it was weird, but she wasn't getting the same nod of approval from the minister.

"So, your groom doesn't know he's getting married today?"

Heather shook her head.

"Then, how does he know to come here?" The preacher punctuated his question with a finger pointed at the floor.

"Because my girlfriend went to get him. I'm sure she made up some fib about my being sick, or needing him for something. She'll drive him to me here. Then, you'll marry us. They should be here any second now. Nachelle is very punctual."

The preacher couldn't take it anymore. His voice rose. "But, you need paperwork, young lady. You can't just show up at the church and expect to get married—and how did all these people know to be here."

Heather maintained her bride's smile. "You should be less linear in your thinking, sir." She turned halfway to the audience and pointed. "You see the man that escorted my mom in?"

The preacher nodded.

"That's Roger Wolfe, Senator, United States. He has a lot of connections."

With more patience than he actually had, the preacher spoke. "I know who he is."

"Good. The man sitting four rows behind him is Judge Canker." Heather waved at the judge. He waved back. "Between the two of them, they took care of all of the paperwork. Don't worry about that." Heather shrugged her shoulders. She wore the same Bob Mackie dress she had selected before. When it came to her wedding dress, Marilyn had refused to sew Heather one, claiming they didn't have the time and that designing wedding gowns was way out of her league. Heather had given in to her mother on that one point since she had graciously agreed to sew three other dresses. "And, as for all these people, they received invitations in the mail, of course. They were asked not to say anything to Gerald."

The minister wiped more sweat from his brow. "I have heard of surprise birthday parties. I have even heard of surprise engagement parties, but never, in my fifty-four years of living, have I ever heard of a surprise wedding. Little lady—"

Reverend Wilking didn't get the chance to finish his speech. The doors banged open and Gerald ran in, took several steps and stopped, looking around the crowded church with the same confused look on his face as the minister had.

Gerald turned around to fully face the front. Heather

wagged a finger at him, inviting him to join her at the altar. Behind Gerald's back, Heather could see a winded Nachelle run in and plop down in the nearest seat.

In a black warm-up suit, trimmed in red and white, and a pair of black Forrester Nike's, Gerald marched down the aisle to his waiting girlfriend and a drenched minister. He returned the waves of his family members as he walked to the front.

Upon reaching Heather, he grabbed her arm and pulled her close. "Nachelle said you were sick, maybe unconscious—and that I needed to come right away. You don't look sick. As a matter of fact"—Gerald stood back a little bit and surveyed his pretty woman—"You look great, honey, beautiful," he breathed. He ran a finger around the neck of Heather's dress, touching skin and fabric. With a small smile, he asked, "You've been busy, haven't you, honey?" His eyes took in the scene before him, the family and guests, the decorated church, the musicians and soloists, the Unity candle, and lastly the minister. "Why did everyone, but me, know I . . . we were getting married today?" There was a hint of hardness in his voice.

Heather experienced a moment of indecision, but squaring her shoulders, she spoke in her normal voice, not caring that some of the guests who sat close could hear her. "You still do want to marry me, right?" A sparkle of doubt entered Heather's eyes.

Gerald looked at her for a long time, trying to clear the confusion in his head. He turned to look at the crowd, then turned back to her. In a lowered voice, he said, "You know I do, but at the hospital you said no, and we've been living together for a month and it's never come up. I thought it was a dead topic."

Heather smiled tenderly at him, wondering how she ever allowed herself to hurt him. Turning from him, she faced the crowd. "Dear friends and family—Gerald and I want to thank you all for coming on such short notice. As you may remember, a few months ago Gerald and I were supposed to wed. However, I got a serious case of cold feet and left him standing at the altar. Since then I've grown up a lot." Heather turned her head, looking at Gerald. "I've come to realize that I almost threw away the most important person in my life. I was blessed with a second chance at happiness and here, now, in front of you all as my witness, I'm asking Gerald if he will marry me."

Tossing her bouquet to her mother, Heather took Gerald's hands in hers. Standing face to face, she continued. "Gerald, I love you and I appreciate you for putting up with me. Months and months ago, I should have talked to you about my fears concerning marriage, but I didn't. I hid them until like an untreated sore, my fears worsened and poisoned my whole view of marriage. With the help of my mother and Nachelle, I've been able to bury those fears and, now, I realize I will not kill our love by marrying you. Rather, like the roots of a tree, burrowing farther into the ground with each passing year, our love will deepen and grow stronger so that no fears, no misshaped conceptions, nothing, will be able to kill it. I love you, Gerald, and I harbor no fears about loving you forever. I want to be your wife. I want to spend the rest of my life with you, have your children and make you happy."

She ran a finger down Gerald's face. Her eyes were filled with tender love. "I'm sorry I've hurt you, Gerald. Please marry me and let me make it up to you."

Gerald's answer was to put his large hands around her waist and pull her to him. Taking his own sweet time, he slowly covered her mouth with his lips, instantly drawing her into his passionate world. The kiss started out tender, seductive, and evolved into raw passion. Breathing deeply, Gerald ended the kiss but kept his lips lightly touching hers. "If you'd have shut up five minutes ago, I would have said yes, way back then."

"He said yes!" the minister reported.

The crowd stood on their feet, clapping, applauding and cheering wildly.

Gerald took that as his cue to gather his soon-to-be wife closer and kiss her mindless. The kiss contained all the promises, dreams, and love two people could produce. It communicated forgiveness, love, and a bright future.

Reverend Wilking cleared his throat and whispered to the engrossed couple in a coaxing manner. "If we don't move on with the ceremony, you won't get to the honeymoon."

That did the trick. Gerald lifted his head and winked at the man. Maintaining a tight grip around his wife's waist, they turned to the front to face the minister.

Gerald instructed the man of the cloth. "Skip all that juke in the beginning and get to the 'I do' parts. You can put the rest on tape. I promise we'll listen to it on our honeymoon."

The minister almost choked in his collar.

Heather laughed and stepped on tiptoe to kiss her husband-to-be. That meager act started a marathon kiss all over again.

Later, once they made it through the ceremony, officially declared as Mr. and Mrs. Gerald Forrester, they ran out of the sanctuary and into the waiting stretch limousine.

With the door shut on the outside world, Gerald pulled his wife into his arms and started the honeymoon in the back of the limousine.

Dear Reader,

WHEW! I did it! Thank God, I was able to finally get Gerald and Heather together. Never, in all my short publishing career, have I had such difficulty getting two characters blissfully wed.

I can't blame it all on the characters. During the writing of this book, I had several personal events going on, but I was determined not to let a new job, new living arrangements, and medical problems upset my plans for Heather and Gerald.

In the writing of this book, I wanted to make sure that you, the reader and supporter of Arabesque, received a quality story that would allow you to escape from those personal and professional events that beat on us—day in and out. I wanted you to cheer for Heather as she beat up Warren in the car and boo for Warren when he abused Mary and cry with Heather and Marilyn as they renewed their relationship and laugh when Gerald showed up at his wedding in a warm-up suit and tennis shoes. I hope I was able to craft a novel that touched your emotions and made the day a little easier to get through. But, I especially wanted to keep my promise that I made to you all in *After Hours*.

After the publication of *After Hours*, I received numerous comments from family, friends, readers, asking: Can't you find a nice gal for Vincent? Did Nachelle quit her job after she married Steven? Did Nachelle have a bunch of babies? Are you sure Harlan died? And what happened with Nathaniel? Was he fired? And what's the deal with Heather? Why doesn't she want to marry that fine man?

Some of these questions I attempted to answer in *Love Everlasting*. Some will have to be answered in a totally different book. But, I hope I satisfied your questions for now. Of course, if there's something that's eating at you . . . If there's something you just have to know right now, write it down on—a postcard, a Post-it, a napkin, etc., and send it to me. Who knows? Maybe your feedback will be the one to generate yet another spin-off book.

Thank you all for supporting me and Arabesque. Without you, the dream would not be real.

God bless.

Anna Larence

Anna Larence
Post Office Box 17875
Dallas, Texas 75217